What the critics are saying…

"If you are in the mood for a touching and enigmatic love story, then SONS OF SOLARIS 2: TAURUS is absolutely the book for you…I was held utterly spellbound by this tale of destiny and true love, as the story moved toward a startling ending." ~ Amelia Richard, eCataRomance Reviews

"An excellent read that will take you on an emotional roller coaster ride. The ending will definitely shock you and leave you wanting more. Jodi Lynn Copeland has done a great job with this book and I look forward to seeing what's next in the Solaris series." ~ Angel Brewer, Just Erotic Romance Reviews

"Jodi Lynn Copeland weaves love and affection into her characters while telling a deeper and more complex story. Sons of Solaris: Taurus gives readers a reason to believe in true love, and also takes us on a roller coaster of events." ~ Cy, Romance Junkies

"The first book in this series was a breathtaking, exciting tale. Again, Ms Copeland has given us a tightly woven tale, full of suspense and passion. The plot flows from page to page, and I could not turn the pages fast enough. This is definitely a series that this reviewer is putting on her auto-buy list." ~ Valerie, Love Romances

RECOMMEND READ. "Sons of Solaris: ARIES is intriguing, suspenseful, powerfully erotic and impossible to put down. This is one series that could have at least twelve more stories to it, I hope for every last one of them. …the story is magnificent and I can't wait to sit down and read it again." ~ Tracey West, Road To Romance

Taurus
Son of Solaris

Jodi Lynn Copeland

SON OF SOLARIS: TAURUS
An Ellora's Cave Publication, March 2005

Ellora's Cave Publishing, Inc.
1337 Commerce Drive Suite #13
Stow, Ohio 44224

ISBN #1419950797

Edited by: *Briana St. James*
Cover art by: *Syneca*

Warning:

The following material contains graphic sexual content meant for mature readers. Son of Solaris: Taurus has been rated E-rotic by a minimum of three independent reviewers.

Ellora's Cave Publishing offers three levels of Romantica™ reading entertainment: S (S-ensuous), E (E-rotic), and X (X-treme).

S-ensuous love scenes are explicit and leave nothing to the imagination.

E-rotic love scenes are explicit, leave nothing to the imagination, and are high in volume per the overall word count. In addition, some E-rated titles might contain fantasy material that some readers find objectionable, such as bondage, submission, same sex encounters, forced seductions, etc. E-rated titles are the most graphic titles we carry; it is common, for instance, for an author to use words such as "fucking", "cock", "pussy", etc., within their work of literature.

X-treme titles differ from E-rated titles only in plot premise and storyline execution. Unlike E-rated titles, stories designated with the letter X tend to contain controversial subject matter not for the faint of heart.

Also by Jodi Lynn Copeland:

Uncharted Waters
Gold Frankincense and Myrrh
Naughty Mistress Nita
Son of Solaris: Aries
Wild Hearts: One Wild Weekend
Wild Hearts: Wild by Night

TAURUS
SON OF SOLARIS

Chapter One

Dear God, how could she have ever brought herself back here, to the one place she vowed to never return?

Necessity, Cara Larsen acknowledged. The need to persevere without having to rely on others, including the one person she longed for. The one and only man she would ever love. The same one she'd left behind along with her spine over two months ago.

She'd done what she had to do. Done what was necessary to survive, to get by. To not fear each and every day what would've happened if she'd followed the path that Tristan wanted and they'd married and had children.

Would their kids have ended up like her brother Joey or would they have taken the road of their father's abnormalities? It didn't matter, because either way they would have been shunned for their differences. The same way both Cara and Tristan had been in their youths, the same way Joey still was. She wouldn't let that happen, and if stopping it meant losing both her spine and the man who'd given her faith, love and hope in a time when she'd desperately needed them, then so be it.

Heels clicked on the tiling of the Red Room gentlemen's club back floor, scattering Cara's wayward thoughts. The woman who'd earlier introduced herself as Maria reappeared from a dark hallway. Cara's belly curled with acid at the knowledge of where that hallway led—to a small, dingy office occupied by Diablo, her one time boss. Her soon to be boss again if she played her cards right.

She laughed at the ludicrous thought. If she played her cards right she would have her old job back, but what about her self-respect?

Right, Cara. As if you had any self-respect in the first place.

For a while she had. For the almost four years she'd served as Assistant to the Art Director for Manseletti Art International she'd had both the respect of her peers and of herself. But that time had passed and she was back to where it all began. Back to one of the seediest joints on the Vegas Strip about to grovel and do whatever else it might take to get her old job back. She'd tried getting in elsewhere, somewhere she would be billed as a performer and not an exotic dancer, A.K.A. stripper, but the places were either not looking for new hires or looking for someone younger.

Younger, Cara thought wryly. She was all of twenty-eight, and with the weight and frills she'd lost since saying farewell to the East Coast, she could pass for a teenager. God knew she'd been carded enough during her stroll into the many casinos that lined Las Vegas Boulevard and the surroundings streets.

Maria reached the row of short stools situated along the club's bar and her gaze narrowed on the one that Cara occupied. According to the placard out front, the woman was one of the top acts at the Red Room. Right now the dancer wore street clothes. A wide-necked, midriff top that hung off one shoulder to reveal a thin red bra strap, and tight fitting nylon pants. Strappy black heels topped off the ensemble. She might be forty as easily as she might be eighteen. So many of the dancers nowadays had breast implants, Botox injections and various other procedures done that age became more a factor of appearance than reality. That her body hadn't been altered by surgery or any other means was obviously the reason Cara had been too old in so many of the casino and club owner's minds.

"Mr. Diablo's ready for you." Maria's voice held an icy edge, and her gaze was one of resentment.

Maria was worried about her being here, Cara knew. Worried she would steal her act and regain the spotlight she'd once claimed at the Red Room. Maria could quit worrying. Cara wasn't here to make headlines any more than she was here to make friends. She was here to earn enough money to keep her younger brother enrolled in school.

The image of Joey's smiling face flitted through her mind and squeezed at her heart. His smiles were rare, as was his speech. It was both unfair and cruel the hand he'd been dealt in life, and she would do anything to see that he was as happy as he could be. Even trade in her hard earned self-respect and revert to her old ways of eating next to nothing and stripping to make ends meet.

As if she knew her thoughts, Maria's glare faded to sympathy. "Hey, don't sweat it. You might not be the new kid on the block any more, but with the body you got you're a shoo-in. Now you'd best get your ass in there before you lose your chance."

Her heart took off with the words. She couldn't lose her chance. Wouldn't. Not when so much was riding on her success.

Passing a weak smile Maria's way, Cara uttered her thanks and started for the back of the club. The hallway that led to Diablo's office exuded cigar smoke and the acrid pitch of sweat, a combination that never failed to wreak havoc on her guts. Today her guts were already so jumbled she had to force long, hard breaths of air into her lungs to keep from being sick.

The hallway ended and, taking one long, last calming breath, Cara pushed against the plexiglass window of the office door. The door swung inward and Diablo stood from a time worn desk and gestured for her to take a seat. Cara knew the action wasn't to set her mind at ease for the events to come, but because he was a short man with a big ego. He refused to look up to someone when he was talking. Least of all a woman.

She closed the door and took the indicated seat. He sat as well, steepling fat fingers on the desk before him as he took a long moment to study her. Black eyes roamed from her face to the portions of her chest visible above the desk. What he could see of her was very little and still his assessing gaze had her stomach ready to take flight.

He returned to her eyes and his upper lip curled. "You've changed."

The words were spoken in a thick Spanish accent marked with a backstreet Vegas drawl. The combination was a cross between greasy and demanding, a tone she remembered well, and yet it managed to alarm her all the same.

Determined to move past her anxiety and prove she was still more than capable of doing this job, Cara came to her feet and stepped away from the desk. She pirouetted before him, showing him her body and that it hadn't changed so much in the time she'd been gone. If anything she looked better. She'd lost weight the last few months, yes, but her figure was still intact. Her breasts still firm and full. Her ass and abdomen tight from the ruthless exercise routine she'd forced herself to do every day for the past six weeks in preparation for this day.

She might be a little on the thin side, but other than that she was in great shape.

She spun back to find Diablo's expression remained unyielding, and croaked out in a tiny voice she hated to realize was hers, "I'm not that different. If anything I'm better."

"Show me."

It was late June and already in the eighties at nine-thirty in the morning. The air inside the Red Room was even more stifling than the sweltering humidity outside. Yet, the second the words left Diablo's mouth, Cara felt frozen. Knowing he wouldn't repeat himself and that if she took too long he would dismiss her altogether, she reached with shaking hands for the hem of her plain white T-shirt. She hadn't bothered with a bra, knowing she would have to take it off once she arrived, and the instant her breasts were released from her shirt, her nipples beaded.

She was cold, scared, hating herself. The flicker of interest in Diablo's eyes told her he believed differently. He thought she was turned on. Good, let him think it. Let him think whatever he wanted so long as he gave her a job.

His upper lip curled again, then turned to a full out smile. The rasp in his voice reflected arousal when he spoke, gesturing her toward him. "Come here."

Cara's stomach tightened with self-loathing, but she did as he asked, rounding the desk with her shirt fisted beneath her neck. He reached out when she arrived at his side and the instinct to shrink from his touch was almost too much to ignore. His warm, stubby fingers touched down on her breast and rubbed across a distended nipple. Tears threatened at the back of her eyes. No one had touched her so intimately in years. No one but Tristan and his touch hadn't felt vile. His touch had been breathtaking. Magical.

Her mind started to roam with the thoughts. She closed her eyes and let it go, hoping to convince herself it wasn't Diablo before her now, but Tristan. It was working, the thought of his large, gifted hands on her body, caressing her breasts, teasing her with their warmth and skill, had the anxiety uncoiling in her belly and her inner thighs heating with expectancy for the rush of power he set free within her. It was working beautifully. And then Diablo cleared his throat and ruined everything.

Cara's eyes snapped open and the coiling in her belly began anew, twisting at her guts and threatening to make her tremble. She bit the inside of her cheek and forced the urge away, as well as the urge to order him to stop. His handling was all part of the job. The inspection. Making sure she was fit for the position. It would end soon. She could last through it even without her forbidden thoughts that it was another man who touched her. She had to last through it for Joey's sake.

Diablo stilled the rubbing of his fingers over her nipple and palmed her breasts, squeezing them, testing their weight and authenticity. She counted backwards in her head, knowing it was almost over. He wouldn't go any farther. Her breasts were what mattered. Her breasts and her face, and their combined ability to reap fistfuls of dollars.

Several more seconds passed and he lifted his hands away. She heaved a sigh that turned to a gasp when they returned to splay along her naked sides. His hands moved downward, his fingers sliding to the waistband of her shorts, and his dark eyes gleamed with excitement as he sank his fat fingers beneath the edge. The twist of his lips was both carnal and lewd. Cara knew if she moved so much as an inch closer, she would feel the press of his swollen cock against her thigh. She didn't flinch, aware if she did brush against his groin he would take it as a sign she was available. Many of the girls were. They claimed there were benefits that came with the role of fucking the boss. She had no longing to find out what they were.

His fingers returned from the edge of her shorts and his thumb stroked over her navel. "Are you looking for side jobs?"

"No!" She hadn't meant to shriek her response, but the thought of the jobs he meant and how much more she'd be doing than removing her top had her doing it anyway.

"That's a shame. There's a lot of money to be had."

She struggled to keep her tone flat this time as his hands moved back upward to fondle the soft flesh of her breasts. *Almost over. Just another few seconds and you'll never have to go through this again.* "The dancing pays fine."

Diablo's gaze wavered from her face to her chest and he caught her nipple between his fingers, pinching it until she wriggled from the acute pain. He chuckled, then finally lifted his hands from her body and sat back in his chair. "Nothing fake about you, is there, Cara? I like that. I also like the changes. They suit you. They'll suit the job even more."

She released a sigh and let her shirt fall back down. Thank God, he approved of her body. Now if only she still had the moves as well. She used to be a great dancer, flexible, graceful. She had no idea what kind she was any longer. The hotel she'd been staying in since returning to Vegas barely had a bed, let alone a mirror where she could watch herself perform. "Then you're ready to see me dance?"

"You know how much I love watching you, Cara. How much all the men love watching you. Unfortunately, we don't need any new girls right now."

The words were like a physical blow. She breathed in a sharp breath and shook her head. Why did he have her strip half-naked and let him touch her then? That wasn't like Diablo. He was slimy and diabolical, yes, but he didn't act this way.

"Then why did you even agree to see me?" Cara asked, not able to keep the anger from her voice. He'd given her hope, damn it! He'd made her believe he was going to take her on. He'd made her think she could stop worrying about Joey's upcoming tuition costs and how she would be able to afford to keep him in the special school.

"I thought you might be interested in taking on side work."

"I'm not!" Damn it, she couldn't! She wouldn't! But what if she had to? What if it was the only way?

"So you've said." He rocked back in his chair and bridged his fingers over a burgeoning gut. "There is an opening in Reno. Mason doesn't pay what I do, but you can work longer hours to make up for it."

"You expect me to move?"

His lips curved in a fickle smile. "I don't expect you to do anything, Cara. You came to me for a job and I'm offering you options. Whether you decide to take one or not is of no concern to me."

Of course, it wasn't. She was a fool to ever have raised her voice to him, to make it sound as though he should care about her well-being. She was nothing to him and never had been anything but a dancer whose body generated income to feather his nest and pay for his many nasty habits. "You're right. You've given me options and for that I thank you."

He eyed her knowingly. "But you won't take them."

The arrogance in his expression suggested he knew her well, that she wouldn't return to her home only to leave it again so soon. He was wrong. He didn't know her. And this wasn't her home. She had nothing and no one in Vegas anymore. The friends she'd had when she left four years ago were either gone or so dead to the world they couldn't remember their name let alone someone from their past. And her mother—her mother she couldn't even work up the energy to track down.

"Okay. I'll take it. The job in Reno, I mean. When can I start?"

"Mason needs someone by Friday. If you don't contact him in person by Thursday night the job will go to someone else."

Two and a half days. It was a short amount of time and still way too long. She had to start working immediately. "Tell Mason I'll be there tomorrow and ready to dance."

He nodded his reply, and Cara started for the door. As much as she'd been hoping to obtain a job in Vegas due to its proximity to Joey's school, she couldn't deny her eagerness to leave the city and the memories associated with it behind. Reno wasn't really that much farther from Joey than Vegas, just another thirty miles or so.

She reached the door and was in the process of pulling it open when Diablo's voice halted her. A genuine affection seemed to tinge his words. "You always were an agreeable girl. Smart too. You haven't been around here in so long I figured you finally cashed in on those smarts. Hoped so even. Guess not."

The unexpected words cut deep and had her belly churning with self-derision. She once thought she was smart too, enough so to move on and cash in on that intellect. And she had for a while, but not any more. Her only skill outside of stripping and stealing was finding, cataloguing and assisting in the restoration of fine art. It was a talent that was only good in one marketplace and that marketplace was so tight the minute she showed her face in it. Tristan would spot her. She wouldn't risk a run-in by taking a job in the industry. She was too weak where he was concerned. One kind word out of his mouth and she would be back in his arms and living her fears all over again.

As much as she ached to return to him, she couldn't go back. Wouldn't when she knew too well a union between them could only lead to future heartache, be it through a mother's eyes or that of a child's.

No matter how much Tristan believed they belonged together, that their eventual union as man and wife had long ago been set in stone, the two of them couldn't be. It was a cold, hard fact, one she knew deep down inside her and was determined to accept. Just as she had to accept the reality she was destined to be a stripper for the rest of her life, or at the very least the rest of Joey's.

"Guess not," she said with as much flippancy as she could muster when tears clogged her throat, and with a final parting glance walked out the door.

* * * * *

Tristan Manseletti wasn't sure of the day he'd stopped being a sharp-thinking, top of the game player who could run a business from six in the morning to ten at night without wearing thin, he just knew it had happened.

Raking a hand through his hair, he cast a weary gaze at the wall clock. Not even five o'clock yet and he was ready to drop down on his desk and catch up on his Zs. While he might not know the exact day he'd stopped being the tireless go-getter everyone in the art world associated him with, he did know the reason. Or rather the person responsible for his character shift.

The woman who'd left well over two months ago and he still dreamt about nightly. The one he refused to believe wasn't coming back.

Cara might claim she couldn't go through life with a man who had the power to not only start a fire of burning need deep within her, but an honest to God fire with a snap of his fingers, but Tristan knew better. Cara loved him just as he loved her. She was his predestined soul mate, and she couldn't stay away forever. He wouldn't allow it. Even if it meant tracking her down and forcing the truth into her stubborn head, he would get her back. He wouldn't resort to that aggressive means quite yet, but he would if another two months passed with no sight or sound of her.

"You ready for something hot?"

At the slow southern drawl, Tristan pulled his mind from its distant wandering to glance at his assistant Janice. The brunette's cleavage-baring and body-hugging outfits never ceased to amaze him. Today was no exception. She wore a tapered black jacket with a matching skirt. The outfit would have looked smart, professional even if she'd had the sense to wear something beneath the jacket and not hem the skirt so damned short her ass stuck out whenever she bent over. And it was her ass. Janice didn't believe in panties any more than she believed in stockings.

What she did believe in was persistence, Tristan thought with an inward groan as she crossed the office and came behind his desk to fill his coffee mug. Pouring him coffee wasn't her job, but he needed the caffeine so damned bad he wasn't about to complain. The rich scent of the strong brew filled his nostrils and had his earlier groan turning to an outward one that resounded through the office, echoing off the painting and artifact-lined walls and clearly giving Janice the sign she'd been waiting for.

She set the coffeepot on his desk and wiggled her hips as she settled back against the rich cherry wood. She shifted to the right and her bare leg rubbed against his thigh. Her lips curved in a wide smile. "Sounds like you really did need something hot. Maybe you could use a little something to take the edge off too."

Not the kind of something she had in mind.

He'd gone through a number of assistants in an attempt to replace Cara. None of them had worked out. Considering Janice's work had been adequate at best before she decided to pursue him and since it was consistently growing sloppier, he had a good feeling he would soon be looking for yet another replacement. One willing to work around the clock to rectify the growing chaos caused by Janice's negligence. One who understood that working around the clock meant on real work and not on easing the boss's frustrations via her hands and mouth.

Even if he didn't have the power to sense the heat of arousal coursing through Janice's body, it would have been obvious he needed only to say the words and she would be naked and ready for him.

Merda, maybe he should say them.

Maybe if he gave in to her advances, he would finally be able to shake thoughts of Cara from his mind enough to sleep at night. Or maybe the only thing that giving in to a woman he couldn't want less would accomplish was making him feel like a scoundrel.

Not that he hadn't had emotionless sex in the past. He just hadn't had it in years. Not since Cara had first entered his life. The cheap thrill that came with meeting a woman one minute and screwing her brains out the next was no longer enough. He craved the thrill only Cara could provide when they linked in body and spirit. Since he wouldn't be experiencing that thrill any time soon, he would just have to keep a lid on his too long deprived libido.

"The coffee will do," Tristan said sharply, his fatigue turning to frustration.

Janice's over bright smile faded. "If you're sure."

Oh, he was. "Thanks," he said in way of dismissal.

She pushed off from the desk and moved toward the door, stopping after a few feet to retrieve a pen he knew hadn't been on the floor minutes ago. She had to have planted it there. She bent slowly and direct from the waist. Her short skirt slid up and the swell of her naked buttocks slipped free. As much he had no longing to take up her unspoken offer of sex, he couldn't stop his body's response to her plump and generously exposed backside. The erection that stirred to life, pressing at the front of his slacks only made his already bad mood all the blacker.

She straightened and shot him an innocent look. "Guess you dropped your pen."

He laughed shortly at her ridiculous behavior. "It would look that way."

She tossed the pen to him and he caught it and set it on his desk. "Thanks again."

She remained unmoving and he sent her a pointed look, growing more tired and equally aroused by her antics with each passing second. She would definitely have to be let go, preferably sooner than later. "Close the door on your way out, and unless it's a national emergency hold my calls for the rest of the night."

"You got it, Boss." The wide, naughty smile that had fallen flat with his earlier dismissal returned, spreading a mischievous glint into her teasing blue eyes. Her tongue came out and dabbed at her lower lip before retreating back into a mouth lined in deep red. "Just let me know if you want anything," she said, purposefully, he knew, laying her sultry drawl on extra thick. "Anything at all."

"You'll be the first to know."

Finally, the door closed behind her and Tristan let out a weary breath. He didn't want her, honest-to-God, he didn't. But if he either didn't fire her fast or she didn't stop with the over the top flirting and barely concealed innuendoes, he might just have to have her anyway.

Not about to digest that thought, he returned to his computer monitor and the most recent string of e-mails. The constant influx of messages and phone calls from buyers and sellers alike never ceased to amaze him. Nor did the company's success.

He'd started Manseletti Art International seven years ago after leaving behind a job as an art purchaser for an eccentric elderly couple. They were loaded and more than eager to shell out a salary that surpassed what he'd be making elsewhere. Anywhere else but for himself, that is. He hadn't left the couple because of money, though. The man had passed on and the woman's love of the finer things in life had died with him. His services were no longer needed even if he had continued to be paid. He wouldn't reap a reward for a job he wasn't doing, just like he wouldn't sit around and let his skills and years of training go to waste. And so began his business.

The first couple years had been slow, but once his name and track record had a chance to circulate that had changed. The business was soon thriving and he'd had to bring in others. Now the company was one of the largest of its kind and his reputation as a world-class art dealer solidly intact. Much unlike the rest of his life.

His thoughts threatened to wander back to where they'd been before Janice had entered his office, and as if she could tap into his mind and didn't care one bit for its direction, she once more appeared at the door.

She popped her head in. "Tristan?"

He bit back a grimace at her usage of his first name. She would be gone soon enough to not bother with reprimanding her. Even if he wasn't planning to let her go, he dreaded the outcome a scolding would bring. Knowing her, she'd take it as a prelude to something far more physical than words and jump on his lap.

His cock twitched with the thought of her shapely ass rubbing against it, and he grunted into the back of his throat. "Yes, Janice?"

"There's a call on line one. I know you said you didn't want to take anything, but he says it's something you'll want to hear. That it would qualify as a national emergency in your mind."

"Did he give a name?"

"Tony Dresdan."

Thoughts of sex died away and he smiled as his long time friend and scout's face entered his mind. Tony moved to Europe five years ago and rarely returned to the States. He also hadn't called in well over six months. That he was calling now, claiming he had news that would qualify as a national emergency, had Tristan sobering in an instant. "Put him through. Thanks."

"No," she said, her voice breathy and lashes lowered. "Thank you, Tristan."

He shook his head at her continued attempts at seducing him. A few seconds ago her coy look and sexy voice might just have been enough to finally push him over the edge and give her what she wanted. Now that Tony was on the line, with what sounded to be highly valuable information, it wasn't even close to enough. "This will probably last the rest of the night. Why don't you take off?"

Her smile fell flat and her forehead knitted. "It's really no prob—"

"Take off, Janice," he said sternly, allowing just a trace of his growing impatience to show. He didn't want to fire her tonight—knowing how long it might take to get another assistant in, he dreaded letting her go her at all, but she wasn't leaving him much choice. He bridled his building temper and returned to the calm state he prided himself on maintaining. "I want some alone time."

She looked thoughtful for another few seconds, then nodded. "Right. See you in the morning?"

He couldn't stop his snort at her hopeful expression or the way she voiced the question. Like this was the end of a date and not a working day at a company she was lucky to still be employed by. "Sure. See you then."

Tristan waited until she closed the door to pick up the phone. His mood lightened and his anticipation built with the prospect of the world-shaking news Tony had for him. "Hey, Dresdan, long time no talk. What's going on?"

"I've got a lead."

Having grown up in LA, Tony's European accent wasn't very distinct, what was distinct was the excitement that marked his voice. It took a lot to get the man riled, and that knowledge had Tristan's anticipation soaring to a whole new level. His pulse sped as he tipped back in his chair. "I'd say a damned hot one by the sound of things."

"L'occhio della Tempesta ring any bells?"

"The Eye of the Storm," he mouthed as his pulse went from brisk to hammering. His heart kicked into his throat and all thoughts of sleep vacated his mind. If he'd thought the sight of Janice's round ass waving in his face had his body on the attentive side, then the thought he could get his hands on the ancient circle of life had his cock rock solid and his testosterone on fire. "No kidding?"

"I wouldn't joke about anything this big."

"Have you seen proof? Photos?" Tristan pressed, more than a little eager to get the details now that he knew what he was dealing with. He worked primarily with paintings and other wall furnishings, but there were exceptions to every rule. This exception was a huge one. He'd been tracking The Eye of the Storm for over a decade, determined to locate the Italian artifact and bring it home. He never believed the day would come when he might actually have that opportunity.

"So far the contact has been via e-mail. There are pictures though. Enough to make it seem like this could be the real thing."

"What's he asking for? Twenty? Thirty?" Hell, he would pay fifty million if that's what the seller wanted. He would pay damned near that much just to see the artifact, to touch it and see if the legend Solaris, Tristan's one time mentor, had told him back when he'd been a temper-driven teenager was true. If *L'occhio della Tempesta* was a direct connection to his past, to his powers. To understanding why he'd been chosen and what he was supposed to do about it, if anything.

"He's asking for you."

Tony's answer brought his thoughts up short. "What?"

"He said he wants to sell it to you, but he won't go through an agent. He wants to see you in person and soon."

He didn't often meet with the sellers, but then he didn't often have a buy like this one presented to him. "Where are we talking about?"

"Reno."

The one word response brought Tristan's racing heart to a standstill. The prospect of getting his hands on the artifact died down in turn.

Why the hell had the man picked Reno?

"He lives there and prefers to do business on his own turf."

Tristan hadn't realized he'd asked the question aloud until Tony responded. If the seller lived in Reno and preferred business to be handled there, then he would simply have to make himself available. The city wasn't really all that close to Vegas—closer than the East Coast where he currently resided, but still not that close—and he had no concrete proof Cara had gone back to her hometown anyway. He prayed to God that she hadn't. She didn't belong in that town, or at least belong there doing the things she did to make a living. She belonged with him, using her natural talent for the arts to help out the company and earn the respect of her peers, and her natural gift to drive him wild with passion and love to ease his currently overtaxed state of mind.

She belonged with him, and while he'd planned on giving her another couple of months to come to that realization, maybe she didn't need that time after all. Maybe what she needed was an up close and personal reminder of just how good they were together. It wasn't a decision to be made in an instant, and neither was trekking out to Reno to meet a man who could be a fraud as well as he could be the real deal. He would decide in the morning, after he'd had a chance to see the photos of the ancient orb and catch up on some much-needed sleep.

"Reno, right. Send me the pictures and I'll let you know."

Chapter Two

Lights glowed and coins clanked and jangled while the neon glow of sex and money colored the thriving Lazy Ace casino. Tristan hadn't been inside the establishment in years. Four to be exact, when he'd flown out to assist Perry in tracking down décor for the casino's renovation. It was the same trip that he'd met Cara. They'd taken the corporate plane down to Vegas for the afternoon to spend some time with Paul, Perry's twin brother who ran the Vegas branch of the Lazy Ace. While Tristan had never been one much for strip joints—it seemed a pointless waste of money to be able to look but not touch—Paul had insisted they rehash old times inside the Red Room. Tristan still didn't know what they'd talked about that day, or if any words had actually made it out of his mouth. Cara had appeared on the club's stage and he'd been lost.

She had the kind of face poets and lyricists had been writing about for years. The slashing cheekbones, mesmerizing jade green eyes, and slightly too wide mouth gave her the look of the ancients. Her tall, statuesque figure held a more aristocratic appeal. And when ancient and aristocratic were combined and topped off with a waterfall of deep red hair, they created a splendor all its own, a splendor that made Tristan, a man who hadn't touched a paintbrush in years, itch to pick one up and capture her beauty on canvas.

And then there was the heat.

The first thing he'd noticed about her might have been an outward elegance as old as time itself, but the crackle of energy that sizzled between them hadn't been far behind. Having been born with the power to detect thermal warmth and the drum of both arousal and emotion in another, the heat hadn't been unexpected. The level of the heat had. Tristan had never experienced anything so solely intense, so all consuming, and it was clear by the flash of confusion in Cara's expressive eyes that she'd felt it as well. He'd known in that moment, known as she swiveled and danced and gyrated across the stage that he'd found the one he was meant to find. His destiny. His soul mate. His lover for all of time.

And then she was gone.

"Sir, if you're not going to play, you'll need to move aside so someone else can use the machine."

Tristan shook free his thoughts to glance into the eyes of a middle-aged woman with a coil of jet-black hair. She wore a red and black tuxedo top that sported the Lazy Ace's insignia and a look as severe as the knot on her head. A woman old enough to be his grandmother stood beside her and the irritation in her eyes made the floor worker's expression seem warm. One gnarled hand fiercely clutched a bucket of dollar coins to her belly and another had a white-knuckled grasp on a cane.

Dio caro! Dear God, he was keeping an old lady from her slot machine. He might not have spent much time in casinos in his life, but he knew where old ladies were concerned blocking their path from a slot was the equivalent of stealing their Friday night bingo spot. Both actions were liable to have her wielding that cane at a location he didn't care to think about.

He smiled, hoping the grin that had earned him more than a few sidelong glances and whispered invitations from beautiful, young women worked on a seasoned one as well. "Sorry, I was distracted."

The displeasure in her gaze melted and her bright coral lips curved upward. "Well now, don't you worry about it none, sonny. I can imagine a fine looking boy like you has all kinds of important things on his mind."

"Thanks," Tristan said, glad to know the grin still worked, regardless of the age of its recipient. "And actually, yes, I do." He glanced at the floor worker. "Can you tell me where I might find Perry Ellison?"

The stern expression that hadn't faltered when the old lady's had, turned keen. "That all depends...are you here on business?"

In Reno, yes. In the Lazy Ace, no. Now was hardly the time for specifics. Not when he had the Ice Maiden herself breathing down his neck. Only she wasn't an ice maiden. Her body was generating some major heat and her aura was shrouded with the longing to be wanted. Sometimes being able to read people's emotion was a real bitch. Times like this for example, where he didn't particularly care to stand around and coddle a stranger and yet also couldn't work up the desire to move on. "Yes, though I don't have an appointment with Mr. Ellison. If you'll tell him Tristan Manseletti would like to speak with him, I'm sure he'll be more than happy to see me."

Her expression made it clear she wasn't sure if she should believe him, but she unhooked a small radio from her belt hoop all the same. She turned away while she spoke into it. After a few seconds, she turned back and rehooked the device. Her eyes and voice were a shade warmer as she spoke, "Mr. Ellison said to send you on up. His office is on the fifth floor." She reached into her shirt pocket and pulled out a red plastic card imprinted with a series of gold-plated numbers. "There's an elevator at the back of the casino, just give the guard this card and tell him Joanne sent you."

"Right." Tristan tried at the grin one last time as he accepted the card, intent on leaving the woman with a smile on her face. It took a long moment of continual grinning, but finally she cracked, giving in to a friendly smile that had her aura shimmering. It also had his already decent mood turning into a far warmer one. Sometimes being able to read people's emotions sucked and sometimes it was an honor he wouldn't give away for anything. "Thanks, Joanne. You've been a big help."

Several minutes later, Tristan stepped off the Lazy Ace's executive elevator and into paradise. While the rest of the hotel and casino sported paintings and adornments he had selected personally, at Perry's request the décor had been done in a modern theme. This floor wasn't just traditional, it was downright antiquated in a way that spoke directly to his artist's soul. While the beige walls and the trimmings that offset them looked aged they weren't cheap. On the contrary, most of the ornamentation and furnishings situated about in the main offices were priceless.

He strode past a sitting area to a desk where a girl who looked to be in her late teens typed diligently. He cleared his throat and she looked up. "May I help you, sir?"

"I'm here to see, Mr. Ellison. Joanne radioed up for me."

"Mr. Manseletti?" He nodded and she indicated a hallway to the left. "Mr. Ellison's office is the last door on the right. If the door's closed, you'll want to knock." Her face colored with a flush of scarlet and she added in a softer tone, "It's lunchtime."

And that was embarrassing because?

Considering how flustered she'd become at the simple words, he decided not to ask. Nodding his thanks, he started down the hall to the last office. The door wasn't closed when he reached it, at least not all the way, but it should have been. Perry leaned against his desk, an expression of pure elation on his face and his lunch all over his lap. At least parts of her were in his lap. Tristan couldn't see much of the woman's face or her hands, but he was guessing they were hidden beneath all that long blonde hair attached to her bobbing head.

Another man might have turned away, but Tristan had known Perry the better part of his life. They'd roomed together the two years Perry had attempted college and, in that time, Tristan had walked in on far more than oral sex. Hell, so had Perry, if the truth be known.

Able to detect the heat radiating through Perry's body and more than a little knowledgeable of the harsh grunts and groans coming out of the man's mouth, Tristan entered the office and took a seat in a chair by the desk. Neither seemed to notice his presence, so he relaxed back, folded his hands over his stomach and waited.

The blonde's head bobbed faster, the sucking of her mouth giving way to throaty sighs. She swiped her hair away from her face giving Tristan a perfect view of the action. While he might have walked in on far more than oral sex in his college days, he hadn't witnessed anybody having sex of any kind in quite some time, and more specifically, he hadn't had sex himself since Cara left. His cock shot to instant life, his heartbeat stepping up in turn, and as the blonde cupped Perry's balls in her hands and fondled them, Tristan's own testicles squeezed tight with the need to let go.

Maybe waiting this out hadn't been such a bright idea after all. Maybe it wasn't too late to retreat to the front area. Only after seeing the young secretary's reaction to her thoughts on lunchtime he was afraid to show her the tent in his pants "lunchtime" had provoked. He wouldn't leave. He could handle this. They had to be almost done anyway. Perry was good, he shared the same extensive lasting power that Tristan had, but he was still only a man. A man with a hot blonde's rosy red lips wrapped around his cock and her big tits slapping up against his thighs with each and every move.

Tristan's penis pulsed with the thought and a moan threatened to escape. He bit back the sound and reached down to adjust, taking pressure off his straining shaft and the engorged sacs beneath it. The heat fanning through him burned higher and he drew in a hasty breath and counted slowly in his head. Tension rocketed through Perry's body and his hands fell to stroke the blonde's bountiful breasts. He palmed her tits roughly, causing a shriek of delight to work its way past her mouth, and her lips pumped even faster. She fucked him fast and hard with her mouth and hand, and finally the heat that coiled through Perry let go, jerking through his body, spasming come into her mouth and, when she pulled back, onto her lush breasts and naked belly.

Tristan hauled in a sharp breath and thanked God that he'd been able to maintain control. He'd come damned close to going off himself, and he had no real desire to walk out of this office with a wet spot lining the front of his slacks.

He waited a few more seconds, time for both himself and Perry to get their wits back about them and for the blonde to stop laving her tongue over the head of Perry's cock like it was her favorite treat, before finally making his presence known. "Nice little dive you've got here."

The blonde shot to her feet and glanced over at him. Her eyes were wide for an instant, then returned to their normal size and she flashed a smile as she went about tucking her breasts back into her top. Nothing shy about her, obviously she did this sort of thing a lot.

Perry sent him a smirk. "Well, I'll be damned, man, you really are here." He straightened and after ushering the blonde out the door went into the small bathroom attached to the office. "When Joanne radioed up," he called through the opened door as water ran and a toilet flushed, "I thought she had the wrong man. Figured you were dead or something, it's been so long since I've seen that pretty-boy face of yours."

Perry exited the bathroom and stretched out a hand when he reached Tristan's side. Though he should have planted a fist in his face for the "pretty-boy" remark, it wasn't Tristan's style, hadn't been in years. Blame it on Solaris' expectations—ones he had made it a point to live up to—or the ridiculous feminine marking on his back that so many took delight in heckling him about, but he was a lover not a fighter.

He pushed Perry's hand away and enveloped him in a hug. After a moment, Perry pulled away laughing. "You haven't changed one damned bit, man. Still living on an emotional high."

Tristan nodded to the door the blonde had left through. "Neither have you."

Perry strode across the room and dropped down behind his desk. "A man's entitled to his lunch break."

"And which exact part of lunch was she? The appetizer or dessert?"

"Candy's sweet, but definitely not dessert material," he said soberly.

The serious tone was accompanied by a way too sedate expression given the man who wore it. Tristan was tempted to question it, but decided to let it go for now.

"So, what brings you here?" Perry asked after several seconds of silence. "It's been...hell, years."

"Four —" like he could ever forget how much time had passed since the day he'd met Cara " — and business."

Obviously his wayward thoughts betrayed his voice as Perry sent him a knowing look. "You know what they say about mixing business and pleasure."

"Yeah," he said dryly, "they make bad bed partners."

"Damn, I guess Lucas knew what he was talking about."

"You spoke with Lucas?" Wonderful.

For years Tristan had bemoaned the loss of Lucas in his life. The two, along with Perry and Paul and several others shared the gift of unexplainable powers. At least how they'd received them was unexplainable. Solaris had brought the men together as teenagers and taught them about their powers. They'd been together for years, joined as brothers in a group known as the Sons of Solaris, then one night it had all died. Or rather Lucas' sister, Alana, had died and Lucas had blamed Tristan for her death. After that, the group had slowly disbanded. Then three short months ago, Solaris had been murdered. Given the man's believed immortality, the death shouldn't have happened. Still, it had occurred and ultimately led to a reunion between Tristan and Lucas, as well as Lucas finding his destiny in the form of Solaris' psychic niece, Amy.

Yeah, for years Tristan had bemoaned the loss of Lucas and at the moment he wished to hell he still did, because then the man wouldn't be interfering in his life now. Lucas and Amy were obviously concerned about him, and given the frustration

Tristan had let show over Cara's leaving, they probably had a reason to be.

"I've talked to him a few times recently," Perry said of Lucas. "He told me the two of you are on speaking terms again. He also told me about Cara."

Merda. Now what? Tristan could just imagine Perry's thoughts on how he might help to ease his restless state of mind and body. While Perry had all the right connections to ease the latter, the former would take a hell of a lot more than a good fuck to set right. "I've been too wrapped up with business the last couple weeks to see him. Did he mention if anything new was going on with Mike?"

Perry sent him a look that told him how poor his attempt at changing the subject had been. Tristan knew there wasn't anything going on with Mike, the man who'd been pinned with Solaris' death, but even sounding stupid was preferable to having a conversation about the woman he was doing his damnedest to not think about.

"Still in the loony bin," Perry said wryly, "though somehow, I think you already knew that. So, you need a place to crash while you're in town?"

Tristan breathed a sigh of relief at the question. He had little doubt Perry would be attempting to get him to talk about Cara again, but for now he was in the clear. "I was hoping you might be able to set something up."

"You've got it." Perry picked up the phone and punched in a number, telling the front desk to set Tristan up with one of the suites. He covered the mouthpiece and raised a blond eyebrow Tristan's way. "You want any special amenities?"

He meant the kind that came with skilled hands and mouths and a ready supply of condoms, Tristan knew. As wise as it might be to take him up on the offer and end his prolonged celibacy streak, the one that had his cock ready to burst out of its skin a short while ago, he couldn't find the drive to do it. "Thanks, but I'll pass."

"Let me know if you change your mind." Perry spoke with a front desk clerk for a few more seconds then returned the phone to its cradle. "All set. You'll be able to check-in in a half an hour. Until then, do you have time for lunch?"

Tristan smirked even as his shaft stirred to life anew at the memory of watching the blonde go down on the other man. "I thought you already had your lunch."

He shrugged. "Like I said, Candy's nice, but more like an appetizer."

The sobriety Tristan detected in the man's earlier words returned, making him wonder again just what or who had put it there. He wasn't about to ask because he knew it would only steer the conversation right back to his own problems. "I don't have to be anywhere until seven."

Perry's grin returned and he stood. "In that case you can buy my lunch *and* dinner."

*   *   *   *   *

What the hell had he been thinking agreeing to meet here, in the Red Room of all the damned places? It might be the Reno location and not the one where he'd met Cara, but it still brought back memories as well as thoughts of where she was right now. If he had the man's number he would call and request they meet somewhere else. Unfortunately, he didn't have the man's number. He didn't have a thing but his e-mail address and last name.

A tall woman dressed in a silver-spangled bikini top, matching miniskirt and very little else appeared by the establishment's open doorway. "Can I help you?"

"I'm supposed to be meeting a B. Stevenson here."

"Oh, right. She's already waiting for you."

She?

Tristan was barely aware of the music that blared around him or the raucous laughter and flashing glow of lights as he followed behind the woman. One single question reverberated through his mind... How the hell had he missed that the seller was a she? He'd obviously followed Tony's lead. His friend had indicated the seller was a man, but admittedly had never spoken with the person over the phone. The only contact thus far had been via e-mail and obviously that contact hadn't been with a man at all, but a woman.

Make that a siren, he thought an instant later, when he was led to a table already occupied by a woman with a face that could bring a man to his knees. A face *and* a voice, he realized with the first of her loudly spoken and highly throaty words.

She stood and extended a hand. Her lush lips formed a radiant smile and her knee-length black dress hugged her curves delectably. "Mr. Manseletti, finally we meet."

He reached for her hand and the zing of awareness that skyrocketed through him with their first touch nearly had him letting it go again. *Jesus,* he hadn't felt that much heat with anyone before. No, not anyone. He'd felt it with Cara numerous times, but no one other than her. He released the woman's hand and spoke as loudly as she had to be heard over the music and patrons. "Tristan. Call me Tristan."

She returned to her seat and he slid into his, not quite able to resist a quick glance at the slice of pale cleavage exposed above her neckline. The dress was snug, but not overly so. The hemline modest and yet teasing. It was just enough to whet the appetite and make a man wonder what lay hidden beneath.

"All right, Tristan, and you can call me Brandy."

"Brandy. It's fitting."

Why the hell is it fitting?

He didn't know the answer any more than he knew why he'd suggested she call him Tristan. He rarely worked on a first name basis, just as he rarely checked out his female business associates' assets. Something about her just seemed to call to him. Something he wasn't sure he wanted to deny.

She lifted a wineglass to her lips and sipped back the blood-red contents while eyeing him over the glass's edge. Her eyes were the color of smoke and loaded with promise. She set the glass back and her smile returned. "I'm so pleased you were able to make it out here on such short notice."

"Let's just say you picked the right impetus."

Her smile grew wider yet, bringing new life into her eyes and an unexpected rousing in his groin. "I thought you might say that."

"Is it here?" Tristan pressed, aware his developing erection had to be about anticipation to get his hands on the Eye. As enticing as Brandy might be with her dark silky hair, radiant face, and gently rounded figure, he didn't get physically aroused by simple conversation. At least, not with anyone but Cara.

She laughed huskily and took another sip of wine. "Do I look like a fool to you?"

Her smile had gained a slightly naughty edge with that laugh, her eyes following suit. She didn't look like a fool in the least. She looked like a woman who knew what she wanted and wasn't afraid to go after it. And as her tongue slipped out of her mouth to rim the lip of her wineglass, he had a feeling that what she wanted was him.

"I thought we might enjoy a few drinks and get to know each other a bit first. You don't have a problem with that, do you, Tristan?"

The question was loaded with sexual intent. He could hear that much even over the din of their surroundings. As much as he should have said yes, that he had a problem with it, a big problem, he found himself saying, "Not at all."

Brandy raised a dark eyebrow. "There's not a Mrs. Manseletti waiting somewhere?"

Only a woman he wanted to be Mrs. Manseletti and since Cara wanted nothing to do with him in return, she wasn't worthy of notation. "There's no one waiting. Not even a girlfriend."

"Now, why do I find that so hard to believe? You're a very attractive man, Tristan. An attractive man with a lot of money."

"Perhaps I don't have the time for a woman in my life."

"Perhaps. Or perhaps you just haven't yet met the right one."

The promise in her eyes grew to new heights with the bold words and a jolt of awareness jetted through Tristan's body nearly too intense to believe. He straightened in his seat and glanced around. Brandy couldn't be stirring that strong of a reaction in him. She simply could not. Only Cara could do that, but Cara was nowhere in sight.

"Is something wrong?"

He glanced back at Brandy's odd expression. Was something wrong? No, he was just losing his damned mind and feeling things that couldn't be authentic. "No. I just… I thought I felt something."

"Felt something?" She mulled over the words a few seconds. " It must have been something awfully strong to make you turn around like that. A sixth sense, perhaps?"

"I'm not clairvoyant."

Her eyebrows danced together with his quickly spoken remark. "What a strange thing to say. Of course you're not."

"Right." *He* was right, that is. He clearly *was* losing his damned mind that he would make such a brash statement as "I'm not clairvoyant." Some of the Sons were, as well as various others he knew. To clarify that he was not among that farseeing group was habit more than anything. It wasn't, however, a habit that he wished to discuss with Brandy anytime in the near future.

Fortunately, that seemed fine by her. She finished her wine in one long drink and stood. She smoothed her dress, rubbing her hands along her hips and back up and over the outer swell of her breasts. Her nipples beaded with the action, pressing into rigid points against the thin material of her dress and making it clear she wore no bra.

She dropped her hands back to her sides and smiled. "What do you say we get out of here and go somewhere a bit less crowded?"

Tristan stayed rooted to his seat, fighting the heat coursing through his body that had only grown worse with her all over smooth down and its resulting effects. His cock grew thicker by the moment, aching with too-long unfulfilled desire. The warmth spiraling through him couldn't be generated by Brandy and a yet to be spoken invitation, and he wouldn't fool himself into believing it could. Determined to keep this about business now more than ever, he asked, "To discuss the Eye?"

She nodded and extended a hand. "Sure."

He stared at her hand, knowing the response to be a lie. The offer was *not* just about business. He accepted her hand all the same. He had to be agreeable if he wanted to get close to the Eye. And he did want to get close to it, more than life itself some days. Brandy's fingers connected with his and white lightning seemed to spear through him. He hurried to his feet and pulled his hand from her grip. Resolved to avoid her face and any telling signs she'd experienced the electric heat as well, he turned his attention to the stage. He could feel her body's response if he chose, could sense her emotions on everything happening between them, but right now he didn't want to know.

The music faded around them and the light sequencing changed as one of the dancers made their way offstage and another came on. The cascade of deep red hair and the scantily covered backside of the dancer leaving the stage is where Tristan's attention and all his energy zeroed in on. For an instant, his heart stood still.

Cara.

No, it couldn't be Cara. It was merely a lush redhead that resembled Cara from behind. A woman he'd obviously somehow seen in his peripheral vision and allowed his body to respond to. It was the reason for the heat. Not Brandy at all, but a case of mistaken identity.

It *was* a mistaken identity. Regardless of how much both his body and mind might have been confused, the real Cara wouldn't be in Reno. He hoped to God she wasn't back to stripping on a stage of any kind. His confidence in the matter wasn't nearly as strong as he would have liked. He knew her motivation behind her career choice and the easy cash it would net. Yet, as much as he knew it and respected her efforts to help out her little brother, it didn't set his mind or his guts at ease. Least of all, when the reality was her money didn't mean a damned thing at Joey's school. It never had. And as long as Tristan kept paying the boy's massive tuition bill, it never would.

"Ready?"

He turned back to Brandy's expectant look and his gut tightened even as his penis pulsed with prospect. Ready. The word could mean so much. Was he ready to talk business? Was he ready to give pleasure with her a try? Was he ready to move on without Cara? He didn't know and he didn't want to think about it. "Yeah, let's get out of here."

* * * * *

Why? Or maybe the better question was how, Cara thought as she changed out of her harem girl costume and into the coaxing kitty one for her next act. How had Tristan found her so soon?

Maybe he hadn't been at the Red Room tonight looking for her at all. Maybe it was just a coincidence his being here. She couldn't tell much about what had been happening at the table toward the back of the smoke and light-filled club, but she guessed it was a business meeting of some kind. The person he'd met with was female, but since the woman's back had been to her the entire time she'd been on stage Cara couldn't tell anything outside of gender and the fact she had black hair.

Unless gender had been all that Tristan cared about her seeing. Was it possible he'd somehow found out she was working at the Red Room and come here with another woman in an attempt to make her jealous?

No, that wasn't his style. Outside of his excursion into the Vegas Red Room the fateful day they'd met, she was fairly certain he'd never even been in a strip club. So why was he here? It had to be about business. The woman he'd met with today must have requested this place, because Cara knew Tristan and he wouldn't have come to this club without some damned good persuasion on another's part.

She hoped to God no one persuaded him to come back.

An accidental brush where she managed to escape without him seeing her was bad enough. If they came so close again and he not only saw her, but spoke with her, bad things would surely happen. The kind of bad things that had to do with her low tolerance and enormous appetite where he was concerned. The kind of bad things where she admitted how alone she'd been since leaving him. The kind of bad things where she forgot her reasons for doing just that and rushed back to him open-armed.

Chapter Three

"This is nice. Don't you think?"

Tristan met Brandy's appreciative look across the small, candlelit table. Did he think secluding himself with a beautiful woman at the back of one of the most romantic restaurants in Reno was nice? He might, if not for the fact he still couldn't shake the surge of heat that registered in him every time the two of them got close. He had honestly believed the sensations had to do with the dancer back at the Red Room, the one who'd reminded him of Cara. If that were true, then why was he still feeling them?

Brandy laughed, the sound high and melodious, and the warmth building within him stirred to a potentially dangerous level. She reached for her wineglass and caressed her fingers along its stem. Her skin was alabaster and her bone structure fine. Her movements as she stroked the glass' stem graceful and yet somehow sensual. It was almost as if he could feel that subtle brush of her fingers on him, caressing his body, his mind.

"It really shouldn't be that difficult of an answer, Tristan. The setting is exquisite, the company superior. What's not to like?"

The company *was* superior. Most notably her ability to carry on a conversation that was both mentally stimulating and physically arousing.

Tristan frowned at the thought, even as he accepted it as the truth. He could pretend, blame the fire flaming inside him on something or someone else, but it wouldn't change the facts. There was something special about Brandy. Something he hated to think might even exceed the something special he'd found with Cara.

Mio dio. My God, was he really ready to move on? It was a question he'd asked himself numerous times over the past two months, and more than a half dozen times since meeting Brandy an hour ago. He'd never known the answer before. He did now.

It was time.

Past time to stop fantasizing about a woman who wanted nothing to do with him. Who would rather give up a job he knew she'd loved, than spend time with him even as a colleague. A woman who Tristan had believed for years was his soul mate, but maybe he'd been wrong. Maybe he was looking at his soul mate.

As if she knew his mind, Brandy's lush red lips grew into a wide smile and mirth glimmered in her smoky gaze. She was so beautiful when she smiled that way, as if it were for him and him alone, that it physically hurt him, pressed pain at his heart. If that wasn't proof enough she was his true destiny, then what was?

"It's nice," he admitted, and was stunned by the thickness of his voice.

The knowing light that flashed in her eyes ensured she'd heard it as well. Heard it and knew how aroused he was by her presence alone. She stilled her finger's movements and lifted her glass to her lips. He watched entranced as her throat worked gently to swallow back the fine red wine she favored. He didn't even have to try to read her body's heat, it automatically registered. She was every bit as stimulated as he was and so far they had yet to talk about anything outside of business and the art world at large. Conversation aside, he held little doubt if he asked her to go back to his room with him she would readily accept the offer. Tristan wasn't quite ready for that. Close, but not quite.

She set the glass back and idly fingered the curly ends of her shoulder-length hair. The ebony strands matched her dress perfectly. "Tell me about yourself, Tristan."

He pulled his attention from her fingers and smiled. He couldn't tell her anything she didn't already know. Everything about his life was a matter of public record. Everything, that is, but his powers and the six years he'd spent learning about them under Solaris' admirable tutelage. "I'd rather hear about you. How did you get into the art industry?"

For a moment she looked surprised by the question, as though she might not respond, but then said, "My mother was an artist. I grew up attending her showings. I guess you could say the bug bit me. But that's boring stuff. My life is boring. Yours isn't."

"I find it exceptionally difficult to believe you wouldn't have examined my background before arranging this meeting."

Her smile peaked for an instant. "I did my research, of course, but I was hoping to go beyond what's written in the papers and on the Net. I want to know Tristan Manseletti the man, not the millionaire or fine arts specialist. I want to know the *real* you."

Something in Brandy's expression or maybe it was her voice hit him wrong. Only it couldn't be her expression because it was one of pure fascination, and it wasn't her voice, how could something that sensual bother him? It had to be his imagination.

Shrugging off the thought, Tristan sat forward in his seat and rested his elbows against the table, bridging his fingers before him. "Why? What is it about me that interests you enough to want to know more?"

While before her smile had been fleeting, this time her lips curved fully into the slightly enchanting, slightly naughty smile he'd witnessed back at the Red Room. "I think you know why."

"Yes, but do you?" he returned, not knowing why at all, but hoping the overconfident words would be enough to convince her that he did.

Amusement lit her gaze. "I guess there's only one way to find out."

"What are you suggesting?" His groin tightened with the question and the expectancy in her eyes, even as the rest of him tensed with the thought he might not be prepared to know the answer.

"Really, Tristan, you strike me as a man who doesn't need things drawn out for him, but in case I'm wrong, allow me to make myself clear."

He waited for her to continue and when she didn't offer more, opened his mouth to question her. No words made it past his lips before her bare foot touched down against his inner thigh. He'd been stimulated since the moment they'd met. Now, as her toes rubbed his flesh through the thin material of his slacks on an upward journey to his cock, he was more than stimulated, he was hard as granite. Her foot found the juncture of his thighs and her toes kneaded against the base of his penis, tightening his balls further with each new stroke. The heat within him flamed higher and he bit back a groan at the pressing need consuming him.

It truly had been too long since he'd last had sex that such a simple fondling could have him ready to come in ten seconds flat. Or maybe it was more about the setting, the voyeuristic edge to it and the idea others might know what was happening beneath the table.

"Are things becoming clearer, or do I need to crawl under the table and explain it a bit more orally?"

His cock pulsed with the breathy suggestion and the visual that formed in his mind. Initially it was the one of Perry and Candy back in the casino's office, of the voluptuous blonde giving his friend head without concern to who might be watching. Then the vision changed, and it was Brandy down on her knees. Her pale breasts bared to fill his hands and her luscious red lips wrapped around his engorged penis. Brandy sucking him back, fucking him with her mouth until every last bit of come drained from his body. He grunted at the effect the vision had on him, hardening his shaft further still and speeding his heart and blood into a madly pumping crescendo.

"They're clear," he said tightly.

"And?" she asked, her voice barely a whisper as her toes continued their ruthless assault, kneading and caressing his cock through his slacks and briefs.

"And I don't make it a habit to mix business with pleasure."

"But?"

"What makes you think there's a 'but'?"

"Evidence." Her lips twitched and humor danced in her eyes. "Rock solid evidence."

"But," he continued, aware of just how accurate she was. The evidence was irrefutable, even if he had managed to hold back the bulk of his moans, "sometimes it's good to break from the norm."

Brandy's foot left his lap without warning, and she pushed back her chair. She stood and raised an eyebrow. "Are you staying nearby?"

Tristan held back his frown just barely, bewildered by how nonchalant she suddenly seemed. The steamy invitation wasn't in her eyes any longer, nor was desire reflected in her tone. The heat still burned in her though, that much she couldn't hide behind indifference. Her composure had to be for the sake of appearance. It wouldn't look good to walk out of this restaurant with their mouths latched together any more than it would look good to do so with their hands buried under each other's clothes. Then again, in Reno it might not be such an uncommon occurrence.

He stood and nodded. "At the Lazy Ace."

"Mmm...just two short blocks away."

She finished the sentence with a lusty lick of her lips, and his moment of wonder passed. Her composure was definitely about keeping up an appearance. She still was eager for him, and he was more than eager for her.

Less than fifteen minutes later, they were inside Tristan's hotel suite. Just inside. They had cleared the door and he was in the process of closing it when Brandy went from selectively reserved to an all out wildcat. With a strength that belied her slender build, she pushed him back against the door, his weight slamming it closed the remainder of the way, and then she was on him.

Her mouth was ravenous, her hands the same as they tugged and plied at his lips and clothing. For an instant, as he adjusted to the suddenness of it all, he was still. Then he too came alive, feeding the fire within him with raging anticipation. Gripping the plump globes of her ass in his hands, he lifted her up and against him. She twined her legs around his waist and rubbed her cunt against his throbbing cock. While the knee-length cut of her dress had seemed modest, what lay beneath wasn't modest at all. She was bare beneath the dress. Bare and wet. A wetness that grew, permeating the air, as he held her ass with one hand and found her damps curls with the other.

He plunged past her lips with the force of his tongue, parting her, diving into her heat, needing to sink even farther, to lose himself completely. To let go of his control. She could make him do that. The crackle in the air around them, the rising temperature of the room. The breeze that seemed to come out of nowhere all made it clear. Brandy was the one. Brandy was his destiny.

As if she too knew the connection meant for them and that knowledge fueled her need to fever pitch, her hands went from rubbing and groping to an erratic chaos. It had been far too hot for Tristan to wear a jacket and tie to the meeting tonight and now she used the lack of those layers to her advantage, sweeping her hands beneath the collar of his dress shirt and sending buttons sailing. Her long nails skimmed past his neck and dug deliciously into the rigid muscles of his back.

She mewled into his mouth, and he rimmed her sex as he released an answering cry. Her mewling faded to nothingness as she used her tongue to feast with wild abandon, suckling, licking, meeting his with a desperation he understood completely because he felt the same way. He had to have her. Had to have this woman.

This woman he loved.

He pulled his fingers from the swollen lips of her pussy and buried them in the thick rope of her hair. *Dio*, how he loved her hair. The deep color. The vibrant strands. So long. So silky. He used to lay awake at night inhaling the scent of her. Strawberries. They were her favorite dish. Strawberries and chocolate. Godiva, of course. Only the best for his baby.

She sighed against him and he gathered her close. He was so hard, so needy, and yet so content just to hold her. She wasn't content to be held though. She wriggled in his embrace, gyrating her damp cunt against his cock, making her ache more than known. His own ache throbbed through him, raising the temperature in the room a notch higher and his control ever closer to the snapping point. He couldn't snap. He had to stay in control. She hated it when he lost control, when he let his power out. She hated that he wasn't normal.

"Please, Tristan…"

The plea in her breathy words was too much. He couldn't deny her. Never had been able to. He tipped his head back and smiled into her passion-hazed eyes. Such expressive eyes. So green. So wide. So seductive. "*Dio*, Cara, you make me want to come so badly, baby."

The words no sooner left his mouth than the siren in his arms went still. She dropped her legs from his waist and stepped back. Tristan shook his head and sucked back a breath at the transformation that seemed to happen before his eyes. It wasn't Cara who stood before him now. Cara would never laugh in a situation like this, and this woman was laughing deeply.

Brandy's eyes lit with rich humor. "So you think I'm cara?"

Tristan dragged a hand through his hair. *Scopata!* What the hell had just happened? He'd tasted Cara on his lips, saw her beautiful face smiling up at him, buried his fingers in her long, thick hair. He'd smelled strawberries on the air, goddammit!

Cara wasn't here. Only Brandy was here. Here and smiling at him. Why the hell was she smiling? "What?"

"You called me cara. That's Italian for expensive or pricey or something along those lines, right? Are you afraid my tastes are too rich for you, Tristan? That I want you for your money and plan to bleed you dry?"

He puffed out a hot breath with the ludicrous question. It proved two things. She had researched him enough to know Italian was his mother's language and one he often used himself, and that he'd almost made one big damned mistake. Brandy might be able to start a fire of need burning deep within him, but she wasn't his soul mate. If she were, she would never need to ask a question like that one. She would know the truth that existed between them. She would be able to feel it.

That being the case, he needed to get her out of here fast, before he soured this deal any more than what he already had. Damn it, he never mixed business with pleasure. Now was a hell of a time to have started. He pulled his shirt together and slid the few buttons that hadn't been popped off back into place. "I didn't mean to imply you were expensive."

The humor died from her eyes, as did the smile from her face with his matter-of-fact tone. He'd meant to put things back into perspective fast and obviously it had worked. "Then what did you mean to imply?"

Exactly what he'd said. That Cara was his baby and only she held the power to make him come undone. That he'd nearly lost control with Brandy was due to his overtaxed mind and the fact that for several long, hot seconds he'd honestly thought it had been Cara in his arms. Not about to put his thoughts into words, Tristan dismissed her question with a shrug and opened the door. As much as tossing her out sounded like the quickest way to end this night, she hadn't done anything to deserve such rudeness. He was the bad guy here. The bad guy who would probably be spending the next week kissing Brandy's ass to ensure he left Reno with the Eye in his possession.

"I don't mean to sound rude," he said as warmly as possible without crossing into sexual terrain, "but I really should get some sleep."

Her eyes narrowed. "It's barely after nine."

"I live on the East Coast. It's after midnight there."

"Ah, jet lag." Her eyes widened again and once more humor sparked there. Her lips curved as she took a step toward him. Had he seen her next move coming in the least, he would have been able to sidestep it. Obviously, he really did need sleep, because his typically rapid reflexes didn't even kick in until her hand was curled around his still swollen cock and pumping. "For someone with jet lag, you don't seem very tired. In fact, you feel quite awake."

Mentally forcing back a fresh surge of testosterone, he lifted her hand away. "I might not seem tired now, but I will be. I have an early morning planned."

"Multitasking while in Reno, how entrepreneurial of you."

"You could say that."

She continued to look at him for several seconds before finally shrugging and stepping out into the hallway. She turned back. "What time would you like to get together tomorrow?"

Tristan was breathing a sigh of relief when the words reached him. He exhaled sharply. So much for ending things swiftly yet friendly. "What do you mean, get together?"

"To see the Eye."

"Oh. Right. Anytime after four."

"Six then—" her smile returned "—at my place. I'll send you directions." She rose on tiptoe to brush a kiss across his cheek. "Good night, Tristan. Sweet dreams."

He stared after her back, as both the parting words and the piercing heat that shot through him with that chaste kiss sank in. It was the heat that he'd felt at their first meeting, but so much more. The heat he'd felt when she was in his arms that had led him to believe it was Cara. It was a heat he didn't begin to understand and had no idea where to look for answers.

* * * * *

Answers. Tristan had gone to bed soon after saying goodbye to Brandy to ponder that very thing. Where did he get answers to explain the sensations Brandy evoked in him? If it were simple sexual longing it would be one thing, but what she stirred went well beyond desire. He'd thought because she questioned his feelings on her motive for wanting him, she couldn't be his soul mate, but maybe he'd been wrong yet again. Maybe his soul mate wouldn't know those things inherently.

Had Cara known? He'd always taken it for granted that she knew his mind just as he knew hers, but maybe she didn't.

If he could just ask her…

His mind drifted to the Red Room and the dancer who resembled Cara so completely from behind. It was ludicrous to even consider that it could've really been her. Yet ludicrous as it might be, he couldn't stop from getting out of bed and pulling on khakis and a short sleeve polo shirt. It was almost two in the morning. The odds the dancer would still be at the club were slim, but he had to try to find her. Had to be absolutely sure that it wasn't Cara.

And if it was…

It couldn't be.

Ten minutes later, Tristan stood outside the Red Room's open front doors. The city was lit up around him so brightly it looked like it was the middle of the day instead of the middle of the night. Music drifted from inside, making it clear dancers were still onstage. The woman might very well still be in there, yet for some reason he couldn't get himself to go in.

It wasn't fear. He didn't get scared. So what was it?

Unsure of the answer and unable to make himself go inside, he sank down on the stone ledge that surrounded either side of the doorway and waited. If the woman was still inside, she would have to come out eventually. Unless she took a back way out.

"You look lost."

The tired voice drifted down to Tristan over twenty minutes later. He'd more or less given up on finding the woman tonight and was in the process of counting the small red and blue diamonds that made up the tiled sidewalk beneath his feet. Breaking from the diamonds, he glanced up and felt his eyes bulge even as heat raced through his body hot enough to start a forest fire. The woman's eyes bulged as well and pallor overtook her face.

No way. No way in hell. "Cara?"

Her mouth fell open and she shook her head as her body visibly trembled. Words stumbled from her lips. "Oh...my...God..."

"It can't be... It cannot be." But it was. He sent his gaze over her quickly, his guts turning at the scanty outfit. Her breasts were barely concealed by a black, sleeveless shirt small enough to fit a child and her lower half just covered in a tiny pair of canvas shorts. The long mass of her hair pulled back in a high ponytail and the loud makeup that donned her face only made her appearance seem all the more trashy. He growled his repulsion even as his cock hardened with pure desire.

Damn it all to hell! It wasn't bad enough she was back on the stage undressing day and night, but she couldn't even find the time to change out of her strip clothes before exiting the club?

The calm Tristan prided himself for hanging onto in the most infuriating of situations evaporated in a flash. He shot to his feet and grabbed her wrist. "What the hell are you doing, Cara? Look at you. You look like a hooker."

Her eyes went from wide with shock to narrow with animosity. She wrenched on her arm, but he held fast. "Thanks for the compliment, now get your hands off me."

"Why are you doing this?" he demanded, not about to let her go. If he did, she would only run. The same way she'd been running her whole life. From him. From her mother. From her past at large. It was her signature, running every time things started to look a little scary.

"You know why," she spat.

He nodded. "Because you're a stubborn fool who's afraid to give life a try."

"Because I love my little brother and he's counting on me to keep him in school."

He couldn't hold back his derisive chuckle. "Joey doesn't even know that school costs money, or hardly any damned thing else. You're lucky if he remembers your name on a good day."

A horrified gasp rent the night and her slitted eyes flew wide only to water with tears. She brought her free hand to her face and swiped at the moisture. "Go to hell, Tristan. Go. To. Hell."

"*Jesus,* I'm sorry, Cara. That was cruel…and stupid." It was also the reason he worked so hard to hang onto his control, to remain calm no matter what. Because when he didn't remain calm he became a real bastard. He loosened his grip on her arm and ran his thumb along her wrist, savoring the rapid beat of her pulse. "I didn't mean it, baby. You know I didn't. I adore Joey. I always have. I just… Damn it, I just can't handle this. You can't do this. You're too smart. You could do so much with your life. You *were* doing so much."

She sniffed back the last of her tears and looked away. "I don't belong in that world."

The words were quietly spoken and yet managed to pack a punch that hit Tristan square in the gut. Hit him square and had him ready to beg if that's what convincing her took. "Yes, you do. You belong…" *With me.* He couldn't say it. She was already resisting him. If he spoke those words aloud, she would be gone from him for good. Some miracle or gift from above had brought them together here tonight and he wouldn't lose her over misplaced words. "Just listen to me. Please."

She turned back and shook her head, her long ponytail bobbing and making his fingers itch to get lost in its weight. "No. You listen to me. I am *not* in your life any more, Tristan. I'm not in that world. I chose to walk away, just like I am choosing to leave now." Her voice rose several notches and she wrenched at her arm again. "Now let me go. I need to get home."

He should. He should release her and allow her to run home and be alone and miserable while he sought out Brandy and gave himself over to the unexplainable longing she aroused in him. He should, but he couldn't. As much as Brandy might be able to pleasure him, he didn't love her. He loved Cara. Too much to watch her throw her life and talent away in some sleazy strip joint. "I'm not letting you go until I've talked some damned sense into you."

"Wrong answer, asshole."

The voice was deep, masculine, and followed by a meaty fist direct to Tristan's face. Pain erupted inside his head and red swam before his eyes. Red that became all the more prominent with the cracking sound of his skull as it collided with the multicolored concrete. Stars danced before his eyes and his brain seemed to spin in circles. He lay still, sucking back clammy air for just a second and then his senses returned, along with his reflexes.

He jerked to a sitting position, and the spinning of his head turned to massive somersaults. He closed his eyes and gave his head a shake, fighting back the pain. "Son of a bitch."

"That was a warm up swing, buddy. You want more, try and touch her again."

Tristan forgot all about his throbbing head and the blood he knew trickled down his face and locked his sights on the man who stood next to Cara. The man was big, at least six and a half feet. Muscles rippled in his arms beneath a stained tank shirt and bulged out in his calves and thighs as well. The gleam in his eyes made it clear he was hoping for a fight. A fight he assumed he would win.

Blame it on lack of sleep, a shitty end to what was otherwise a pretty damned good day, or something else altogether, but Tristan could only laugh. Laugh and then ask a question he had no business in hell asking. "You really think you have what it takes to kick my ass? If so, bring it on. I'll start on the ground to make things easier on you."

The big guy broke out in a toothy grin. "You just pressed the wrong guy."

"I think you're in for an eye opener, bozo. Or maybe I should say a spine cracker."

Cara gasped and stepped in front of Tristan, her eyes wide. "Don't," she mouthed, then swiveled back to the other man. "It's okay, Craig. Honestly. He's my...friend."

Craig shot her a disbelieving look. "What kind of friend holds a lady against her will?"

"It wasn't like that," Tristan said, though he knew damned well it was exactly like that.

"It wasn't," Cara backed him up. "We just had a disagreement. It's over now."

Craig looked from Tristan to Cara and back at Tristan, his expression one of malice. "You so much as make her raise her voice, buddy, and you'll be eating that shirt instead of wearing it."

Tristan nodded. "Thanks for the tip." He waited until the guy disappeared back inside the club's door and his temper was in check before standing and looking over at Cara. "Is that what we are these days? Friends?"

She met his eyes for a second, then looked away and hugged her arms to her body. "You know I just said that to appease him."

No, she'd said it to stop Tristan from beating the other man into a bloody pulp, which is likely what would've happened had things continued on the course they'd begun. He was more than a little thankful it hadn't come to that. "Then we aren't friends?"

"We're…" With a shake of her head, she started walking. He followed behind her, unsure where they headed and not really caring if it was anywhere so long as they were talking or at the very least spending time together again. She stopped after a few feet and turned to him. Sympathy coated her features and she reached to his face and gently probed the skin surrounding his left eye. "You really should get something on this soon. It's already starting to swell."

And it wasn't the only thing, Tristan though wryly. The instant her fingers touched down on his face, his entire body had come alive, his blood hummed and a fire of arousal charged through his body. His cock damned near stood on end with excitement. He realized in that moment just how much he hadn't felt with Brandy. She had aroused him, yes, but not nearly so intensely as what Cara could do with only a friendly brush.

He reached up and caught her fingers in his hand. *Dio,* it felt so good to be touching her again. To have her standing in front of him. He couldn't let her walk away, not even if he knew where she worked and could see her most anytime he wanted. He brought her hand to his mouth and kissed the tips of her fingers. He smiled automatically. She tasted like strawberries. "I'll put something on it…if you help."

She jerked her hand from his and stepped back. Her eyes held wariness, but the heat steaming off her body and lighting up her aura gave away her true feelings. She didn't want to leave. "It isn't that difficult a job, Tristan."

"I'm feeling dizzy." It wasn't a lie. She made him feel lightheaded, like his feet weren't quite touching the ground. She felt it too, he knew, that sense of euphoria, of connection.

Her lips twitched. "I know you better than that, Trist. It takes more than a fist to the face to make you dizzy."

He brought his hand to his face and felt sticky, warm liquid. He showed her the blood that lined his fingers. "I might not be a lightweight, but it still hurts like hell."

The sympathy returned to Cara's gaze. Her lips pressed together and her right cheek sank in slightly. He knew what she was doing, chewing on the inside, thinking. Deciding if she dare go with him. He could push that choice, sway her thoughts in his favor if he wanted to. He wouldn't do that. He needed her to want to go with him on her own, not because he'd used his powers to convince her of that fact.

Several more seconds of silence passed before her cheek filled out. She dropped her hands to her sides. "All right, Tristan. Five minutes, but only because I somehow feel responsible for this."

He didn't want her going with him out of guilt either, but at least it was better than metaphysical persuasion. "Long enough for room service to bring up a steak? My eye is stinging like a bitch, and I might need help keeping the meat pressed to it."

Her lips twitched again, then turned to a full out smile. She shot him a "you are such a bad liar" look. "Fine. Long enough for the steak to arrive and to see if you're up to the daunting task of pressing it to your eye all on your own, but not a minute more."

Chapter Four

"What is wrong with you?" Cara stilled her furious scrubbing to question her reflection in the bathroom mirror of Tristan's hotel suite.

She had no business coming here. No business in hell falling victim to Tristan's sexy smile and the boyish way that one strand of sandy brown hair fell across his forehead. And then there was the soulful look in his deep brown eyes. She knew he'd used that look on purpose, just as he'd used his smile and teasing to get her to come upstairs with him. No matter how much she knew she should say no to him, all he had to do was give her that look, that smile and she would say yes.

And that's exactly why she shouldn't be here.

They'd agreed to five minutes, or however long it might take to have a raw steak brought up to the room. She wasn't staying an instant longer. If she did stay, Tristan would talk. He would soothe her, he would ask questions. He would make her talk in return, and eventually they would quit talking and revert to touching, kissing. Loving. She wouldn't allow that to happen. She couldn't. She'd meant what she said downstairs. She was no longer a part of Tristan's life. As far as his derogatory thoughts on her appearance and career choice, she didn't care. Let him call her a hooker, let him think she enjoyed playing out that very role, it didn't matter.

Right. And that explains why you're in here scrubbing your face so hard it hurts, a little voice piped in from the back of her head.

She narrowed her eyes and returned to rubbing her face clean of the garish layers of rouge, mascara, eyeliner and glitter. "I am not doing this for him," she assured that voice.

Tristan might not care for the overloud stage makeup, but neither did she. She hadn't been gifted with much in this life, but she had been given a clear complexion, defined cheekbones and eyes that were expressive enough all on their own. She didn't need the makeup Mason insisted they wear to look attractive and neither did most of the other dancers at the Red Room.

The last of the smudges of mascara gone, Cara turned off the water and blotted at her face. She set the towel down on the sink basin and pulled her hair free of its ponytail. After a quick finger comb, she again met her reflection, and groaned.

She blew out a hot breath at the deep color she'd managed to work into her cheeks with her scrubbing. Add that to her wildly tousled hair and vibrantly glowing eyes and she looked— "Like I just spent the past five minutes standing in this bathroom preparing myself for sex. Wonderful."

The ponytail was going back in. Now.

She grabbed a brush from the shaving kit on the back of the toilet seat and was starting to gather her hair behind her head when Tristan knocked on the door. "You okay in there? If you need help with anything, just let me know."

"Fine," she called back, rolling her eyes.

The last thing she needed was his help, least of all with brushing her hair. The man was a master at hair brushing. Something about the way he ran the brush gently against her scalp, the small beaded tines over the sensitive curve of her neck and down further still was soothing yet sensual. What he'd done for her on a whim one night after they'd shared a long, steamy shower that was more pleasing than cleansing had turned into a nightly routine. One that she savored. One that the moment she closed her eyes and gave in to the arousing sensations and liquid heat the simple strokes ignited deep within her core, she never wanted him to stop. And he never did. At least not until he was ready to replace the brush's firm strokes with far more satisfying ones.

57

Her eyes drifted shut as the memory of those far more satisfying ones filled her mind. His hands were magical, mystical, and far beyond the power they held in reality. All he had to do was touch her, tease his clever fingers along her flesh, be it her arm or a far more intimate part of her body, and she'd come alive; her mound flooding with the juices of desire and her breasts throbbing to feel his exquisite touch. Her nipples hardened at the thought of his masterful mouth taking them in and drawing them tight. Her pussy pulsed with a heated wetness that was no longer in memory but actuality.

It had been so long…so very long…

"The steak's here."

The deep sound of Tristan's voice resonated through Cara's mind and knocked her from her forbidden thoughts in a flash. Her reflection stared back at her, more flushed than ever, and her eyes narrowed with scorn. Maybe it had been a long time since they'd made love, but that didn't mean she wished to bring that streak to an end. The only thing she wished to do was to leave this hotel suite and Tristan behind for good. And now that the steak was here, that's exactly what she would do.

No longer concerned about her appearance and how Tristan might interpret it, she replaced the brush and allowed her hair to fall back around her shoulders. Two minutes from now he would be out of her life and mind for good. "Thank God."

"Did you say something?"

"I said… I said thank God, I'm sure your face hurts."

* * * * *

The smile that Tristan had ready for the moment when Cara stepped out of the bathroom fell flat the second she materialized before him. She'd gone into the bathroom looking like a prostitute and come out looking like the angel he knew and loved. Her green eyes were wide and luminous and her skin alive with natural, glowing color. "*Mio dio*, you're beautiful."

Her pace faltered for an instant. Wrapping her arms around her body, she continued across the room. She pinned him with a frosty look. "Well, that's a step up from a hooker anyway."

He bit back an apology. He didn't have anything to apologize over. She had looked like a hooker. From the neck down she still did. Now, at least, she looked like a hooker in the privacy of his hotel suite. Remembering his plan for when she walked out of the bathroom, he smiled and gestured to the wheeled cart positioned next to a small round table in the dining area. "Looks like they brought more than just a steak."

Cara glanced at the uncovered cart, which held a vat of simmering chocolate surrounded by fat, red strawberries. Her eyes went from narrowed to adoring. "Oh, God, is that Godiva?"

The breathy quality of her voice ensured he'd hit his mark. If there was one thing that could turn Cara's head, or in this case stop her feet from walking out his door, it was Godiva chocolate. The strawberries were a bonus, one he hoped reminded her of their first night together.

He allowed his smile to grow into a knowing grin. "Is there any other kind?"

She looked back at him and a myriad of emotions crossed through her gaze. Finally, she shook her head. "You are an evil man, Tristan Manseletti."

Maybe. Or maybe just a man who knew the right strings to pull. "It's here now. It would be a shame to let it go to waste."

She glanced at the cart and back at him. "I'm supposed to be leaving, remember?"

Judging by her tone, she'd spoken those words in an attempt to remind herself she was supposed to be leaving as much as she had to remind him. She hadn't needed to, because she wasn't going anywhere. They both knew it. It was a simple matter of acceptance on her part.

Tristan crossed to the cart and dipped a lush strawberry into the dark chocolate. He brought it to his lips slowly, licking the sweet substance away from the berry, savoring the rich flavor aloud. Cara watched him with trembling lips and a knitted brow. In her eyes was want. A desire that Tristan could feel burning deep within her. One that went far beyond chocolate and fruit.

He selected a second juicy strawberry from the plate and dipped it into the chocolate. Holding it above his opened palm, he crossed to her and offered the berry. "What's a few more minutes between old friends? Go ahead, enjoy."

She looked from the berry so near to her mouth and back at him. Her eyes watered and her words came out terse. "I can't!"

Frustration charged through him with her declaration and Tristan fought the urge to toss the berry across the room. He drew several calming breaths and asked a question he was already too aware of the answer to. "Because I'm paying for it, right?"

Her eyes watered further. She sniffed back tears and shook her head while her full lower lip quivered. "No. Because I already had my chocolate this morning."

Both the destituteness of her expression and the absurdity of her response had laughter bubbling up in his throat. He checked the humor, and asked calmly, "You're on a once a day diet?"

She nodded, sniffing back more tears. "I have to be to stay in shape."

The amusement he'd known with her first sniff vanished, rage returning in an instant and boiling through his blood as loathing. He looked away in an effort to check his temper, but when he looked back it was still there. "So you can undress?"

Cara's tears seemed to dry in an instant. Defiance entered her eyes and she set her chin in a stubborn gesture he'd come to know well through the years. "So I can dance."

No. So she could undress. So she could flash her breasts and most of the rest of her body to drunks and lowlifes who would go home and fuck themselves to sleep while thinking of her raunchy show.

Damn it, how could she do that to herself? She was too damned smart and talented to degrade herself that way. She'd claim she did it for Joey, but if seeing to her little brother's welfare truly meant so much to her then she would have stayed working for Tristan even after they'd broken up. There had to be some other reason.

Did she find it stimulating? Would he? "Show me."

Her eyes went wide and she took a step back. "*What?*"

"Show me how you dance. If it is just dancing, then you won't mind."

She shook her head wildly. Her long red hair swished over her shoulders, giving him an idea how it would look when she was undressing. The ends of the thick, fiery strands caressed her breasts and drew his attention to her nipples. They were erect beneath her thin black shirt, the shape of them too definable for her to be wearing a bra. Definable and truth telling. Clearly she did find stripping stimulating. And as his cock throbbed restlessly beneath his slacks and briefs he realized he too was suddenly looking at her undressing in a whole new light.

Cara crossed her arms firmly, blocking his view of her breasts. "Absolutely not. You've seen me dance before, you know how I do it."

"Only once, years ago. I wasn't watching your body that night, but your mind."

Her lips pinched tight. "Stay the hell away from my mind."

Tristan sighed at the anxiety he felt storming through her. She would agree to stay with him tonight, he could already sense her relenting, but would one night of pleasure make a damned bit of difference in the long run? Her expression said it all, as had her words. She was scared of him. It wasn't a surprise, he'd always known she was scared of his powers at times, but the strength of her fear concerned him. How could he ever compete with it?

All he could do was try, and keep trying. "Please dance for me, *mia bella signora*. Just once."

"Tristan…"

There was warning in the word, but more than that was acceptance. He stepped toward her slowly, deliberately, giving her every opportunity to flee. She remained unmoving, her body and eyes heating a little more with each inch he traversed. He stopped and touched the briefest of kisses to her nose. "I won't ever ask again."

He drew back slightly and she sighed. "You shouldn't be asking now."

"You know how I hate taking no for an answer," he responded in a teasing voice, then as if to prove his point, lifted the strawberry he still held to her mouth. "Open up, baby." She did out of instinct and before any words could make their way out he fed her the juicy berry.

Her eyelids drifted shut as she chewed, and breathy moans of sheer ecstasy escaped her lips. Moans that had the erection Tristan had had since first spotting Cara swelling to a painful level. Her pink tongue darted out of her mouth to lick away the chocolate that had found its way to her lips and the action was simply too much. No longer able to have her so close and not touch her, he pulled her into his arms and caught her tongue with his. Her eyes flew open and her mouth stilled beneath his. He closed his own eyes and parted her lips wider, relishing the sweet taste of berry and chocolate and her own natural flavor.

He pulled her closer and her arms uncrossed from her chest. He accepted the unspoken invitation gladly, aligning the softness of her body to the hardness of his. She was tall, almost even with his six foot two frame in her chunky stage heels. Her hard nipples came to just beneath his chest, chafing his sensitized and quickly overheating flesh through the thin material of his polo shirt. That heat kicked up several notches as she mewled into his mouth and arched her pelvis against his groin, revealing her want with a demanding rub. Her hands came up and into his hair, and her mouth came alive, licking and feasting at his while releasing the same breathy sighs she had for the chocolate-covered berry. Only these were sweeter, far more indulgent. These were the sounds of desire that ensured she would eventually come around, that she still needed him as much as he needed her, and fear could never be enough to stand in the way of that need.

He savored her mouth and the urgency in her kiss for several long, hot seconds, and then pulled away, breathless and yet more alive than he'd felt in ages. Stepping back, he skimmed his hands along her sides and over the swell of her rapidly rising and falling breasts. Her eyes darkened with his touch, and the heat inside her threatened to explode. The heat in the room around them went from balmy to sizzling and the thickness of her hair lifted from her shoulders with the force of the rising breeze. "Dance for me, Cara."

"I shouldn't," she said, sounding as breathless as he felt.

"And you probably shouldn't be here either, but I'm glad you are. I want you here." *Where you belong.* Tristan couldn't say it, but he could show her. Or at the very least, encourage her to see things the way they were meant to be.

Taking her hand, he led her across the open sitting and dining area and into the adjoining bedroom. He dimmed the room's lighting and released her hand to sink back on the large bed. She stood in the center of the room, looking at him through uncertain eyes. She wasn't a woman of doubt but purpose, he knew. Just as he knew how little it would take to convince her to take that final step. Two simple words. "I'm ready."

Her cheek sank in for an instant, and then puffed out and she nodded. "Okay."

* * * * *

Even if she shouldn't be doing this, it wasn't a big deal, Cara reminded herself in an effort to still her stampeding heart. She danced for hundreds of men as well as women every day and night, and besides, this man had seen far more than her bared breasts. Be that as it may, she couldn't stop her hands from trembling or her voice from shaking. "Do you, uh, want music?"

"Sure." Tristan reached to the alarm clock on the end table beside the bed and tuned into a station playing a smoky Blues song. "I hope this is okay."

"It's fine." She could barely hear the music over the pounding in her head anyway.

She drew in a deep breath and exhaled it slowly. The sooner she started the sooner she would be done, and when she was done she would have proved her point and she would leave.

What was her point? That her dancing wasn't derogative the way Tristan thought? That couldn't be her point, because it was derogative. She hated it, hated every minute of it, but she would never admit that to Tristan. If she admitted it, he would demand she come back to work for him or find a job with another art dealer or supplier, and that would put her right back to square one. Seeing him, if not every day, then often enough to keep memories of the two of them and the four amazing years they'd shared together fresh in her mind and heart. She couldn't tolerate those memories when she knew it was all they could ever have together. And so she was doing this to prove a point. One she didn't even believe in.

"Do you need some inspiration?"

Cara's thoughts came to a standstill with the huskily spoken question. She shook her head. She didn't need inspiration of the nature he had in mind. "I'm preparing."

"That involves thought?"

The nerves that had bunched in her stomach the moment she agreed to dance for him turned to a pit of anger. Her job might be degrading, but it was also damned hard work. "Yes," she snapped. "It involves thought. Do you think dancing just comes naturally? We work hard at our routines. We have to exercise our asses off to stay in shape, not to mention practice for hours on end. If we miss a step, we could end up hurting not only ourselves, but those around us."

Tristan raised an eyebrow. "My mistake. I never realized the life of a stripper was so trying."

"Dancer," she corrected, struggling to keep her frustration at bay.

"Right, dancer. One who has yet to prove to me she knows how to dance." He skimmed his gaze down the length of her body as he finished the sentence, his gaze lingering on her mound and her breasts before returning to her face. "Move, Cara. It will soon be dawn."

She urged back the heat his intense look churned in her, the way his drifting gaze had her remembering the desire she'd felt in his arms seconds ago. The wetness and want his touch, his kiss made her ache with. She urged it all back, closed her eyes, and began to move.

Tristan's smile fell flat with the first rotation of Cara's hips. Her arms were in the air above her, her hair hanging long and thick down her back, and her face tipped toward the ceiling. The drapes were parted behind her and the lights of Reno gleamed electric shades of sex and sin off her glowing flesh. She looked as if she were in another place and time, as if some other being had overtaken the woman he knew. She continued to sway for several long seconds and then she opened her eyes and leveled an excited look on him. A look that had him sitting up straighter in the bed and holding his breath in anticipation.

She brought her hands to her thighs and then slid them down slowly, caressing her long, bare legs as she sank nearly to the ground and then gyrated up again. Her palms flattened over the silky smooth skin exposed between her top and her shorts and then moved upward as her hips continued to move to the music, swaying and grinding, thrusting toward him in action too erotic to ignore. Tristan didn't even attempt to do so, but allowed the energy and lust each of her moves stirred in him to take their toll on his body, tightening his balls with painful pleasure and making his cock ache to be released from the confines of his clothing.

Cara smoothed her shirt up and over her breasts and palmed the plump, naked mounds. Her gaze constant on his, she fondled her hard dusky nipples, teasing and tugging at them until a moan of pure rapture escaped her tongue-moistened lips. Her expression changed from concentrated desire to all out ecstasy as she released her nipples to rub her breasts together. She yanked the shirt free of her body completely and once more gathered the heavy mounds in her hands, rubbing, caressing, fondling the puckered and sensitized flesh. His shaft pulsed with the need to get lost between them, to feel her loving him with the bounty of her ample breasts.

Her hands left her chest and she twirled and bent, flashing her shapely ass in his face, grinding it slowly and more effectively than what his assistant, Janice, could ever hope to accomplish. The sight of her rounded butt cheeks peeking from beneath her shorts had his cock on the verge of exploding. He wouldn't explode. He'd lasted through watching Perry receive a blowjob earlier today and he would last just as well now. He had to last, he had yet to see where Cara planned to take this. She'd already bared her breasts to him and showed him more of her dance moves than what he'd ever before witnessed, he had to see if she would stop at that or continue into far more dangerous territory.

She turned back to face him and, grabbing her foot, brought her leg up parallel to her body, then slowly folded it back out. Pleasure built in her eyes and on her face with each of her gestures, each of her moves, and when she settled her leg back to the floor and started to unbutton her shorts that pleasure threatened to spiral out of control. The warmth in her body heated to the boiling point and her eyes darkened and glazed over with purpose.

Tristan felt the effects of that look and so much more as her fingers found their way inside the opened fly of her shorts to stroke her mound. The shorts slid down her slowly swaying thighs and exposed her petting moves to his view. She wore a white G-string that was already soaked with the juices of arousal. The wetness of the material grew with each of Cara's caresses, as did the heat in her eyes. Her tongue came out and danced along her lower lip, and her fingers stilled their slow, torturous moves to skim back to the hemline of her barely-there panties and then beneath.

He drew in a ragged breath with the rapid move. They had been together for four years and yet he'd never seen her masturbate, never seen her touch herself with the lights on. To watch her fondling herself, burying her fingers deep into the damp lips of her pussy, was beyond words. The idea that others watched her doing this same thing wasn't. The heat that smoldered through his body arced into a frenzy of turbulent passion and he shot to his feet and spat, "You call this dancing?"

Her eyes widened and her hand and legs stilled with the question. She opened her mouth, but no words came out. She tried again... "N-no. I don't do this at the Red Room."

Thank God, but then why was she doing it for him? Because she wanted him, Tristan realized, wanted him the way he'd been all but certain she did from the start. He could have asked her if that was the reason or looked into her emotions for the answers, but finding out through actions was far more appealing.

He went to her and attempted to pull her into his arms. She jerked away and restarted her slow, mesmerizing dance. Her hands went back to work under the small patch of material that made up the G-string's front and the sultry sweet scent of her sex filled his nostrils and had his pulse accelerating to an unhealthy level. His cock pulsed with the need to replace her fingers, to plunge into her wet cavern and make her remember just how good it was between them, how magical. How the moment they became one, the world itself seemed to stop spinning and the room around them came alive with a vitality all its own. He reached for her again, yearning to touch, to taste.

To savor the woman he'd only been able to dream of for way too long.

Cara pulled away and shook her head. "Hands off, Trist."

The words stopped him for all of a second, then he saw the teasing glint in her dark eyes, the knowing light and burning need in her expression as she slid her fingers beneath the thin straps at her sides and slid the G-string down her legs. He eyed her bared cunt with elation, the neatly trimmed red curls parted from her petting to expose the sweet pink flesh of her pussy.

He wanted to drop to his knees and sink his tongue deep into her center, lap up the juices he knew gathered in her sex. He stood his ground instead. "Hands off? Is that the rule at the Red Room? No touching? No handling the merchandise. No filling my hands with your breasts. No burying my tongue into your pussy. No licking away the come I know you're just dying to share with me. None of that, *mio bello*? Not even a single kiss?"

"N—no. None of that is allowed."

"What about here? Is it allowed here?" He chanced reaching out to her and when she didn't move away, he came closer still. He rubbed his thumb over a distended nipple, touching the rosy tip with just enough pressure to make her arch toward him. "Is this off limits?"

She glanced at his hand and then to his face. Her throat worked visibly and the breath rushed from between her lips. "It should be."

"But you don't want it to be." He continued to tease the peak of her erect nipple, aching to touch so much more, but refusing to do so until she spoke the words.

Cara stared at him in silence, their collective heavy breathing and a smoky Blues tune the only sounds to pierce the sudden stillness. Several seconds passed and she shook her head and moved into his touch, pressing the fullness of her breast against his palm. "No, and neither do you."

"Never," he admitted, allowing the emotion that surged through him to enter his voice.

He filled his hand with her breast and pulled her naked body firm to him. He moved his free hand between them and found the lips of her sex, heavy with desire and wet with the need to let go. More than eager to give her that release, he eased a finger inside the opening of her pussy and stroked. The breath whistled from her lips and she ground her cunt against his hand, needing so much more than that one digit. He needed more than that, too. He needed her, his everything. His soul mate. His destiny.

Tristan nuzzled the hair away from her neck and kissed the sensitive flesh below her ear, smiling at the expected shudder. "Let me make love to you, Cara. I promise not to scare you."

The writhing she'd begun with his entry stilled and she went rigid in his arms. His own body stiffened and he cursed under his breath. He already knew what her next words would be. That is, if she spoke at all. She might just disconnect herself from him and run, the way she was so good at doing. He wouldn't allow her to run. Not without an answer.

Catching her chin in his hand, he forced her gaze to meet his and silently demanded her response. It would be no, of that he was certain, but at least she owed it to him verbally.

She wet her lips and slowly nodded. "Okay."

The one word answer hit him hard. His heart took off, crashing madly against his ribs. The air around them screamed to life, swirling with energy and lifting the papers he'd left on the bedside table to circle in the room around them. He didn't have to look to know the papers weren't all that was moving, everything would be alive. And that meant he'd broken his promise. He was going to scare her. Scared or not, he wasn't taking back his offer, not when he needed her so badly.

"Yes?" Tristan questioned, desperate to hear her agreement one more time, fearing he'd misunderstood. Or that if he had heard Cara correctly, she would change her mind now.

She didn't change her mind, but pressed her hips against him insistently and sighed. "Yes. I need this right now more than anything else in the world."

Chapter Five

Cara needed to make love with Tristan. Needed the closure one last time in his arms would provide. She believed she'd left him behind both mentally and physically over two months ago, the day she'd told him that things were over and rushed out of his condo before he could stop her. It had taken his tracking her down in Reno and convincing her to come up to his room, but she now knew that she hadn't left him behind at all. She wouldn't leave him behind. Not until she paid one last visit to his mind and body.

"You're sure?" he asked.

She forced her smile to grow wider, while her belly twisted with anxiety. No, she wasn't sure. She hoped, prayed, believed this would work, but she was not one hundred percent sure. Of course, that wasn't what he'd meant. He meant was she sure about having sex with him. That he'd continued to ask the same question struck a chord of guilt deep within. She had to ignore that guilt and the idea he believed she was not only agreeing to make love with him, but agreeing to be a couple again. She should tell him exactly what this would mean to her. She couldn't do that because if she spoke those words he would never go through with it.

Pushing back her uncertainties, she took hold of his hand and started slowly toward the bed. "I'm sure, Trist. I want you. I want to feel you inside me. I want to taste you on my lips."

He didn't respond and he didn't need to. Cara could feel the probing heat of his gaze on her ass as she walked, could sense his growing need to get lost in her, as well as witness it in the air around them. Papers flew and the opened curtains danced in the dimly lit room as wildly as if the gusting winds of a summer storm blew through the night-darkened window. Only the window was closed and the scorching winds that surrounded them weren't those of a summer storm, but a storm of an altogether other kind. The kind that only happened when the two of them touched, kissed. Loved.

Tristan swore it was her and her alone, that only she could make it happen. That she was his destiny. That he believed it so completely and allowed his emotions to become tangled up in that idea made this all the harder to stomach. She had to stomach it, had to have her fill of him one last time, and then walk away for good.

The bed covers hovered above the bed, swaying and rippling like a sheet twisting in the breeze. She breathed a sigh of relief to know this would be the last time she witnessed it, the last time she took him into her body and felt as though she ascended to a different time and place entirely. Even if it weren't for the many outside factors — Joey's problems, Tristan's endless marriage proposals, the fact he wanted children and she refused to chance bringing more not-quite-normal people into this world — she still would be walking away after this.

She simply couldn't handle the bizarreness of it any more. Returning to her roots had reminded her only too well how disturbing her youth had been. How troubling her so-called family still was. She'd grown up in a setting as far removed from the family ideal as possible: with a mother who solicited her body to make ends meet and a father she'd seen less than a dozen times in her life.

Cara might solicit her body, but not in the physical sense and not with every stranger who waved a little green in her direction. She did it legally and for the right reason, to cement a foundation for herself and her little brother. To find the simple life they both deserved. One where she didn't fear tomorrow any more than she feared a man who with a single kiss could start an internal fire of burning need and an external chain reaction of extraordinary events that grew stronger each time they touched.

Cara reached the side of the bed, and blocked out her thoughts as she turned to Tristan. She knew a moment's sympathy for the swelled flesh that surrounded his left eye and the small, jagged slash over his cheek left behind from Craig's ring, and then dismissed it to focus on the heat in his gaze. His eyes were as dark brown as the chocolate he'd taunted her with and alive with mixed emotions of desire and love. The latter squeezed at her heart and inflated the guilt eating at her belly.

Pushing the sensations away, she released his hand and sank back against the bed. The covers fluted up at her sides and shimmied around her naked body. She ignored the abnormality of it and opened her arms and legs, beckoning him to come to her. "Make love to me, Tristan."

"Yes." He'd spoken the word before, but this time it was done with meaning. An acceptance that crackled the air with energy and warmed the room ever more.

His gaze locked on hers, he stepped back from the bed and pulled the polo shirt over his head. She sucked in a gasp at the beauty of his bared chest. Bronzed, muscled, lightly furled with sandy brown hair. A lazy trail of hair tapered down his abdomen to come to a halt at the waist of his slacks. And then, he unzipped those slacks and peeled them down his thighs along with his briefs. His cock jutted out thick and long from a thatch of pubic hair darker than that of the hair on the rest of his body, and her mouth went dry while her inner thighs heated and her pussy ached.

Tristan was an artist, one who had taught Cara nearly everything he knew. She knew a masterpiece when she saw it, and she'd also believed it would stay in her mind. She'd been wrong. His body had stayed in her mind, but not enough. Looking upon him standing naked before her now, she seriously doubted her tactics here tonight. This was to be goodbye, but all she saw in his eyes as he knelt on the bed between her bent legs was homecoming.

"I've missed you, *mia bella signora*." He cupped her buttocks in his hands and tipped her hips upward. She sucked in a breath, aware of his intentions well before his tongue touched down, slicing once across her center and awakening every nerve ending in her body. "I've missed your sweet taste." He bent his head and buried his nose against the lips of her pussy, inhaling deeply and bringing a shudder racking through her frame she couldn't stop any more than her moan. "I've missed your scent." He pulled back slightly and once more found her sex with his mouth. He laved his tongue across her swollen cunt and then plunged deeply inside.

Her eyes snapped shut with the force of his entry. She arched up and blinked at the explosion of color dancing through her brain. "Oh, God, Tristan! I've missed this too."

His nails bit into her buttocks with the admission and his tongue went from seeking to explosive, rimming her wet pussy, chafing over her clitoris, taunting her with demanding strokes that shot from her center to her curled toes and back again.

She shouldn't have admitted to missing him, his masterful mouth or any other part of him, but she hadn't been able to stop herself. Just as she couldn't stop her body's reaction now. Heat sizzled through her, beading her flesh with perspiration. Her heart pounded and the breath wheezed from her lungs. She didn't have to open her eyes to know he was covered in sweat as well, that his own breathing was labored, his sense of here and now becoming fogged. She could feel the energy radiating through them, feel his control slowly slipping away, the strength of his tongue growing ever stronger, more inhuman, more magical and more intense.

His grip on her ass turned almost painful and the thrust of his tongue chaotic, lashing at her, branding her, divesting her of the ability to concentrate. The colors that flashed through her mind grew brighter. Her pussy throbbed and her frame shook with the beginnings of a soul-bending climax. She fought the urge to let go and fall over the edge, aware her trembling was too intense, the fire flaming within her too powerful. It wouldn't be simple pleasure, but so much more.

Yet, as much as she knew it, she was powerless to stop it. The orgasm overtook her, rippling through her body, firing her blood to the boiling point, transporting her if not in body, then in mind to a place and time far removed from this one. Images filled her mind, images that felt more like reality. Scattered flashes of her and Tristan and many others, garbed in flowing layers of white and gold, of children laughing, of fields of rolling green and gold, of the summer sun streaming down upon them. And of that look, that look of Tristan's she could never say no to, as he professed his everlasting love.

She hated this place, hated the fact it could never be, that it was nothing more than an altered state of her mind. A part of her also loved it. Loved to think that if only for the short while she was in his arms, she could go here, to this place where there was warmth and light, laughter and music. No evil, no sorrow, only happiness.

Tristan released his hold on Cara's buttocks and breathed in a disconcerted sigh. He hadn't meant for that to happen, to push her that far, into a realm he knew she hated to traverse. Her body had ceased its trembling, but her eyes were still closed and her lips pressed into a harsh line.

"Cara, baby, are you here with me?" Her expression remained unyielding and he moved to the bed beside her and pulled her into his arms.

Merda! Why couldn't he have held onto his control a bit longer? At least until they were joined as one, when he would have gone with her into that other place and helped to ease her troubled thoughts. She would still have been angry with him, but she wouldn't have been alone.

"Cara," he soothed near her ear, "come back to me. Tell me that you hate me."

Several more seconds of silence passed where he continued to berate himself and his stupidity, and then her eyes flickered open. He smiled his relief and rubbed his thumb over the high arch of her cheekbone. "I'm sorry for that. It's just been such a long time and I told you I've missed you."

"It's okay."

The words were barely a whisper and, between that and the sorrow reflected in her heavy gaze, ensured what he'd already guessed. It wasn't okay. "I know you hate going there, and I never meant for it to happen. At least, not by yourself."

"I said it's okay, Tristan," she said louder, shaking away his hand as she came up on her elbows. "I know it was an accident, but I didn't mind."

"Honestly?"

The remorse left her expression and she set her chin and nodded. "Honestly."

He wanted to believe that look, that in the months they'd been apart she'd become accepting of all that happened when they touched, of what they were truly meant to be to one another, and was now ready to embrace it fully, but he knew better. Even if it weren't for his ability to see that she was lying reflected in the dimmed rays of her aura and the turbulent emotions that tumbled through her body, he could tell by her physical response. The way the tip of her nose twitched and her voice became just a bit strained.

Tristan was tempted to question why she bothered to lie to him about her feelings now when she'd never done so in the past, but he couldn't bring himself to speak the words. They would only end in argument and whatever progress he'd made here so far tonight would be lost. He wouldn't lose the progress any more than he would lose her.

Easing her back on the bed, he nibbled a kiss at the corners of her mouth, then sank his tongue between her lips, making love to her mouth slowly until he felt the tension within her turn from anxiety to anticipation. In those moments when she'd been gone from him and then when she'd returned to him, he'd forgotten about his own needs. Now as he tasted her renewed desire, the heat in him was restored. The air around them returned to its erratic nature, crackling, sizzling, filling the dimly lit room with flashes of dazzling color and a spiral of effects lifted from tables and chairs and the floor throughout the suite.

Cara's mouth turned from languid to needy and her palms settled on his back, her nails edging into his muscled flesh and pushing his resolve to go slower this time, to ensure if she went to that place again it would be with him at her side. She arched her hips against him and his cock rubbed against her pussy. He sucked back a hard breath and drew away from her mouth. She was already so wet, so swollen. He could drive into her with one long thrust and explode just as easily.

He wouldn't do that yet, not when there were questions still left unanswered. Namely, the question that had urged him to go back to the Red Room and discover if it had indeed been Cara he'd seen earlier in the night.

Tristan came up on an elbow and smiled down at her flushed face, her eyes dark jade and full of expectation, her lips rosy red and swollen. Always so beautiful, his Cara. A beauty that didn't hurt as Brandy's had done to him. Brandy. He'd all but forgotten the woman and the unexpected sensations she evoked in him. He couldn't forget her any longer. Not until he had his answer. Not until he knew if Cara could read him mind and body the way he'd always believed she could.

"What am I thinking?" he asked.

The anticipation in her eyes died and she frowned. "What?"

"What do you think is going through my mind right now?" he pressed. He didn't want to ruin this moment, the progress, but he had to know, had to try to understand what it was that he'd experienced with Brandy. If it were anything at all, or merely his imagination. Most importantly, if it even begun to come close to what he felt with Cara. "Tell me what I'm thinking right now, *mio bello*. I know you can."

Her cheek sank in slightly and she hesitated a long moment before shaking her head. "I...I don't know."

But she did. The twitching of her nose, the momentary gray shimmers in her aura, the flicker of panic in her eyes, they all spoke the truth. She knew what his thoughts were, not in exact definition but in general, just as he knew hers. She held back telling him so out of fear. "Please tell me, Cara. I need to understand how you're affected by me. I know what happens in your body, but I can't begin to understand your mind. Not unless you help me."

She looked thoughtful, troubled almost, and then dismissed it all with a shrug. "You're thinking of how much you want me, and you're afraid if you don't start doing something about it soon, I'll leave. You're right, Trist, I will."

He laughed shortly. That wasn't what he'd been thinking and she knew it, just as he knew how sincere her words were. If he wished to keep her here with him, then he needed to put his questions to rest for the night. He could do that, there would be other days to find answers and in a way she'd already given him the most important one. She could read him, mind and body. She knew his intentions without having to ask, and that meant what he'd always believed to be true was accurate. She was his destiny, his soul mate, and whatever he thought he'd experienced with Brandy had been nothing more than a mistake conjured up by his loneliness.

Tristan settled back between her thighs and found her mouth in a long, hot kiss meant to disorient. "You're not leaving, Cara." *Because you know you belong here with me.*

The sudden stillness of her lips guaranteed it, she could read him all right and it scared the hell out of her. Before she could attempt to pull away, he applied more pressure with his mouth and sank his cock deep inside the wet folds of her pussy. He pulled back and thrust deep once more. With a throaty mewl, her mouth came to life, as did her body. Her hands moved wildly, gripping, rubbing, fondling. Her tongue the same, suckling at his, gliding over his damp, salty flesh, then dipping into the hollow of his ear. He shuddered at the feel of her hot, wet tongue licking at the sensitive skin and the pumping of their joined bodies increased to a whole new level, the tempo chaotic and signaling the beginning of the end of their control.

Images spun through his mind, fragments of the same unknown time and place Cara had been moments ago. The same place Cara was now, Tristan knew as her teeth found his neck and bit into his flesh while her nails pinched deep into his back. On some level he was conscious of the pain, of the fact he too was being too rough, his hands palming her ass too hard and his own short nails biting into her soft flesh until moans of anguish filled the air. More, though, he was aware of Cara beneath him on the golden fields of a land with no name. The sun beat warm upon his naked back and her breathy cries of ecstasy filled his senses as her pussy contracted around him. Her dark eyes held his with a devotion that went well beyond the thresholds of space and time.

Her cries died away, and Tristan rolled her until she straddled him. Her waterfall of deep red hair crowned the classical beauty of her face and her full, supple breasts heaved inches from his mouth. He pulled an aroused nipple between his lips, biting down at the swollen red crown. She arched her hips in response and took his cock deeper yet, enfolding him completely within the tight, wet walls of her cunt, milking his shaft with near painful pressure. The sun beat down on his face, its growing brilliance threatening to blind him as the orgasm built within him. He refused to close his eyes and shut out the pain. He had to see Cara's face, had to see her passion, her ecstasy when he came inside her. He had to know she felt as he did.

"Say the words, Cara," he ordered, his voice not quite his own, but his all the same.

Her pussy opened wide and then squeezed tightly around his cock, shuddering around his shaft with the subtle demand in his tone. Once more climax overtook her and had her gripping his forearms and riding him hard, pressing his back into the softness of the lush field, and bringing his own orgasm to the surface.

He couldn't hold back any longer and when she responded to his command with a broken, "I love you, Tristan. You are my destiny, my partner for all of time, my everything," he gave in to the heat and need boiling through him completely.

His seed filled her and her own release washed over him, cleansing him, bringing him salvation he'd been without for too long.

In this time and place there had always been magic, happiness, and yet in this moment he also knew sorrow. Remorse that he couldn't define. Before he could think on it any further or question her heavy gaze, he left that place behind and opened his eyes to find himself staring up at the bedroom ceiling of a steamy, dimly lit hotel suite.

For an instant as he lay there catching his breath, Tristan thought it had all been a dream. Then he heard Cara's sleepy sigh and felt her weight on him, her sex still encircling his own and knew it wasn't a dream at all. They'd gone back to that place, that place she hated. Only this time it had been different. This time something had happened in the end. There hadn't been any long, lingering looks or happy moments of afterglow bliss. They hadn't returned to their home where they were loved and revered by adults and children alike that they didn't know outside of that place. They hadn't exchanged words of adoration aside from those he'd commanded from her. Something had been very different this time around. Something that frightened him beyond logic.

What did that say of Cara?

She would have experienced it as well, and while he hated to linger on a subject that in the past she never wished to speak of, he had to question her. He glanced down at her body, so still over his, her breathing so deep, and realized this question, like so many others, would have to wait. She was asleep and he wouldn't wake her. Not at the risk of having her leave the moment he did.

Holding her against him, Tristan reached for the tangle of covers that surrounded them. One of the sheets had found its way to the floor and lay in a jumble of disarray along with scattered paperwork, a handful of glasses, a detached phone cord, and a few errant strawberries that had made their way in from the other room. He would worry about the chaos their loving had caused in the morning. For the next few hours he would concentrate on only one thing, the woman in his arms and how he would keep her there. And he would keep her there.

"*T'amo, mia bella signora.* No matter what it takes we will end up together."

* * * * *

Cara woke to find dim sunshine streaming in on her through an opened window. She only had one window in her apartment and that was in the kitchen. It didn't feel like a kitchen table beneath her. It felt like a man. A warm, virile, magical man who held the power to rob her of her better judgment and make her do something so rash as to not only come up to his hotel suite and succumb to the allure of Godiva-dipped strawberries, but to succumb to the man himself.

Her mound heated with the memory of feeling his tongue within her, lapping at her aroused sex, then his cock overtaking it, sliding into her, driving her on, pushing her to that place that was theirs and theirs alone. The place that she'd left behind for good last night. She knew Tristan had felt her pulling away, that by rescinding her emotions from the moment she'd managed to alter the outcome of their joint imaginings. It had been nearly impossible to separate her feelings from her actions, particularly while removed from this plane, but she'd had to do it. It was the only way to fully disconnect herself from him, and in time he would understand what it had meant.

This morning he wouldn't, and so she had to get of here before he woke.

Cara glanced at the alarm clock that dangled by its cord from the end table next to the bed. It was still before seven. If she hurried home, she would have time to both get more sleep and deal with her feelings before driving over to Joey's school this afternoon. As much as she might have been able to separate her emotions from her actions last night, she couldn't do so permanently. This morning her belly twisted tight with guilt and self-loathing. It would be so easy to forget everything—why they couldn't be together, why they would both be so much better off alone—and climb back into bed with Tristan. She couldn't do it. Not in good conscience. Her leaving would hurt them both, but in the long run they would be better off for it.

Sniffing back tears she refused to cry while still in his arms, she slid from the bed and sorted through the chaos on the floor for her abandoned clothing. Remembering the way she stripped for Tristan last night brought warmth careening into her cheeks and an empty longing deep into her sex. Her pussy throbbed and she had to force herself to shut out all thought, all sensation and hastily tug her clothes on. She found her high-heeled sandals among the jumble, one under the bed and one in the windowsill, then moved soundlessly to the bedroom door.

"Cara."

She froze at the raspy sound of Tristan's voice and her heart took off. Slowly, she turned around...and sighed. He had rolled over onto his stomach, but he was still asleep. Asleep and dreaming about her, she thought on a heavy sigh that squeezed pressure on her heart and threatened her tears to break free. She was doing the right thing. It might not feel like it now, but it was. They would both come to realize it. They had to.

She took one long last look at his body, naked from the knees up, committing to mind each angle, each muscle, each hard line. And then raised to the dark, beautiful marking on his back, the glyph that spoke of who, or rather what, he was and therefore why they could never be. Even though she was on the opposite side of the room she reached out automatically. Her fingers itched to trace over the circle and descending cross that joined to form the shape of femininity. She yearned to open her mouth and ask him to tell her the tale that surrounded his birth—a tale Cara loved to hear recounted, even if no one knew for certain that it rang true.

She let her hand fall back, knowing she wouldn't hear it ever again and that she should be happy for it. The story might be mystical, it might even be beautiful in its own right, but it was also sorrowful. It was the sorrow she couldn't handle, wouldn't allow others to go through. It was the sorrow that threatened to overtake her as she slipped from the suite and quickly made her way back to her apartment across town.

Cara breathed a sigh of relief when her apartment door came into sight. The building was rundown and the walls covered in graffiti. It was never a sight that brought her relief in the past. This morning it did for the express reason she was about to break down. The emotions she'd managed to bottle up last night and hold back this morning, now welled to the breaking point. Her eyes stung with unshed tears and her belly crimped with ache and remorse. She had to get inside, and fast.

She was unlocking the door when a familiar voice called out from behind her, "Hey, stranger."

Damn it. There was no way she would be able to hide her sorrow from her friend. She and Brandy might not have known each other long, but it only took a short while to know when another was in misery. She turned and said as nonchalantly as possible, "You're up early."

"Or you're in late, depending on how you look at it." Brandy tipped her head to the side and frowned. "I was hoping it was a good night, but by the looks of things I'm guessing it was more like a rough one."

"Honestly, I think it was a little of both."

Her black eyebrows darted together and it looked like she wanted to say more. Instead, she shrugged and asked, "Are you working tonight?"

No, thank God. Cara couldn't stomach dancing again so soon. Not when she knew the moment she started, she would think of Tristan, see the hot look in his eyes, remember he didn't approve of her job and even though she shouldn't care, she would. "I have the night off, but I plan to drive over and visit Joey this afternoon, so I don't know when I'll be back around."

"In that case maybe I can get you to take a rain check. I know how much you love chocolate and I just got my hands on my mother's famous Death by Chocolate cake recipe." She licked her lips. "Let me be the first to say it's truly sinful."

"Oh, God, it sounds heavenly." And exactly like the pick-me-up she needed.

Brandy smiled. "More like to die for."

"All right. I'm convinced. Put me down for that rain check please."

Her smile kicked higher. "You betcha. Just give me a couple hours notice and I promise I'll make you a cake so killer you'll never eat anything else again."

Chapter Six

"'Bout time, man. I was beginning to think you weren't going to show."

Tristan made it a point not to make eye contact as he settled into the seat across from Perry in one of the Lazy Ace's several restaurants. He needed coffee damned bad, before he could talk or even think about all that had happened last night, with both Brandy and Cara. He signaled to the waitress pouring coffee at the table next to them and waited for her to fill his mug and retreat before responding with a shrug. "I had some cleaning to do."

"Cleaning? What the hell do you think I'm paying the housekeeping staff for."

Not to clean up the chaos caused by an indoor tornado, Tristan thought humorlessly as he pulled back a long drink of strong black coffee. Obviously the time and distance he'd spent away from Cara had factored into the turmoil left in the wake of last night's lovemaking. The suite had been nearly beyond repair: chocolate sauce spread from one end to the other and strawberries smashed into the pale tan carpet and embedded in walls and doors throughout the place.

He set the mug down and met Perry's gaze for the first time since entering the establishment. "I didn't think they'd quite understand how I managed to not only rip the cord off my phone, but bury the cradle so far into the ceiling it would take supernatural strength to get it back out."

Perry had started to look away. His attention now zinged back to Tristan's face. "Whoa! Nice shiner, man. I take it the deal went sour?"

"I wish." If only this were about the Eye. He wanted to get his hands on it damned bad, and yet his need to figure out what he'd experienced with Brandy versus what he felt with Cara was even greater. More than that, he needed to know what had happened last night in that moment before he returned to the world of the here and now, why the vision had ended so differently this time.

"Then what the fuck hap...?" Perry droned off and his eyes narrowed shrewdly. "Lucas, right? He called and you ended up arguing? It's got to be him, he's the only one I know who can set your carefully composed control off."

Almost the only one. One other person could do it. And Cara could do it far better and easier than what Lucas could even imagine. "Lucas and I are fine. And even if we weren't, how the hell do you think he could give me a black eye over the phone?"

Perry dismissed the question with a shrug. "Knowing you two the way I do, I wouldn't put it past either of you. If not Lucas, then who?"

"Cara." The name was out of Tristan's mouth before he could stop it. He groaned inwardly and his gut twisted with derision. He wasn't yet ready to think about her. He sure as hell wasn't ready to talk about her.

"Cara's here?"

He nodded stiffly, hating having to speak the words aloud, knowing he had no choice now that he'd started talking. The twisting in his gut intensified with the idea she'd be back onstage and sharing her body with the world in just a few short hours, dancing for countless strangers the way she had for him. His cock stirred with the memory of her undressing before him, her fingers sliding beneath the white G-string, the smell of her arousal coloring the sweltering air. His erection pulsed to full attention and his heart took off at a gallop.

He shook the images away and forced his attention back to the matter at hand, back to Cara's stripping. "She's back working at the Red Room. The one in town."

Perry gave his head a disbelieving shake. "No way, man. Why would she do that?"

Good question. One he would kill to know the answer to, preferably that bastard of a bouncer who he had to thank for his throbbing face. Only the guy wasn't a bastard, he'd just been doing his job. The fact Cara had a man like that looking out for her was a blessing if anything.

Tristan took another long drink of coffee, then set the mug back and picked up his menu, hoping to turn from this conversation before it went any farther. "She says she's doing it for Joey. That she needs the money to pay his tuition."

"Last thing I knew you were paying the kid's bills. Or did you stop when she moved out?"

"Hell, no, I didn't stop," Tristan returned too sharply, smacking his menu back against the table. He drew a calming breath and cursed under his breath. Yeah, only Cara could rattle him this badly, destroy his tranquility like no other. "I never plan to stop paying them. The thing is she still doesn't know I ever started."

The cutting words he'd spoken about Joey last night returned in a flash and demolished any remaining lust the memory of Cara's stripping had stirred. He loved the kid, and he'd been an idiot to ever allow her to believe differently. Only she couldn't have believed it. She had to have taken his apology last night sincerely, or she'd never have come upstairs with him.

"So what's with the face then...and the phone?"

"Bouncer. And sex."

Tristan expected a laugh, but instead Perry's forehead knit with lines and he asked soberly, "You're back together?"

He stared at the other man for a long moment, reading into his body, his emotions. The gravity of his expression. Someone had done him wrong, or perhaps it was the other way around and he'd lived to regret it. Whatever the case, Perry was hurting and doing his damnedest to hide the fact. "I don't know what we are," he admitted. "Cara was gone when I woke up this morning and…"

"Yeah?"

"Nothing." By the looks of things, Perry already had enough on his platter. Even if he didn't, it wouldn't matter. Nothing was to be gained by Tristan revisiting last night aloud, and trying to explain the vision or the world or whatever the place was he and Cara went in the midst of their lovemaking. It wasn't going to help one damned bit to dwell on the fact he hadn't gotten to wake up with her in his arms and spend the morning showing her how much he truly had missed her, how much he loved her. How much they belonged together. The only thing that was going to help right now was more coffee and a plate of fresh grilled grease in the form of sausage and eggs.

Tristan returned to perusing his menu. "Outside of the waitress who poured my coffee, I haven't seen a server since I sat down. How's a guy go about getting some food in this place?"

"It doesn't seem like her style."

He glanced over the edge of his menu at Perry's words. "What?"

"Cara. I obviously don't know her as well as you and haven't seen her in years, but she never seemed the type to fuck a guy just for laughs."

"We don't…" *Fuck.*

Jesus, that sounded so cold, so unfeeling. But if it wasn't fucking, then what had last night been? He'd called it lovemaking. But if it had been lovemaking would Cara have disappeared with the morning light? Damn, he didn't need more questions.

Tristan dragged a weary hand through his hair and reached once more for his now nearly empty coffee mug. "Look, I don't know what she thinks it was about, and I also don't really care to talk about it, *capische*?"

It didn't look like Perry understood; not when worry lines continued to etch his forehead and his lips were set firmly. The severe expression passed and he shrugged. "Whatever you say, man. But if you do decide to talk, know that I'm here for you."

"The feeling's mutual."

"And by that you mean?"

"That I don't think I'm the only one with woman problems."

A smirk claimed Perry's face and he glanced down at his menu. A menu Tristan knew he'd read a thousand times over. After several seconds of silence, Perry tossed the menu to the side of the table and looked back at him. "What the hell makes you think that?"

"What doesn't? Your emotions are twisted up in knots, you scowl more than you crack jokes, which is totally out of character, and your aura has 'big goddamned mess' written all over it."

Perry's typically light blue eyes darkened a few shades as annoyance passed through them. He laughed shortly then and glanced away, looking around the restaurant. "You're right, man. The server should have been here long ago." He pushed back his chair and stood, already starting for the back of the establishment. "Grab some more coffee from the burner against the wall there-" he nodded to the right side of the room, " —and I'll see if I can make a few heads roll in our direction."

* * * * *

"Cara."

Cara breathed a sigh, letting free the breath she'd been holding since walking into Joey's room a half minute before. He looked like a normal eight year old, laying belly down on his bed watching T.V. She knew once she made her presence known the façade of normalcy would fade. That he would look at her with vacant eyes that ensured he hadn't been watching T.V. at all and if he had, he probably hadn't understood the cartoon currently on the screen. Only the joyous light in his green eyes as he looked at her now and the sound of her name on his lips made her believe he might have been watching and comprehending every word.

Smiling, she crossed to a twin bed decorated in a Dragon Ball Z sheet set and matching comforter and pulled him into a hug. Her heart squeezed tight and emotion clogged her throat when he put up a token fight.

Today was going to be a good day.

The days that Joey not only knew her name, but that he was getting too old to be treated like a baby, were always good ones.

"Hi, sweetie." She ruffled his short reddish-brown hair, laughing at his scowl. "How are you?"

"Good."

"I spoke with your teacher. She said you've been asking about me."

He nodded shortly, then returned his focus on the T.V. "Yeah."

"Did you miss me?"

"Yeah." He responded without looking back at her.

She sat on the bed beside him and glanced at the television where a talking pink starfish blew bubbles at a talking yellow sponge decked out in pants, shirt and a tie. "I missed you too."

"Yeah."

She turned away from the antics on the television set and frowned. Joey had moved into one word sentences that consisted of yeah and very little else. In other words, this visit might not go so well after all.

Desperate to distract him from the T.V., which seemed to be sucking what little attention span he had away from her, she stood and went to the wall decorated in various paintings and drawings. He would never be Picasso, but Joey's works were masterpieces all the same.

Her attention wavered to a picture of a woman with long red hair and a tall man in a suit holding her hand. "That's new, right? I don't remember seeing it last week."

"Yeah." Once more he responded without looking up.

"Who is it of?" she asked louder, trying to force his gaze on her.

"Cara."

He still stared at the T.V., but his response told her he was listening. It also brought the emotions in her throat to the back of her eyes. "You drew a picture of me. That's sweet." She pointed to the man holding her hand in the picture. "And is this you?"

"Trist."

She swiveled back around sharply, guessing she'd heard him wrong. "What?"

Joey finally looked her way. His mouth curved into what she knew to be his happy smile, though it barely turned his lips at all. "Trist," he repeated.

Cara's heart sped, beating against the walls of her chest painfully and rehashing every one of the thoughts and emotions she'd managed to force back earlier this afternoon. "It's Tristan?" she asked, hating the way her voice quavered, praying he hadn't heard it as well.

His smile hiked up slightly. "Yeah. Trist."

Oh, God. It wasn't enough Tristan had tracked her down and was infiltrating her life, showing her how good it was between them, how much she still loved him and not even blocking her emotions out could take that away, but he was moving in on Joey as well. "Has Tristan been here to see you, Joey? Has he come by the school?"

His smile remained locked in place, his gaze constant on the picture, but no words made their way out of his mouth.

"Joey?" she pressed after several long seconds of silence.

"Yeah."

"Tristan came here to see you?"

Again silence greeted her. She puffed out a hot breath, frantic to know the answer. "Joey, was Tristan here or not?

"Yeah," he replied once more, the same monotonous tone, his gaze still constant on the picture. His response about as reliable as the weather forecast.

Damn it! She wasn't going to get an answer. At least, not from Joey. The school staff would know if Tristan had been here, if he'd come to this place he had no right being.

He has every right, the little voice in the back of Cara's head shouted. Not only was he the one to help you find this school and work out an affordable payment plan, but he loves Joey and Joey loves him.

They were good for each other.

The truth in the thought chased away the tension in her body. She smiled automatically and returned to the bedside. "Tristan does love you. And you seem to do better after he visits. Maybe if he hasn't already come by I can ask him to."

Joey's eyes brightened with rich light. "Yeah. Tristan's nice."

Yeah, he was. Especially his mouth, his hands, and every other part of his wonderfully honed body. She pushed the inappropriate thought and accompanying desire aside and focused on what mattered most. Joey. If bringing Tristan here, presuming he hadn't already come himself, would make her little brother happy then she would do it. "Would you like it if I brought Tristan by some time?"

"Yeah. Tomorrow. Bring him tomorrow."

Not tomorrow. It was way too soon to see him again. The emotions would still be too fresh, the memories of last night too close to the surface. Next week…if he were still in town by then. "I don't know about tomorrow, but maybe soon, okay?"

"Yeah. Soon. Bring Trist soon."

The happiness in Joey's voice and on his face was too much to deny. She would bring Tristan here before the week was over, even if seeing him again so soon destroyed any chance she had of completely saying goodbye to him in both heart and mind. "What do you say we go outside for a while? The air will be good for us both."

Joey leaped off the bed. "There's air at the park. Lots of air."

The exuberance in his actions, the clarity of his words, reminded Cara once again of a normal kid. The doctors had said when he was born there was only a one in one hundred chance he would ever move past his disabilities, that the effects of the substances their mother had put into her body during his pregnancy were likely irreversible. In her heart, especially at moments like this, Cara believed that Joey would overcome their mother's stupidity and be that one in a hundred. She believed one day they would both have the simple, normal life they deserved. The kind they could never have with Tristan. At least, not with Tristan as part of their family, but maybe as a friend there was still hope.

"The park, is it?" she asked quickly, before her feelings could once more rise up to choke her. "All right. One park coming up. Anything for you, kiddo. Anything at all."

* * * * *

Tristan stood at the opened front doors of the Red Room, determined to remain calm no matter what happened here tonight. In a way, he should be happy. Brandy had changed her mind about meeting at her place tonight and had e-mailed to say they would meet at the Red Room at seven and decide where to go from there. And in a way, he was happy. Relieved he wouldn't be spending the evening mere feet from her bedroom after the way last night's meeting had unfolded and his ensuing refusal to have sex with her. In another way, he wasn't happy in the least.

His muscles were disturbingly tight and while he'd yet to experience the charge of heat he felt whenever Cara was within fifty feet of him that didn't mean she wasn't working tonight. Then there was the other reason he wasn't contented. Not going to Brandy's place meant not seeing the Eye.

He had another week before he was due back in Ashton, a week he could easily extend to more if necessary, but that didn't mean he wanted to wait that long to get his hands on the Eye. The orb was the sole reason he'd come to Reno. While that purpose might have since grown, it was critical that he realigned his priorities. Last night and this morning he'd been certain that getting to the bottom of his reaction to Brandy and subsequently how it might affect him and Cara was priority number one. As the day progressed and he'd had to time think things over more clearly, he'd realized just how wrong he'd been.

If *l'occhio della Tempesta* proved to be all that he had been told in his youth. If it could indeed reveal the truth of not only his past and present, but of his future. Then he wouldn't need to discover what was meant for him or anyone else. He would simply know.

"In business mode I see."

Tristan turned at the lilting feminine voice and found himself looking into Brandy's smoke gray eyes. A beguiling smile curved her full pink lips. He grinned back before the realization of how she might interpret the action hit him. It was a friendly smile, he ensured himself, and hoped she took it the way it was meant. "Guilty," he lied. "I was wondering how they were holding out back in Ashton."

"Ah. The old 'when the cats away the mice will play' syndrome." Her mouth tipped higher and her thick black lashes batted coyly, in a way that was as old as time and completely unexpected of her. "Or maybe in your case, tiger would be a better choice of euphemism. A tiger who spent last night on the prowl by the looks of things."

She brushed her fingers over the bruised flesh of his left eye and he bit back a grunt at his body's response, the internal warming, the external hardening. His eye still hurt like hell and her touch should have hurt even more so, instead it felt almost therapeutic. Her caress turned more insistent and his skin heated even as his shaft swelled further.

The extensive reaction might have confused him, might have made him second guess his belief Brandy couldn't read him the way he'd once thought, if not for the fact he finally understood what it was about her that called to him, enough to hit on his control. It wasn't that she knew him, or that she was destined to be his anything, it was precisely to the contrary. She didn't know a thing about him outside of what was common knowledge. She thought he was an aggressor, a tiger who saw what he wanted and went after it. She thought of him in a way that no one outside of his business colleagues ever had and he was momentarily reveling in her confusion.

Enjoying her misunderstanding and the effects it had on his body or not, it was time for the gratification to end and business to begin.

Doing his best to ignore his expanding erection, Tristan lifted her hand from his face and nodded toward the strip of casinos and businesses that extended in either direction. "Where do you suggest we go?"

"Your choice, I live here. Besides I told you last night I wanted to get to know Tristan Manseletti the man. Seeing how you react to your surroundings and the choices you make is the best way I can think of."

The words confirmed his deduction. She wanted to unveil the tiger she believed he was and for reasons that were far removed from business.

Her persistence should bother him. Things would be far easier if Brandy accepted him as a business associate and nothing more. His own attraction should bother him even more. It should worry him a hell of a lot that as much as he loved Cara and wanted to be with her, he could still stand here and be aroused by the simple presence of another woman. And maybe it did bother him. He honestly didn't now.

He did know one thing. They needed to get out of here. If Cara was working tonight, the last thing he wanted was for her to see him with another woman. She had never been the jealous type and yet he had a feeling her seeing him with Brandy would be all the further motivation she needed to remove herself from his life permanently.

"What do you say we walk until I see something that grabs me?" he asked.

The look she shot him as she slid her arm through his suggested she could think of a thing or two that might do so. He didn't question that look and she didn't speak on it as they made their way along the light-brightened, bustling sidewalk.

After several minutes of casual walking conversation, Brandy came to a standstill. "Do you dance?"

Tristan glanced at the pink and blue canopy of the dance club they stood in front of and his gut tightened. Pressing himself so close to her supple curves was the last thing he should want to do. Yet the mere thought of her breasts rubbing up against his chest, her pelvis gyrating against his own had his erection returning full force and his temperature rising. Dancing was a damned bad idea, and he ached to do just that.

He shrugged, effectively removing her arm from his in the process, and freeing himself from temptation. "I can dance, but a quieter environment would be more conducive to business."

"You're right, of course. But then it's early and business can wait."

He should say no, that business couldn't wait. But what if no wasn't any longer an option? What if a transaction he'd once believed to be based on money alone was now contingent upon his agreement to sleep with her? Was he up to the challenge? Physically the answer was apparent, but mentally could he go through with it?

He forced humor into his tone. "I suppose it can, but what happened to my calling the shots?"

"I changed my mind." Flashing him what could only be termed a naughty smile, Brandy took hold of his arm again and tugged him into the club and directly onto a revolving hardwood dance floor.

It was early enough in the night that the place had few patrons and that gave Tristan all the more reason to want to turn back before it was too late. Feeling her rubbing up against him in a crowded, smoky bar was one thing. Feeling her doing so in the heated intimacy of a room that was mostly theirs alone was a whole other.

The overhead speakers blasted a fast-moving beat and strategically placed strobe lights flickered splotches of yellow, blue and green onto their bodies. The colors seemed unnatural, in that they took the elegant lines of Brandy's face and turned them into a thing of etherealness. Her lips had been a soft pink in the lights of the strip. Now they were a muted shade of red and pouty. Her eyes held the same secret promise they'd contained last night and her body was already moving to the music.

He watched her sway and gyrate her limbs encased in a flowing gown of pale yellow silk, and was taken back to the previous night, watching Cara strip. Her clothing had fallen away piece by piece until she stood before him, naked and glistening. Her legs longs and shapely, her ass rounded perfectly and her breasts full and waiting to fill his palms. The scent of her sex had hung heavily in the sweltering air. He couldn't stop himself from sinking between her splayed thighs, burying his tongue deep into her pussy, licking at the sweet taste of her come. Just as he couldn't stop his cock from straining with heady need at this moment.

The pressure on his balls had more to do with his thoughts of Cara than the woman dancing before him now, but when Brandy stopped her dancing to jerk him into her arms and whisper loudly, "Give it a try. You'll like it," he gave in all the same.

Tristan pressed his pelvis flush against hers and gave himself over to the pulsing music. It was nothing he would ever have listened to himself, but here tonight it felt right. The slide of Brandy's hands over his body, under his shirt to chafe along his heated flesh felt more than right. The insistent press of her breasts against his chest and the grinding of her cunt against his cock had him ready to explode. One small graceful hand snaked beneath the edge of his khakis and past his briefs to grasp his engorged shaft and a moan escaped before he could stop it.

Her mouth returned to assail his ear with hot, teasing breath. "I was right. You do like it. But I know something you'll like even more."

The warmth that boiled through his body, weighting his limbs and setting his blood afire told him she was right indeed. She might not be his destiny, but she could affect him in a way no other woman outside of Cara ever had. Mentally he might live to regret it, but the reality was she had something he would like very much, something he burned with the need to experience. Something they would experience together on this dance floor for everyone to witness if they didn't stop their actions damned soon.

Tristan set her back and whimpered as her skilled palm left his cock.

She raised a black eyebrow. "Tired already?"

"No. It's just...hot in here." It wasn't a lie. It was hot in here. The temperature had risen several degrees from the moment they'd stepped onto the dance floor and he could feel sweat beading his forehead and the rest of his body. It glistened over her flesh as well, giving him all the more motivation to strip her clothes away and bare her smooth skin to the kiss of the air and that of his lips.

"Very hot," Brandy agreed. "I have something that will cool you off at my place."

"I thought you didn't want to go there?"

Her mouth tipped wide and she extended her palm, offering so much more than just a hand to hold. "I changed my mind again. Unless you don't want to go there."

He shouldn't—God help him, he shouldn't, but he did. "I do."

Her lips curved higher and excitement gleamed in her eyes. "Then let's move."

"Let's." The sooner they did, the sooner he would have some answers. Be they the ones he'd originally come to Reno to find or merely the ones his body now craved.

Chapter Seven

The slamming of the apartment door at his back was the only sound Tristan acknowledged outside of that of his and Brandy's heavy breathing. She lived in a rundown tenement in a far from safe looking neighborhood on the opposite side of town as the casino district. He'd expected so much more from a woman like Brandy. A woman whose tongue was currently buried deep in his mouth and her skilled hands finessing their way into his pants, and this place had taken him by surprise.

If it weren't for the incessant press of her pelvis against his, the mad way her hands tore at his clothing in a burning endeavor to end what they'd begun on the dance floor of the club twenty minutes ago, he might even have asked about her living situation. He couldn't ask with his mouth full, and honestly right now he didn't care.

He just wanted to taste, to savor, to push up the silky folds of her thin dress and cup the softness of her naked ass in his hands. He knew she wasn't wearing panties or a bra again. There was nothing but smooth, hot flesh beneath her gown.

On the cusp of making contact with his swollen cock, her hand jerked free of his pants and she tugged her lips from his to mouth a breathy, "Bedroom. Now."

Bedroom. Door. Floor. It didn't matter. The heat charging through him, splintering his sanity, destroying his state of mind more and more with each of her deep, wet kisses had him on the verge of coming. The moment he entered her, sank his cock deep into her pussy, he knew he would be a goner.

With a husky mewl of desire, Brandy dipped her hand back into his pants. Her small palm snaked into his briefs and fisted around his erection. And then she tugged, backing her way across the room, forcing him to follow or risk having his throbbing genitals removed permanently.

"Bedroom. Now," she repeated in a louder, harsher voice when he didn't move fast enough for her liking. A voice that was as much violent demand as need.

Cara never spoke to him that way. She ached yes, was impatient to feel him inside her yes, but she never made it sound like a command.

Cara. The name stormed through Tristan's mind, through his scattering thoughts, and planted his feet firmly to the floor.

Merda! What was he doing? How could he even consider having sex with another woman regardless of how much her touch might make him ache? How could he allow that woman to be dragging him to her bedroom by bodily force?

He opened his mouth to tell Brandy to stop. That he'd made a near fatal mistake, but no words made it out before she'd turned and sank her tongue back between his lips. Her palm pumped his cock and his body tensed in return, his blood heating, churning. His thoughts threatened to scatter once more. His mouth seemed to respond on its own, his tongue licking, seeking, tangling with hers. His palms followed suit, dragging maniacally down her sides to clutch the dress in his hands and yank it upward until she was bared from the waist down.

For an instant she pulled away from his mouth, long enough for the forbidden view of her neatly trimmed pussy and the blistering scent of her damp sex to fill his senses. Long enough to register the crackle of excitement in the air. The sprinkling of items that hovered around them, swirling with an energy that a woman who wasn't his soul mate shouldn't be able to bring about. And then she was back, filling his mouth, pillaging his reason. Assaulting his mind and body completely.

His hands continued their siege without his permission, taking the twin globes of her ass into his palms and squeezing them harshly as he lifted her to meet him. She pulled his cock from the open fly of his slacks and then rocked her wet cunt against the swollen head of his penis. A moan of ecstasy ripped from his lungs at the feel of her damp pussy lips gliding over his cockhead. A moan that he loathed, because as much as it was his, it wasn't a sound he desired.

What the hell was it about this woman?

He'd convinced himself his attraction to Brandy was based on her belief he was a sexual aggressor, a tiger. If that was truly all that there was between them, then why was the air alive with energy and effects lifted from the floor and walls of the room that surrounded them? Why was he responding to her so intensely and she responding back in a way that only his soul mate should be able to do?

He had to break this connection, this hold she seemed to have over him. He refused to allow this insanity to go any farther, to a point where he wouldn't be able to forgive himself any more than Cara would be able to forgive him.

With the strength of his mind alone, Tristan willed his head to turn away, his mouth to break the connection with her lusty, demanding one. His palms to slide from her buttocks and his penis to ignore the sweet heat of her cunt open before him and ready to take him deep into her body. And when finally his lips and hands relented, he forced himself to look away, knowing if he looked into her eyes, if he saw the dark passion that burned in their smoky depths, all hope would be lost.

The objects that hovered around them fell to the floor and the heat of the room cooled instantly. In the midst of inhaling much needed air, his gaze landed on the painting that occupied the center of the wall…and he choked.

All thoughts of Brandy and whatever power she held over him were forgotten and it was all he could do to hold himself in one place and fight for normal breathing. "*Dio mio.*"

"Yes," she cried, her hand grasping his cock, angling it to meet her open pussy lips, to take him into her wet, willing body. His salvation came in the form of his height. He was too tall for her to mount without him bending his knees. He wasn't too tall to stop her from dropping to her own knees and taking his erection between her lips.

He groaned at the feel of her lush lips encircling his cock, pumping him with the force of reality. He was on the edge of his threshold, able to come so easily, be it Brandy or any woman on her knees, but there was no way he would. He pushed at her shoulders and her lips slipped from his cock, suckling as they went, with an intensity that nearly took more strength to ignore than what he possessed.

She returned to his penis immediately, not taking him into her mouth this time, but running her lips over the head of his cock, spreading the pre-come that lined its tip over her soft pink flesh and making the internal heat of his body thrum back to dangerous life.

Licking at her glistening lips, she rocked back on her heels and met his gaze, her own dark and turbulent. "This is too good, Tristan. We can't stop. You know it's right. You can feel it, just like I can."

Could he? Is that what he felt? Was that what all this was? Had he been wrong yet again? Was she the one? Had it never been Cara? Or was he not the one who was wrong at all, but his one-time mentor Solaris? It had been Solaris who'd assured him there would be only one woman for him, but maybe the old man had been mistaken. Maybe there was more than one woman and maybe he should be happy for it.

Whatever the case might be, now wasn't the time to worry over it. Now something far more unbelievable lodged in his mind and rumbled indefinable emotions deep into his chest. That something being the painting that hung on the room's far wall and bore a too perfect likeness to a woman whose visage thrust him into the long ago past.

He wrenched his gaze back to the portrait, and inclined his head. "What is that?"

Brandy came to her feet and said in a tone edged with frustration, "A painting."

He swiveled back to face her. Her eyes no longer held desire, but open aversion. Was it his reaction to the painting that disturbed her? Did she know more about his past than what she had allowed him to believe, or was it merely his once again rejection. "Of who?" he pressed.

"Just a woman," she responded in a tone as fervent as his own.

He softened his voice, aware the sudden rage burning in his blood would do neither of them any good. He might have more questions than ever, but he wouldn't be getting the answers to them with anything less than a level head.

Tristan returned his attention to the young woman in the painting and his gut tightened with a guilt he had no reason to feel, and yet he felt it all the same.

Scopata! It was too goddamned unbelievable!

The Alana recreated in the portrait was exactly as he remembered her from more than a decade before. Young, vibrant. Full of life. He hadn't hurt her. No matter what anyone had believed then or now, he hadn't been even unintentionally responsible for her murder. He'd merely been in the wrong place at the wrong time and blame had been directed at him as a result.

His gut clamped painfully with the memory of the night of Alana's death. Of the anger, the friendships lost and those recently restored. Of endless pain and grief.

"Do you know who she is?" He lashed the words out at Brandy, and the depths of his intensity shone in the pallor of her face.

Her eyes lost their dark edge and she looked suddenly meek, as if she were frightened by him. She shook her head. "Just...someone I painted from my mind."

He dragged a hand through his hair and glanced away, forcing air into his lungs with steadying breaths. He was acting like a bastard once again. If Brandy were truly a woman who was meant for him, the way the events here tonight seemed to suggest, then it was very possible she had painted the picture from her mind and nothing else. And even if she wasn't a woman who was meant for him, then she might very well still be innocent of every crime save for one—that of wanting to fuck a man who had no right wanting to fuck her back.

But if the latter were true, then how did it explain the painting? Alana had died more than ten years before it was done. "What do you mean, in your head?"

She smoothed her hands over the wrinkled folds of her dress, looking as far from the red hot vixen he'd come to think of her as, as she could. "You, of all people, should know how unexplainable artists and their habits can be, the way things sometimes just come to us and we have to capture them on canvas or in clay or whatever substrate it might be. It was like that with her." She asked in a quieter tone, "You don't like it?"

"No. Maybe." *Merda.* This made no sense. No goddamned sense in the least. Not unless he was to accept that Solaris really had been wrong about his destiny resting in the hands of one lone woman. He wasn't ready to do that. Not so easily.

Tristan took a step back, putting distance between them, needing to be free of her now more than ever. Needing time to think. "I have to go."

The anxiety that had overcome her expression turned to speculation. "She reminds you of someone? An ex-lover, perhaps?"

"A friend. An old friend." And it wasn't a close resemblance, but an honest to God replica of Alana. "I have to go," he repeated, hastily tucking his semi-erect cock into his slacks followed by his shirt and then refastening his zipper.

The Brandy he'd come to know reappeared with the action, naughty smile and all. She closed the short distance between them in a flash. "You don't have to go, Tristan. It's okay if you're still hung up on someone else, we'll deal with it together."

It wasn't okay. Not now, while too many questions went unanswered. Not so long as he continued to love Cara and believed deep down they truly were meant to be together. "Yes, I do. I shouldn't have come here."

"Because you're the consummate businessman," she said with as much knowing as derision. "You don't mix business with pleasure. What happened to stepping outside of the norm, Tristan? You said last night it was good to do so every once in a while."

"It is. Just..." Not for him. Not now when his life was becoming more disturbing by the hour. "Not tonight."

Hope flashed in her eyes. "Tomorrow then?"

Hell, no. Not tomorrow either. But he couldn't say that. He had more reason than ever to spend time with Brandy, unveiling his destiny and if she somehow figured into it by way of the Eye, and understanding how she could possibly have painted his best friend's dead sister from her mind when she'd never even met the woman. "Maybe."

"If that's all you're offering, then I guess I'll accept."

He should have left then, turned and walked out the door, but instead he lingered, reading into her emotions that were nearly as turbulent as his own but otherwise indefinable. At least for those first few seconds they were. They become more than definable after those seconds. Her aura lit with rich color and humor flashed in her eyes. She rose on tiptoe and brushed the softest of kisses to his lips. Soft and yet heat inducing. Her fingers came to his mouth, trailing with the same subtlety over the fleshy pad of his lower lip, the same flash of heat igniting deep within him, coiling want and a forceful need he couldn't begin to understand.

"Sleep well, Tristan. Think of me..." Her index finger pressed past his lips and into his mouth for a breath and then her hand fell away and she turned from him and started to the back of the apartment. She stopped mid-stride and flashed a deliberate smile over her shoulder. "...and tomorrow."

The implication of her hot look would have been enough to make him spend the night worrying over how he would learn anything from her when it was apparent all she wanted to share with him was sex. She didn't stop with an implication though, but unbuttoned her dress and allowed it to slide over her hips and puddle in a cloud of yellow silk near her feet. Then with a final recalcitrant smile, she shimmied her naked body into the darkness and shadows that enveloped the back of the room and those that adjoined it.

* * * * *

"I don't know what the hell to think," Tristan admitted into the barely visible receiver on his cell phone. He knew his voice was edged with a frustration he rarely let be heard around Lucas or anyone for that matter, but he couldn't do a damned thing about it. He strode across the hotel suite and stared out unseeingly into the fading rays of the sun, drew a long breath before continuing. "You're probably right and it was my imagination making it seem like it was Alana, but what if you're not?"

"I'm not even going to pretend like I'm always right, you know me too well, but, Trist, it's a goddamned impossibility. If anyone wants my sister to be alive," Lucas added in a calmer tone, "it's me, but she isn't. She died thirteen years ago. We were both there. We both saw it with our own two eyes. End of story."

"Right. I just…had to call."

"Something else eating at you?"

Tristan almost laughed at the irony in the words. The question shouldn't have been, "Is something else eating at you?" It should have been, "Is something in your life not eating at you?"

He'd accused Perry of being an emotional mess this morning at breakfast. The truth was Tristan was the mess. Next to nothing in his life currently made sense. He wasn't even one hundred percent certain Cara and he were meant to be together any longer. Though clearly Cara was the reason Lucas had asked the question. "If that's your not so subtle way of telling me you know I've seen Cara, it's a pretty shitty attempt."

"You've seen Cara?"

The shock in Lucas' voice registered with Tristan and had him growling into the back of his throat. Obviously the question hadn't been asked for Cara's sake, but merely in general. Either that or Lucas was sandbagging in an attempt to learn more than what he'd already found out from Perry. "Perry hasn't called you?"

"Hell, no. I haven't talked to him since last week."

Wonderful. Perry hadn't said a word to Lucas about Cara and if Tristan had kept his damned mouth shut the other man still wouldn't know he'd seen her. He hadn't kept his mouth shut and he knew Lucas wouldn't rest until he had at least a few details. Part of the man's probing nature came from his law enforcement background, the other part was left over from their youth.

Lucas had a year on him and while it might not make a difference now that they were both heading toward their mid-thirties, it had made a big difference when they'd been teenagers. Lucas had believed it was his job to look out for Tristan back then and with the recent restoration of their friendship, apparently that protective edge was firmly back in place. "She's back working at the Red Room. The Reno location."

"Ah, hell, that's a bitch."

"Tell me about it. So, how's married life?" he asked quickly, hoping to change the subject before Lucas pressed for anything further and sent Tristan's thoughts roaming to Cara. He might not have seen her at the club earlier tonight, but it was just now creeping toward nine thirty and she could very well be about to take the stage.

His guts churned with the idea and his thoughts took off in her direction against his desire to stop them from doing just that. The visual of leering and groping drunks that formed in his head threatened to take the frustration he'd been feeling all evening and turn it into a dangerous force.

"Ask me next week and I'll let you know."

Lucas' unexpected response brought Tristan's mind flashing back to the present. He'd asked about married life as a joke. Amy and Lucas were engaged, but a wedding date hadn't even been set as of last week. "You guys are seriously getting married?"

"Wasn't that always the plan?" Lucas asked dryly.

"Yeah, but next week? It's great, don't get me wrong, but you couldn't wait until I was back in town?"

"Well hell, Trist, if I knew you were going to cry about it, I would've made Amy hold off on the bridal shower so you could attend that too."

Every ounce of tension that claimed Tristan drained away with the ribbing remark, and he chuckled. Only Lucas could toss his emotional nature in his face and have him laughing as a result, instead of making him ache to do bodily harm. "You know what I meant, Donnigan. If you two are in such a hurry you can't wait a few extra days, then by all means go right on ahead and rush to the altar without me."

Lucas' short bark of laughter came over the receiver. "You can quit your blubbering, Manseletti. Nothing's official yet. When it is, you'll be the first to know."

"I'd better be," Tristan tossed back, meaning the words completely even if they came out in a bantering tone. Amy and Lucas were one of the only constants in his life right now. He cared about them too much to miss out on something as important as their wedding. Particularly when it was looking more and more like he might never have a wedding day of his own.

His thoughts threatened to wander back to Cara. Before they could drift, he went to the bedroom and slipped his wallet from the dresser to his back pocket. After leaving Brandy's place, he'd made plans to meet up with Perry at ten. Showing up early was suddenly looking like the best idea he'd had all day. "Unless you have some other big news, I need to get moving."

"Almost twelve thirty here, which makes it nine thirty there. Hot date?"

"How did you guess? He's tall, blond and blue eyed. And too damned cheap to pick up the tab unless he's in his own hotel's restaurant."

Lucas' laughter drifted over the phone line once more. "Tell Perry I said hi, and I'll do the same with Amy." He paused for a moment then added in a sober tone, "Call me if anything else odd turns up."

In the midst of crossing to the suite's front door, Tristan halted. "I thought you said the resemblance was my imagination. That it being her was an impossibility."

"I did and I'm sure in this case I'm right, but then it never hurts to keep an open mind. Lot of strange people in this world, you know?"

It was Tristan who laughed this time, the sound as metallic as it was hollow. He wished he didn't know, he wished to hell and back he wasn't one of those strange people. Things would be so much easier if he were normal. Not only might he still have Cara at his side day and night, but the rest of his life would be far saner as well. "Do I ever, Lucas. Do I ever."

* * * * *

"Cara."

The too familiar voice reached Cara from where she waited in the wings of the Red Room's stage for her next routine. A routine she would never be able to go through with knowing Tristan was in the building, eyeing her with disdain. Instinct told her to turn back to the safety of the changing room. Self-preservation wouldn't allow it. There were still words to be spoken, an understanding to be reached—one that hopefully would result in friendship.

Steadying her nerves for the jolt she knew they would receive the moment she made eye contact with Tristan, she met his gaze. He wore that sexy smile he'd tossed her way two nights ago and that one errant lock of sandy brown hair fell across his forehead in a way that brought her attention directly to his swollen left eye.

His smile grew, warming his deep brown eyes and her belly tightened into knots of anxiety even as a desire only he could stir so effectively warmed her insides. She moved from the stage's wing and down the platform to his side. The jagged cut and bruised flesh surrounding his eye was even worse looking up close, and she reached for the injury instinctively, drawing back just when she would have made contact. Touching him with such open compassion would never convince him of the words she had to speak. Only the truth could accomplish that.

She led him to a dark corner of the club where the music still filtered loudly, but not so much to make shouting necessary. "You know you shouldn't be here, Tristan."

His look suggested that she was wrong, that she was the one who shouldn't be here. Instead of stating what she knew him to be thinking, he reached a hand out and cupped her face. The kiss came too quickly for her to stop it, and his mouth retreated just as fast, leaving her lips tingling and her blood humming from the subtle brush. "I missed you yesterday. I wanted to see you."

Cara's heart ached with the honesty in his words, the genuine affection he could never disguise. She'd missed him too, missed his touch, his kiss. His warmth. Seeing Joey yesterday had only made things worse. Returning to an empty apartment that lacked for so much as a TV, she'd had nothing to do but sit and think. To regret what she'd done, though she knew it was the right thing. If they were ever to move on and be happy and love others, then they needed closure from their pasts.

Closure he obviously still didn't understand. "Tristan…"

Her voice broke and emotion clogged her throat. She couldn't even get his name out while looking into his soulful eyes, how the hell was she supposed to get out the words she needed to say? Or maybe she didn't need to get them out. Maybe just that one word had made things clear, the collapsing of his smile seemed to indicate such.

Tristan's gaze sharpened, going from warm to direct, and she knew he was reading into her, reading the truth she couldn't speak. He couldn't interpret her exact thoughts, only the tip of what she was thinking and where her emotions lay. It was enough, the sudden severity of his stance, the coldness that seemed to wash from his body and into hers, ensured it. "What is that tone, that look, Cara? What are you trying to say?"

"I think you know."

He shook his head. "Don't. Take time to think it over. Be sure—"

"I am sure," she cut him off in a rush, needing to end this fast, before it became any messier than what it already was. "I have thought about it. I only wish…" She glanced away, unable to finish the sentence while he watched her so intently.

He once more cupped the side of her face, forcing her to look back at him. "What do you wish, baby? Tell me so I can make it happen."

The emotion in her throat rose, weighting the backs of her eyes. She caught her inner cheek in her teeth and bit at it, urging the tears to pass. What she wished was that he wouldn't call her that, it only made this all that much harder knowing he still thought of her as his baby.

Cara lifted his hand away from her face. She took a fortifying step back and set her chin. "I wish you'd never tracked me down, Tristan."

"I didn't track you down. I came to Reno on business."

"And just happened to show up in the Red Room, where I just happened to be working? I don't buy it as a coincidence for a second."

"Well, you should, because that's what it was."

The flash of heat in his look and tone told her how close he was to losing his temper. He rarely lost his temper and yet she had managed to make it happen with only a few words both tonight and two nights ago. It was one more reason they were not good together for the long run. Tristan prided his ability to remain calm under the most dire of circumstances and lately she could upset that calm in seconds flat.

Her objective here tonight restored, she forced back her emotions and stated matter-of-factly, "Fine. It doesn't matter how we happened to run into one another. It doesn't change anything."

"Anything?"

"I'm still not in your life."

"Not in my life? We made love two nights ago, Cara, I'd say that's about as far into my life as you can get."

"No, we had sex, Tristan. Goodbye sex."

"Goodbye sex," he mouthed the words slowly, disbelief drawing his eyebrows together. His gaze narrowed, and the temper Cara had felt brewing before became visible in the hard lines of his face and the sudden heat that claimed her body. Not heat of a good kind, but that of a storm unleashing.

She couldn't fear that storm and if he might go off here, in the club she relied on to make a living, she had to finish. "Yes. I told you I needed you that one last time. We needed to say goodbye once and for all, and we did. You had to feel it. The way the vision ended…you had to know."

As much as she'd forced her emotions back, they still emerged with the last words, at the finality of it all. Her heart squeezed painfully tight and her insides curdled with loathing. A loathing that was reflected in Tristan's eyes.

"We made love," he repeated, his tone darkening and the heat within him building with each syllable. "You goddamned told me that you loved me."

"Only in your mind, and you made me do it."

"We are not through, Cara. I need you, damn it. I love you!"

And whether she'd spoken the words in reality or only in the vision two nights ago, she loved him. Too much to see either of them miserable in the future because she'd let herself take the easy way out and return to him now. "I'm sorry."

"You're sorry?" Rage burned in his eyes. He shoved a hand through his hair, sending the strands that were always so orderly into chaos. "You come up to my room for a goodbye fuck and let me believe you still love me as much as I love you and all you can say is you're sorry?"

Oh, God, it wasn't just a meaningless fuck! But if she corrected him and told him how much their lovemaking had meant to her it would give him false hope. She couldn't give him hope of a future with her, at least not a future as lovers. "I want for us to be friends. Joey—"

"Don't even think about bringing your brother into this," Tristan cut her off, grasping her elbow in his hand and dragging her to his body. "I love that kid. You know I do, but he is *not* the reason we can't be together." His gaze pierced hotly into hers, accusing, blistering. Frightening her with the depths of his intensity. "*You* are the reason, the only damned reason. You're afraid. Scared to have anything good in your life. Well, that's too bad, because we belong together, Cara. Only you and me. We're meant to be together. We're soul mates."

His grasp turned biting and she whimpered at the pain. He'd never hurt her before, never used his strength against her. She struggled to shake her arm free of his grip, but he held tight. "I—I need to work."

He laughed bitterly. "You mean act like a slut, don't you? Toss your naked body around that stage because you love the rush that comes with all those men watching you undress and imagining taking you home and fucking you."

The fear that came with his harsh handling spiked into anger. She didn't feel a rush, she felt hatred, self-loathing that she had no other talents to fall back on outside of her art training and that she would never rely on, not so long as he were in the industry. "I don't feel a rush. I feel…" *ashamed.*

"Bullshit! I was in that room the other night. I saw the pleasure you took in stripping for me. I know how much it turns you on." Finally his grip relented, only to set his hand at her back and shove her in the direction of the stage. "Go do your job, Cara. Sell your body the same way your mother did. Make Joey proud of his big sister the whore."

Fury and hatred melded with the accusation, tears sprang forth in her eyes. Tears she couldn't hide. She swiveled back and lashed out at him, "You bastard! I am not like my mother. I'm nothing like her. I am *not* a whore!"

The mocking expression Tristan wore ensured she could repeat those words a million times and right now he wouldn't believe her. He opened his mouth to respond, but before any words could come out, Craig was on him. Grabbing him by the arms and pinning them behind his back.

Tristan shrugged the bouncer's beefy hands off as if they were no more than a featherweight embrace. He sneered at the other man. "I'm leaving, *arruso*, so I suggest you back off if you want to keep your hands attached."

"You never should have come here," Cara stammered, hating how weak she sounded, how defeated she felt.

Tristan smirked as he made his way past her en route to the door. The force of his ridicule, the depth of his anger was completely uncharacteristic of the man she loved, and she hated herself all the more for making him act this way. "Don't worry, *baby*, I won't ever again."

Chapter Eight

"Tristan. What are you doing here?"

Wasn't that a damned fine question? What was he doing here, at Brandy's front door? Less than a minute ago he'd known the answer easily—he'd come here to give in to every one of her not-so-subtle advances. Looking down into her hopeful eyes now, he began to doubt himself.

Giving in to Brandy as a way to spite Cara seemed not only juvenile but potentially harmful. What if Brandy took his agreement to sleep with her as more than one night of sex? What if it turned out that it truly was more? Was he ready to thrust himself headlong into a relationship when he was still aching from the last woman's rebuttal?

Damn, he shouldn't have come here. Not so soon. "I can leave."

Anxiety flared in Brandy's eyes and she shook her head, sending her dark silky hair swinging wildly around her face. "No! You'd said you had plans tonight. I'm surprised to see you is all."

"They changed." He struggled to keep the bitterness out of his voice with the reality of just how much his evening's plans had gone awry. Struggled and failed judging by the way her eyebrows knit with concern.

"Not for the better by the sounds of things. I'm sorry."

Doing his best to ignore what seemed to be genuine sympathy on her part, Tristan shrugged and lied, "Don't be. I'm not."

The fine lines that marred her otherwise flawless complexion abated and her full lips curved. "Well, then, I'm not either."

The heat that registered in his body with that simple inviting smile sent every doubt he'd encountered since Brandy opened her door into oblivion. He'd come here for the right reason, to forget Cara via the skilled hands of one very willing woman. A willing woman who held the power to tangle his mind into knots and make him question everything he was and had spent his life believing in. A woman who, if last night's slightly abnormal encounter was to be believed, might well be the perfect replacement for Cara.

Dio caro. He might just be looking at his soul mate.

The knowledge eased the tension he'd been feeling since leaving the Red Room behind and he had to fight the urge to yank Brandy into his arms and strip her bare. To plunge his cock deep into her warm, wet body and see if she held the power to not only light the air with energy and effects, but send them both spiraling to that one special place he'd only ever been with Cara.

"This isn't a bad time, is it?" he asked.

Her smile tipped higher and she moved back from the door, so he could pass into the apartment. "Not at all. Come in."

She followed him inside, then shut the door and swiveled around to face him. The raw desire that burned in the depths of her gaze ensured she knew why he was here, even if the next words out of her mouth were merely friendly ones. "So, can I get you something to drink or eat?"

"You."

"Pardon me?"

Tristan found himself grinning at her response. The words themselves might have been coated with surprise, but the anticipation in her expression belied it. She knew him, truly knew him in the way he'd convinced himself the previous night that she could not. She wasn't just after him because she viewed him as a sexual aggressor, a tiger, but because she was his one true destiny.

Solaris had been wrong. There was more than one woman who could be his soul mate, or at the very least more than one woman who could appear to be his soul mate. Cara had put up the pretense, but she hadn't been the real thing. The real thing would never walk away from him out of fear or anything else. The real thing was waiting for him now, waiting for him to make his move.

"You once accused me of being the kind of man who doesn't need things drawn out for him. Well, you were right, I'm not. Just as you aren't the kind of woman who does." He advanced in a flash, drawing on a supernatural speed he rarely employed, and pulled Brandy into his arms. She wore a loose fitting sweatshirt that hid her breasts, but not their outline or the hard points of her nipples abrading his chest.

The persistent chafing of those two erect buds and the heat of expectancy that rolled through her smoky eyes had his blood pulsing and his cock hardening. There was so much visible in her gaze now, his past, his present...his future. How could he have missed it for so long? How could he ever have been so blind?

Tristan brought his hand to her face and cupped the smooth rise of her cheek in his palm. Her breath cruised out in uneven pants and he could feel the excitement building within her, the expectation charging through his own system. He should take things slow this first time, take time with her and cherish her now that he knew the truth, but he couldn't. And if the demand in her eyes was to be believed, she also couldn't handle the waiting that taking things slow would mean.

He trailed his hand lower to rim her full lips with the pad of his thumb. They would be sweet, like...strawberries. The thought momentarily stilled him, and he shook his head, chasing it away. Not strawberries, that was Cara. Brandy would be far sweeter, far more potent, drugging, like the liquor she was named after. "Now in case I'm wrong about that last part and you do need some explanation... I'm here for one reason, Brandy, and it isn't business."

Her lips parted in response and he took that moment to seize them, to fill the warmth of her mouth with his tongue and lick at her intoxicating flavor. His brain buzzed with each needy stroke of tongue against tongue, his mind fogged with the electric slide of palms over flesh, wandering, stroking, tormenting with sinful delight. His cock pulsed, expanded, throbbed to be set free to claim this woman who was to be his forever.

Brandy was every bit as needy as he. Her hands tugged his shirt from his slacks and her nails fastened onto his back, biting into sinewy muscles and pushing his control on a blind journey to one end. No longer willing to take things slow, he lifted her in his arms and carried her to a worn couch that centered the apartment's sitting area. He set her back on the faded cushions and pushed the bulky sweatshirt up over her breasts. They were nowhere near as full as Cara's, the nipples almost brown whereas Cara's were a rosy shade of pink, but then this wasn't Cara, and he wouldn't allow himself to be confused to the contrary.

Tristan buried his head between her breasts, indulging in their silky weight on his face for a long moment, then drawing one aroused nipple into his mouth. He pulled at the sensitive flesh and she arched up beneath him, rubbing her mound against his groin and sending shooting stabs of desire straight to his cock. Needing to take this faster, so much faster, he bit down on her nipple and pushed his hand past the elastic waist of her sweatpants and panties.

His shaft throbbed at the wetness of her pussy, the lather of juices that soaked the lips of her cunt. He slid two fingers deep into the slickness of her swollen hole and she sucked in a hasty gulp of air and moaned out his name.

He released her nipple with the sound and raised to meet her gaze. Her dark eyes were aglow with passion and her face shimmered with a layer of perspiration that could only appear so quickly by one means. That means was just past her head, past the end of couch, where objects spiraled on a hot, hazy current that whipped at his face and had his own flesh sticky with sweat, his hair standing on end. That means was the final proof he'd been right for the first time in a very long while.

Cara had never been the one. Brandy was.

"Not that...I'm complaining..." Her breath puffed out in hot, steady streams. "But...why the sudden...change of heart?"

Because he'd been a damned fool. For years he had been. Tristan wouldn't explain that to her. Not yet. She had much to learn about him, about what they were meant to be to one another. Later he would teach her. Tonight was for pleasure, for the joining of two bodies and minds that should have been joined long ago. "Do you really care?"

Her smile peaked into the lusty one that pierced pain into his heart, a painful pleasure that he was quickly developing an unnatural fondness for. Her nails bit once more into his back, soundlessly urging him to return to her breasts, his fingers to renew their deep, hot thrusts into her sex. "Not really."

"Good," he returned, bringing his mouth back to lap at a greedy nipple, his fingers to plunging into the silken folds of her pussy, "because neither do I."

* * * * *

She would be lucky if she still had a job come morning.

Cara released a frustrated breath as she ascended the stairwell to her third story apartment. She shouldn't be coming home at eight o'clock on a Friday night. She should be at the Red Room dancing. Or undressing while getting her cheap thrills from knowing how badly all the drunks in the audience wanted to fuck her.

The thought, one planted in her head by Tristan, turned her frustration back to the joint forces of fury and hurt she'd known since he'd walked out of the club a little over an hour ago. How he could think that about her, that she enjoyed stripping, made no sense. He was too insightful, too able to read her mind and body to believe such things. She should have set him right. She should have explained the real reason they couldn't be together. She hadn't done either, and instead allowed him to believe the worst and subsequently blow up in her face.

Maybe it was all for the best. He was out of her life now, the way she'd wanted him to be over two months ago. But what was she going to tell Joey? He would be so disappointed when he learned Tristan would no longer be coming around. The words might be more than disappointing to him, they might be enough to set him back in any progress he'd made over the past few years.

Tears welled in Cara's eyes. Tears she'd sworn she'd already cried at the club, in front of the manager no less. Tears that had been her motivation for running out of the Red Room without any explanation. Tears that she shouldn't be crying over Tristan and would quite possibly lead to her termination.

Cara attempted to sniff back her emotions, knowing it was pointless, but needing to get inside her apartment before she further shamed herself by having yet another breakdown in public. She reached her apartment door and dropped her backpack-style purse off her shoulder to search for her keys. Her fingers made contact with the cool metal of the key ring the same moment noises erupted from the doorway across the hall. Loud noises, the sound of things breaking, or maybe of someone breaking.

Her own problems fell away with that last thought and her heart lodged into her throat. What if someone was hurting Brandy? Oh God, what if someone was killing Brandy?!

Her pulse hammering, she crossed the short distance to the hall and turned the door's knob. The door swung inward easily and she moved inside, prepared to sacrifice her own life if that's what it took to save her friend.

All thoughts of heroism died at the sight before her, as did the erratic beat of her heart. For a moment she couldn't breathe, couldn't even feel or hear. She could only see. See the air alive with a sweltering heat, with objects strewn from the apartment's floor and walls and ceiling. See the man she loved and the woman she'd become very close with in the last few weeks together on the couch, mindlessly groping each other's barely clothed bodies.

Cara's breath came slamming back at the same time she found her voice. Her feet wouldn't cooperate though. All she could do was stand and stare and repeat her silent chant until it became audible. "Oh...my...God..."

Tristan's head jerked up from where his mouth was latched firmly onto Brandy's breast and his eyes bulged as recognition sailed over his face. "Cara!"

Brandy's head tipped back and she stared at Cara with the same shocked expression. "You know her?"

"I—"

"You said you loved me!" Cara couldn't let him speak, couldn't let any words come out of his mouth. She also couldn't stand here another moment. The tears she'd fought off in the hallway were back in full force and about to leak down her face. All she had now was her anger to cling to. Anger and disbelief. This man, this man she loved and had nearly given into her fears for, had lied to her. Had spent four long years lying to her. "Y—you said it was just you and me. That only I could do...do this. It was all a lie. It was all just one big fucking lie."

Her entire body shook with deep-seated emotions she hadn't given in to for years. Tears streamed down her face, stinging her eyes. Her heart clamped in a painful vise. Everything seemed to break over her in that instant, all her hopes, her dreams. She couldn't handle it any more. She couldn't stand here and watch it all die. Without another word she turned and ran.

"Cara, wait," Brandy called after her, as she stood out in the hallway fumbling with her keys, trying to fit them into a lock that suddenly seemed impossibly tiny. "It doesn't have to end like this."

The words were too much, too laughable. She returned to Brandy's doorway and stared in at them. Tristan now stood beside the couch and was hastily working to set his clothes back into place. Brandy seemed oblivious to her nakedness.

"Then how should it end?" the question was for Brandy, but she directed her attention on Tristan, on his face that seemed so remorseful and yet she knew better. Knew what a liar he was. He opened his mouth to speak.

Brandy's voice cut him off. "We can share."

Cara's gaze zipped to her with the words. "*What?*"

"You and I, we're good friends, right? And we're both obviously attracted to Tristan. Why can't we both have him...together?"

"Oh, God! You're joking." She could never do that. Never share a man she loved with another woman. Maybe if it wasn't Tristan...maybe...

"No. I'm not." Brandy's lips tipped into a smile, a smile that reached into Cara and ignited a spark of something she barely believed. A spark of desire. The smile deepened and the desire that swelled within her followed, dampening her body with the excitement that filled the room and making her inner thighs ache for release.

"It's not so bad." Brandy's voice beckoned to her, sultry, hot, asking her to come to her, to touch her in a way she'd never considered touching another woman. In a way she refused to touch other women at the Red Room. "Just give it a try."

The little voice in the back of Cara's head told her something about this was wrong, that she should walk away, but her feet were already moving, her body heating further, her pussy filling with heady need.

"Yes," she breathed in a voice that was hers and yet it wasn't.

She reached Brandy's side and took her outstretched hand, bringing it to her breast without hesitation. Brandy's smile grew further, spreading into her eyes, coloring them an inebriating shade, a nearly translucent hue. Her fingers closed over Cara's breast, kneading the fullness through her shirt and bra, and the liquid heat convulsing deep in her womb spiraled out of control. She needed this woman's touch. Needed her hands everywhere. Her mouth melding with her own, her tongue stroking her to completion.

Brandy's hand left her breast for an instant, then resettled beneath her shirt and tugged away the thin material of her bra. Her finger rasped over Cara's erect nipple and she sucked back a shallow gasp at the sensations that careened through her. She felt ready to explode, to come with that single touch.

"It isn't so bad, is it, Cara?" Brandy's voice slid over her heated body, her stroke growing as it chafed along her breast, teasing, tugging, tearing at her core. "It actually feels quite good."

"Yes," she sighed the word as the pressure built higher, ready to spin out of control. One touch, just one touch of Brandy's skilled fingers or even better the warm, wetness of her tongue on her clit and Cara would go off. "I want—"

"What do you—"

"Cara?"

It was Tristan who cut Brandy's question off. Tristan's questioning voice that had Cara falling from the trance that had overtaken her. She broke from Brandy's gaze and met Tristan's disbelieving eyes. A disbelief that suddenly ignited in her own mind and body. The heat within her died as reality returned, gripping her belly with anxiety. She jerked free of Brandy's touch even as her thighs shook for more.

Dear God, what in the hell was wrong with her? What had possessed her to let that happen? To want to feel another woman's hands on her, another woman's tongue suckling at her?

Her heart pumping a mad crescendo, she looked from Brandy to Tristan then back at Brandy and shook her head. "I...I can't. I just can't!" And then she ran.

"Cara, wait!"

It was Tristan who called after her and she knew he would follow her with more than just his voice. She stabbed the key into her lock this time, tossed open the door and shouted back out as it slammed shut, "No, I can't! I can't do this!"

"Cara, open the damned door! We need to talk!"

She raced to the alarm clock that doubled as a radio and turned the volume dial until music blared through the room and sound of Tristan's voice faded. She couldn't face him now. She couldn't face anyone now. She couldn't even face her own reflection after what happened in that apartment. After what she almost let herself do.

Long minutes passed and finally she went to the door, peering out through the peephole. No one stared back. Thank God. Her breathing finally returning to normal, Cara turned the radio off and sank onto her couch, still struggling to make sense of what had nearly occurred between her and Brandy. She never even considered kissing another woman, to think she could be so physically turned on by one. It had to have been Tristan's presence that excited her, the thought that he'd been watching.

Only in those moments when she'd been so close to coming it hadn't been Tristan on her mind at all. It had been Brandy.

A knock sounded on her door breaking her from her thoughts. Her heart sped once more as she went to the peephole. Brandy stood outside. She didn't want to open the door to the woman, but then she had no choice. They had to talk, about Tristan and about what had happened between them.

Drawing a steadying breath, Cara opened the door.

Brandy smiled back at her as if nothing was out of the ordinary. "He's gone."

"Good."

Brandy's smile fell and she looked guilty. "If I'd known about you two, I never would have started seeing him."

Seeing him? She made it sound like they'd been dating a long time. How long? And was that the real reason Tristan had come to Reno? Had their running into one another at the Red

Room that night really been a coincidence as he'd claimed? If it was and he had been seeing Brandy already then, why had he convinced Cara to have sex with him. Why had he told her he loved her just this afternoon?

Because he's a liar, Cara. A liar she had beat herself up over for hurting. She forced a small smile for Brandy's sake. "You didn't know. You couldn't. It's not your fault."

"No, it isn't. Tristan told me he wasn't seeing anyone. He never once mentioned your name."

Even as Cara had begun to accept the fact Tristan had lied to her, to hear he hadn't even thought to bring her up around Brandy hurt all the more. Her belly pinched tight with ache and she fought back her tears for one of many times tonight. "He was telling the truth. We aren't seeing each other. We haven't been together for months, not as a couple. I just never expected to walk into your apartment and find him...you..."

"I know what you mean. I didn't expect things to happen the way they did either." She offered a weak smile and extended her hand. "So, we're still friends?"

Cara stared down at her open palm and gulped back a sharp breath. The last time she accepted that hand it had led to feelings she'd never imagined she'd have, to unnatural urges that even as they sickened her, heated her body all over again. She pushed those sensations away and quickly took the other woman's hand, gave it a fast shake and released it before any further damage could be done. "We're friends."

Brandy's smile returned full force, the concern that had filled her eyes, parting away like clouds on a summer day. "In that case, what do you say I whip up that cake for you now? I'd say after tonight you deserve a good overdose of chocolate."

Cara's own smile surfaced with the question. Brandy wasn't acting flirtatious now. She wasn't acting even the slightest bit interested in her sexually. Perhaps what had happened in her apartment had been a heat of the moment kind of thing for both of them. She could only hope it had. "Thanks,

Brandy. You really are a good friend, but right now all I want it some alone time."

"Okay. But the rain check's still good. Just let me know when you're ready to die."

Cara's heart pounded at her rib cage with the last of those words. *"What?"*

"Death by Chocolate. It's the name of the cake, remember?"

"Oh...right. The name of the cake. I'll let you know."

Chapter Nine

It was the last place she wanted to go and the one place she had to.

As much as Cara wanted to brand Tristan a liar, and after seeing him with Brandy last night and the effects it had on the room around them, it was hard to think of him as anything but, it didn't make sense. He stood to gain nothing by telling her that she was the only one for him, his soul mate. Had he told her that after they'd been together for a couple years and he'd already known about her fears where he and his powers were concerned, then yes maybe he would've had a reason. He might have told her to make her see she had to stay by his side. Only he hadn't told her after a couple years. He'd told her she was his destiny soon after they'd met.

That left the possibility that he really hadn't been lying to her, that he honestly hadn't known the truth any better than she had. Even if that were the case, it didn't change the fact he'd already been seeing Brandy the night he and Cara had made love. It did, however, change the morality of her reaction to what happened in Brandy's apartment last night.

Cara was the one who had ended things between her and Tristan, not once but twice. If he wanted to see other women, sleep with other women, then she had no right becoming emotionally involved when he did so, even if that woman happened to be one of her only friends. After all the years and memories they'd shared she sure as hell had no right tossing accusations his way without getting answers, and that's why she had to come here today. To his hotel suite in the hopes of having a normal conversation that ended with answers instead of shouting and tears.

The elevator dinged, announcing her arrival on the top floor of The Lazy Ace casino and hotel. She drew in a steadying breath as she stepped out onto the plush green carpeting and started down the hallway to the second door. They could have a civil conversation, she assured herself again. They had been best friends for almost half a decade. They could attain that again, maybe not the "best" status, but the friendship.

She continued the silent litany of reassurances until she reached the second door. A door that was opened. A door that when she peered inside brought every one of her reassurances to a crashing halt.

Her belly knotted and cold fury washed over her. Fury she had no right to feel. Tristan stood several feet from the doorway and wrapped in his arms was Brandy.

Cara struggled to form words, to cough, anything to make her presence known before the embrace turned to something more, something she knew would turn the knot in her belly to tears in her eyes. Damn it, she'd told herself she could handle this! She'd told herself she was over him, that they were better off alone. If it were true, if any of it were true, then why when she spotted the two together last night had it hurt so badly and why now did it feel like her heart was breaking all over again?

"Cara?"

She blinked at the sound of her name and met Tristan's eyes over the shoulder of the woman he held. She tried once more to speak, but nothing came out. She couldn't do this. She couldn't stand here and pretend everything was okay, that they could be friends. They could never be friends.

"I'm s—sorry," she managed, and then turned and fled.

A strong hand grabbed hold of her arm mere feet from the safety of the still open elevator doors, forcing her to swivel around and meet Tristan's deep brown eyes. Eyes that were weighted with sorrow and what looked to be pain. The knowledge that he was hurting, for whatever reason it might be, momentarily warmed her, and then she heard a feminine voice calling from down the hall. "Did you catch her?"

Cara turned, expecting to see Brandy watching them from the suite's doorway. The woman who looked back at her had black hair, but that's where the similarities with Brandy ended. This woman's hair was far longer, nearly to her waist, and her body much taller and lithe. Eyes of an entrancing blue seemed to see right through her.

She shivered with the thought, and then shivered again as reality hit. If the woman Tristan had been holding wasn't Brandy, then who was it?

Cara jerked her head around to stare at him. "Who...?"

"Amy. You met once in passing, the day you ran out of my condo."

"Oh." The woman came back to her now. They'd never even exchanged words that day, just a passing look. Cara hadn't given the stranger's appearance much thought at the time—it had been the day she'd left Tristan, but looking back now things quickly fell into place and in doing so turned the knot in her gut to a painful burning sensation. "You've been seeing her, too?"

For an instant, Tristan's eyes narrowed and then they filled with mirth and he laughed. "She happens to be my best friend's fiancée."

"But you were holding her like—"

"I was hugging her like the good friend she is. They just told me they came out here to get married."

"They?"

A smile stole over his face. "Lucas and Amy."

"Lucas." The name slid from her mouth leaving a bitter taste in its wake. Lucas had been at the source of Tristan's agony for years. He'd blamed him for committing a terrible wrong, for murder. She might not know how honest Tristan was these days, but she knew he could never be a killer. "Lucas is here? But I thought..."

"That we hated each other?" His smile grew into the sexy grin that held the power to do more damage to her state of mind and body than was healthy. "A lot's happened the past couple months." His hand snaked out and grabbed hold of hers while she was still entranced with his expression and the warmth the look stirred deep within her. "Will you come inside and let me introduce you?"

Cara forced her attention from his too tempting mouth and stared down at his hand, holding hers as if it were the most natural thing in the world, as if it were the right thing. It felt right. It felt more than right to be this close to him, to feel the energy that sparked between them each time they came within twenty yards of each other. It felt too right.

She shook her hand until he released it, and she immediately regretted the action. Refusing to acknowledge the emptiness that filled her with the simple action, she said, "I don't think that's a very good idea."

Annoyance passed through Tristan's eyes and his grin fell flat. "Then why the hell did you come over here in the first place?"

Cara bit down on the inside of her cheek and counted to ten. She would not get upset this time, she wouldn't let his frustration affect her. For whatever reason it might be, he couldn't keep a level head around her these days and so it was up to her to be calm for the both of them. "To apologize," she said softly. "I had no right lashing out at you last night. I'm the one who walked away, if you want to see Brandy or any woman it's none of my business."

His gaze narrowed and for several long seconds he only stared at her, then he said in a tight voice, "I didn't lie to you."

"I'd guessed as much." And yet as much as she had, hearing him speak the words aloud still brought sweet relief.

Once more he stared at her, silence lengthening between them. Silence that took her moment of relief and turned it to unexplainable dread. When the seconds turned to nearly a full minute, she hugged her arms to her chest and spoke words she already knew she'd live to regret. "Tell me what's on your mind, Tristan. I can see it's something important and it's only fair to both of us that you say it."

He nodded and the sorrow she'd detected when he'd first come after her returned. The words rolled out of his mouth slowly. "I honestly do love you, Cara. I will always love you. But I now know you aren't the one. It took your walking away to show me that." He put on what she knew to be a forced smile and continued in a quieter tone. "I'm sorry things have to be this way. You have to know it's not what I'd wanted for us."

The bone deep remorse that clung to his words, his expression twisted Cara's heart with regret. If only she hadn't left him that first time he might never have met Brandy. And he also might have met her one day in the future and lived to rue the day he'd ever wed Cara.

As much as it hurt, and at this moment it hurt more than anything else she'd ever experienced, giving him her blessing was the right thing to do. Sniffing back emotions, she unwrapped her arms and took his hand into hers. She forced a smile of her own. "I'm sorry too. But it's for the best." Tears pricked at the back of her eyes and she bit down hard on her cheek to quell them. "You're special, Tristan...more so than I could ever fully understand, and you deserve to be with the one you were born to love."

The Adam's apple bobbed in his throat and moisture welled in his eyes. Tristan had always been emotional, it was his calling to be so, but she'd never seen him cry. He wasn't crying now either, but he looked as though he might and that brought her own tears gushing to the forefront.

"You two planning on standing there all day yapping, or do you think you can come in here and toast with us?"

At the energetic sound of Amy's voice, Cara released Tristan's hand and swiveled away to wipe at her tears. This was supposed to be a happy day. She had no right barging in on a celebration and ruining it.

"Will you go in?"

She turned back with Tristan's softly spoken question. His eyes no longer held the evidence of his sorrow, but she could still feel it, weighting the air between them, destroying the warmth that had always been theirs and theirs alone. "Will we still be friends?"

He smiled with the question and the light of relief danced through his eyes. "Always, Cara. You will always be my friend."

What about his best friend? Would she ever be his best friend again, or now that he'd found the woman he was truly meant to be with, was that nothing more than a fond memory? It was a question only answerable in time, as was the truth of his response. Less than ten minutes ago she'd been certain they could never be just friends, and as much as she wanted to be, she still wasn't certain they could.

She would try. With all her heart, she would try to stand by and be happy while Tristan gave his love and his life to another woman.

She pushed that thought back to concentrate on the here and now, on the hope in his eyes. "Okay. I'll go in, so long as you explain what happened between you and Lucas."

He nodded and placed a hand to her back, guiding her to the suite. "I'll tell you everything, as soon as we're alone again."

Those words filled Cara's head for the next hour as she was introduced to Tristan's friends, as glasses were raised and toasts made, as love sparked the air between Amy and Lucas and made Cara's heart squeeze painfully tight with jealousy. Then the men fell into conversation about their jobs, and Amy stole her off to the opposite end of the suite with a fresh bottle of champagne and two glasses.

Amy poured the clear, bubbling wine into the glasses and handed one to Cara. She'd already drunk plenty and the last thing she needed was more, but at the same time the alcohol was slowing her thoughts down and her mind from wandering to places it had no right to go. Thankful for any kind of intervention where her thoughts and Tristan's place in them were concerned, she lifted the glass to her lips and took a long sip.

"I have a favor to ask of you," Amy said, twirling the stem of her glass. "I know we don't know each other well, but I suck at making female friends, so I'm hoping you'll be my maid-of-honor. With Tristan being the best man, it only seems right."

Cara's throat seemed to close off with the words, and she slapped a hand to her chest and choked on the champagne now burning its way down her throat. "Tristan and I aren't together any more," she finally managed.

"But you're friends, and that's close enough. So, will you?"

Tie herself to Tristan's side in such an intimate setting? It might not be a big wedding, but would that matter? Could she be that close to him and watch a couple so in love take their vows and not yearn for the same? "I don't know."

Understanding filled Amy's eyes, then quickly turned to disappointment. "It's not a big deal. I gotta pick out a dress and flowers is all, and was hoping not to have to do it alone, but, hey, I understand. We're strangers and I'm not exactly girlfriend material, which probably explains why the only female I've ever gotten along with was the cat I had when I was—"

"Okay," Cara said quickly, bringing the other woman's words to a halt. If it meant so much to Amy, then she could handle standing by Tristan's side for a few minutes. It wouldn't be totally painless, but if living through the heartache and loss she'd suffered in the hall an hour ago were any sign, it wouldn't kill her either. "I can help as long as we do it during the day."

"You work nights?"

The sudden snappiness of Amy's words and the smile that stole over her face had Cara wondering how authentic her rambling spiel had been. That wonder faded as her response filled her head.

Did she work nights? Yes, she worked as a whore by Tristan's way of thinking. A woman who got her kicks from undressing for strangers. Amy's bright smile fell flat and she directed a glare toward where the men sat talking. The suddenness of her mood change pulled Cara from her thoughts and had her responding. "Actually I do work nights, as a dancer."

"And she has dynamite legs to prove it."

Tristan's enthusiastic words were as unexpected as they were impossible to ignore. Heat welled up inside her, making her ache to change things between them. To beg him for one more chance, a chance where she would be strong and not fear tomorrow and its possible outcomes. A chance she knew would never happen.

"Tomorrow at noon then," Amy said, clinking her champagne glass against Cara's, "and bring your appetite. I just happen to know of a shop that makes the world's best Godiva-dipped strawberries."

* * * * *

"You have a lot on your mind."

Cara frowned at the way Amy said the words, as if they were a statement more than a question. Was it that obvious? She re-hung the dress she'd been eyeing and glanced at the other woman. The intensity of Amy's expression was startling and caused the same odd shiver she'd felt yesterday when they'd first exchanged looks. "Yeah. I guess I do. Life's been pretty crazy the last few months."

Amy raised a black eyebrow. "Care to talk about it? I've been told a time or two that my listening skills are among the best."

"It's nothing." Nothing but everything, Cara thought on a sigh.

She'd had the night off work last night and had been coerced into staying for a late dinner, which effectively meant spending the evening staring across the table at Tristan and wishing she could simply get over him. Lucas' surprising warmth and insight into the more amusing moments of his and Tristan's past didn't help anything. Every moment had drawn her closer to Tristan, closer to wanting to say to hell with his supposed destiny, to hell with her own fears, to hell with it all, and just be together consequences be damned.

"Did it ever freak you out?"

Cara shook her thoughts away to stare blankly at Amy. "Hmm?"

She nodded toward the shop's exit and started walking. "You know the way they are...their powers."

How could it not? Cara questioned silently as she followed Amy out of the store and along the busy sidewalk. The first time she'd experienced the bizarre events that occurred when she and Tristan made love it had sent her running out the door and refusing to take his calls for nearly a week. She'd gotten used to it in time. Mostly.

She shrugged. "Sometimes. I guess it's something you get used to over the years."

"I guess."

Something about Amy's tone was off, as if she didn't quite believe the words. "You obviously got used to it, if you're marrying Lucas."

"I love him. I know we're meant to be together, that doesn't mean it doesn't scare me. Not knowing what the future might hold is scary as hell."

"That's why I left Tristan." Cara sucked in a hard breath as the words reached her ears. How had they made it out of her mouth? She never talked so candidly about her relationship with Tristan. Not even to Tristan!

Amy laughed shortly. "Don't let it bother you. I told you my listening skills are top quality. I have an uncanny way of getting people to open up whether they wanna or not."

Uncanny as those skills might be, Cara wasn't ready to share anything further. She *was* ready to learn. "How did Lucas and Tristan end up friends again? Tristan said he'd tell me, but then he never got around to it last night."

The humor in Amy's eyes fell flat and she nodded toward an Italian restaurant several shops ahead. "It's a long story, thankfully one with a good ending, but I still wouldn't suggest you hear it over an empty stomach."

An hour later, with a belly full of the types of greasy, fattening foods she hadn't allowed herself to indulge in for weeks, Cara sat back in her chair and shook her head at everything Amy had told her. "My God, that's amazing. I can see how you know you belong with Lucas after going through so much to get that way."

"Like I said, the future is uncertain, especially when we don't know if Mike was responsible for Solaris' murder and the threats on the rest of the Sons or not, but we just gotta try to move past our fears and live."

Smart words, if only they were so easy to follow. If only it wasn't for Joey…

Tristan had said Joey wasn't the reason they couldn't be together, but he'd been wrong. If Cara hadn't spent the past eight years dealing with Joey, seeing his many bad and pain-filled days up close and personal, it might have changed everything. If she didn't have to live with the fear that giving Tristan the children they both longed for would result in more disabled kids like her brother or ones with both Tristan's strange powers and Joey's problems, everything might be different. Or maybe nothing would. Now that Tristan believed she wasn't his soul mate and never had been, maybe nothing made a difference.

"Do you want kids?"

Amy's direct and very close to her thoughts question had Cara sitting forward in her seat and glaring. "Excuse me?"

She lifted a slim shoulder in a shrug. "Just curious. Lucas and I often wonder if we have kids if they'll end up with powers or be normal. In a way we hope they're normal—it'll be one of heck of a lot easier on them when it comes to fitting in, but then in a way we hope they have them, to carry on his legacy."

"That's one way to look at it."

"And the other?"

They never fit in and end up miserable and alone, the way she too often felt and the way she feared Joey would always feel. "I don't know. I'm just sure there is one."

"Hmm…probably. I guess we'd better get moving. Outside of that one possibility first thing this morning, I haven't seen a single dress that belongs anywhere but hidden in the back of a closet."

* * * * *

"What the hell, I'll have one of everything on the menu. You are picking up the tab, right?" Lucas shot Perry a smirk, then added, "By the way, I hear you're having some woman problems."

Perry's smile fell away and he glared at Tristan. "Gee, I wonder what makes you think that. Or should I say who?"

"If anyone knows about woman problems, it would be him," Lucas retorted.

As much as Tristan was enjoying this reunion and the return of the laid back camaraderie the three had once shared, he couldn't escape his thoughts. As much as he also knew he'd be better off not voicing them, he needed answers. The kind only the men gathered here today could provide. "I have a serious question."

Perry's eyes lit with interest. "Shoot."

"This pertains more to Lucas, since you have nothing to base it on. Solaris told us how we'd know when we found our soul mates, that it would be obvious. He told each of us it would happen in a different way, but always during lovemaking—"

"I believe his word was sex," Lucas interrupted with a mocking laugh, "but whatever you say, Romeo."

"He told us it would only happen with one person," Tristan continued, determined to get this out wise cracks and all, "and that's how we would know, but do you think he could have been wrong? That there might be more than one?"

"What makes you so damned sure I don't have anything to base it on?"

The agitation in Perry's voice was practically tangible and momentarily knocked Tristan from his purpose. He and Lucas shared a questioning look, then glanced at Perry. "So I wasn't wrong then?" Tristan asked.

"I'm not saying yes or no, I'm just saying I don't think Solaris was wrong."

"I don't either," Lucas said soberly. "I don't think a thing he ever told us was anything but one hundred percent reality. Why?"

"I just… I was hoping, I guess."

"Care to enlighten us a bit more?" Perry asked, placing his elbows on the restaurant's table and leaning forward with interest.

Did he want to try to explain what was happening with Brandy and how as much as he now believed they were meant to be together, his heart still ached for Cara? Not on either of their lives. Was he going to? If the glowering look Lucas shot him was anything to go by, he'd damned well better. "Do I have a choice?"

"Not if you want to live to see morning." Lucas' scowl melted to a half grin. "Besides, it's damned nice to be the only one out of us who's got their life figured out for a change." He made a show of cracking his knuckles, then sank back in his chair. "Open up, Trist. Tell big brother Lucas all about it."

* * * * *

"I come in peace and bearing the morning paper, so quit with the suspicious face already," Amy said when Tristan answered the early morning knock on his suite door to find her standing there.

He peered past Amy into the hallway, glancing in either direction, then looked back at her. "Where's Lucas?"

She rolled her eyes and pushed her way past him into the suite. "Sleeping. I swear the man thinks just because he works the night patrol back home he's allowed to stay on a daytime sleeping schedule here too." She situated herself in a chair at the small table that sat off to one side of the sitting area and frowned. "Rough night? You look like hell."

Tristan forced a laugh while inside he felt like shouting. Rough night was an understatement. He'd lain awake most the night thinking of Cara and how they could ever make it as friends, and the rest of it dreaming about Cara doing things to his body that were anything but friendly. More like erotic as hell as evidenced by the throbbing erection he'd woken up with and the semi he'd been sporting ever since.

Amy snorted. "That is seriously wayyy too much information, Trist."

This time his laugh was authentic. He shook his head and sank down in the seat across from her, scooping up his half-emptied mug and downing a long drink of strong black coffee in the process. None of his damned friends were normal any more. He'd spent most of yesterday with men who knew him inside and out and shared his supernatural abilities, and this morning he had the pleasure of sharing breakfast with a psychic whose biggest thrill as of late seemed to be drilling into his thoughts.

He set the mug back and passed Amy a flippant grin. "If you can't take the heat, I suggest you stay out of my head."

"Now where's the fun in that?" She shot him a smile of her own, then sobered. "So, do you wanna hear?"

Tristan's gut turned over with the question, the breakfast he'd just eaten weighing in his stomach like a brick regardless of the fact aside from the coffee the meal had been about as heartsmart as one could get. He'd asked Amy to use her abilities to glean some information on Cara and the way she truly felt about him — if she wanted him out of her life as she let on or was just pretending that way for some reason he'd yet to figure out. It was foolish to care what she felt for him when he believed his future was with another woman, but damn it, he did care. And after yesterday's talk with Perry and Lucas he cared all the damned more.

He shrugged. "I don't know. You tell me."

"The truth is... Cara doesn't know why she ever got involved with you in the first place. She's never truly cared about you, only the advantages you can bring into her and her little brother's life." Amy hesitated for a second before laughing, he was guessing because of the way his mouth fell open and his eyes bulged with the words, then added with a shake of her head. "Not! I can't believe you actually bought that, Trist! She loves you. She's never stopped loving you."

He closed his mouth and fought back the urge to reach across the table and wrap his hands around her neck. It wouldn't do to be killing his best friend's future wife. Instead, he drowned his joint feelings of frustration and relief by taking a long drink of coffee. He set the now empty mug back and once more met Amy's gaze. "Tell me something I don't know."

"She hates the thought of you with someone else, but believes it's for the best."

He'd guessed that much from her tears last night and her reaction to finding him with Brandy the day before. Still hearing it stated as fact brought a fresh wave of relief crashing through him. "Nothing new there. I'd guessed as much."

The flash of humor that passed through Amy's eyes ensured she'd been listening to his thoughts and no matter how nonchalant he'd made the words sound he felt anything but indifferent. The amusement vanished as she added, "She wants children."

Tristan frowned, trying to place the concern that came into her eyes with the words. Why was that such a big deal? They both wanted children, they'd agreed on that from the beginning, even before she knew about his powers. "So do I."

"*Normal* children. The kind she believes the two of you could never have."

The stress she'd placed on the first word hit home and turned the leaden feeling in his gut to aversion. "Because of Joey," he said dryly.

She nodded. "Yes. And who their father would be."

"It shouldn't surprise me," he retorted, not bothering to keep the anger out of his tone because if there was one thing he couldn't do a damned thing about it was this. "I know how much my powers scare her, but damn it, I don't get how she can throw everything we have away out of fear."

Amy reached a hand across the small table, taking hold of the one he'd fisted on the glass, and squeezing. "She doesn't want to, Trist. In fact, if her thoughts are anything to go by, she was ready to get over her fear when you admitted she wasn't the one."

He closed his eyes as the words assailed him, the idea Cara had truly been ready to return to him. It was all he'd wanted for so long, to have her back in his life permanently and now that she was ready to come back, he'd made it clear she was no longer welcome. At least, not in the capacity of his lover.

"What's really amazing to me is how she can still feel that way about you after the things you've said to her, the way you treated her. God, Tristan, you called her a whore. That's in Lucas' league maybe, but not yours. You never talk that way."

She was right. He never did, not since before Solaris had taken him in, back when he'd been an angry teenager. He also never spoke negatively about Joey or anyone else close to Cara — her mother included. He'd always been the one to able to find a bright spot where the mass of society was concerned, to bring smiles to the faces of those who were clearly having less than sunny days. But lately, he hadn't made anyone smile. Lately, he'd been confused more than anything else. Lately, he'd been saying things to Cara he never would've said to any woman — be she his friend or enemy.

Blowing out a frustrated breath, Tristan dragged a hand through his hair and stood to pace. "I don't know why the hell I said those things to her. I don't know why I've been doing a lot of things lately. I just…I haven't been myself." And when would he be himself again?

"I have to get my hands on the Eye," the words tumbled out his mouth before he'd even had a chance to think them over. They were accurate though. The Eye would hold the answers, it would end his confusion. He had to get hold of it and damned soon.

"And that means working your way past Brandy."

He glanced back at Amy's speculative expression and smirked. "Is that Lucas' idea of pillow talk, telling you all my secrets?"

"Get with the times, Trist. We don't have pillow talk, we have pillow think."

Right. They talked to each other telepathically. Strange as hell and yet he'd do anything to share those powers with Cara. Maybe then he'd fully understand her. Just being able to touch on her thoughts sure as hell wasn't helping. "Yes, it means getting past Brandy or getting with Brandy. Whatever it takes."

A tick started up near the corner of Amy's left eye and her gaze narrowed with disapproval. "Do you honestly believe it's worth it? Sleeping with someone you don't give two shits about in order to get at something she might or might not have to reveal what you might or might not already know?"

"There's more than the Eye at stake now," he answered quickly, refusing to let her questions sink in too deeply, to consider how Cara would respond if he did sleep with Brandy and then ultimately learned Cara really had been the one all along.

Amy nodded. "Right. Alana's picture."

Tristan snorted, aware she hadn't been reading his thoughts, but drawing on more of the aforementioned pillow think. "I swear to God, I'm never telling Lucas another damned thing so long as I live."

She smiled with the accusation, the light of affection filling her eyes. "Sure you will, and it doesn't matter anyway. Little hint, Trist, I can read your mind."

He wanted to smile back, wanted to allow the warmth of friendship that passed between them to cloak his dark thoughts entirely. Only he couldn't. There was a reality to be faced here. "Then you already know what I plan to do."

Her smile fell flat and she nodded grimly. "Whatever it takes to find the truth, even if it means losing Cara in the process."

"It's a chance I have to take," he said resolutely, knowing the words were for him as much as they were for her. He had to do this. He had to know, because if he didn't get to the bottom of this, if he didn't at least try to understand who he truly was and where he was headed by way of the Eye's guidance, then he could never be completely happy.

"I understand," Amy said softly, her smile returning just enough to tell him it was for his sake and in truth held no joy.

"I know you do. Thanks for your help."

"Any time." She stood and started to the door, turning back when she reached it. "You might not have time to care about it, but Cara's planning on driving out to see Joey in the morning. She wants you to go with her, but she's afraid to ask."

Tristan smiled despite the myriad of emotions that now claimed him mind and body. Cara would never have said those words to Amy and so Amy had obviously learned that from reading her mind as well.

He shook his head. "I never realized how damned much that woman thinks."

Amy laughed. "Oh, honey, you don't even wanna know all the things that go on in a woman's mind. We're *always* thinking.

And it's only about men and how much they can piss us off and yet we can still love them, eighty-five percent of the time."

Chapter Ten

Cara sat on a weather-beaten bench in the park near Joey's school. Thoughts spun through her mind, thoughts of just how good Tristan really was with Joey. How even now, he had her little brother chasing after a soccer ball with him and acting like any other boy his age would.

She had no idea what propelled Tristan into dropping by her apartment last night and asking about Joey and if she'd mind if he spent some time with him. She only knew his timing had been impeccable. She'd been planning a trip out to the school this morning and so she'd invited him along for the ride.

Joey's high-pitched giggling reached her followed by Tristan's much deeper laugh as the two fought to gain possession of the ball only to land in a pile of tangled arms and limbs while the ball shot off in another direction completely. Her own laughter bubbled up, tugging her lips into a wide smile and making her realize just how long it had been since she'd laughed. At least, since she'd laughed and truly meant it.

An instant later, as Tristan's contented gaze connected with her own, she also realized how long it had been since she'd been truly honest with him. Not that she'd ever lied much and when she had it was always for a good reason. Still, she had lied or at least withheld information, about the real reason she'd left him, about the way she felt about her job at the Red Room, about the fact she could never handle friendship.

She'd been so angry with him the other night, devastated to think he'd spent all those years lying to her about what they were meant to be to one another, and in all that time she'd never stopped to think how his lying was justified. After all, she'd been withholding just as much truth from him. Only she hadn't been withholding as much truth as he had, she'd been withholding one hundred percent more, because he'd never lied to her in the first place.

No matter where their future might lie, one thing was certain. She owed him the truth. The entire truth. Even if admitting it meant chancing the last of the fine threads that still held them together.

The mirth left Tristan's eyes and he pushed himself to his feet and frowned over at her. "What's the matter?"

Cara forced a small smile back into place. Everything was the matter. But now wasn't the time to tell him that. Her gaze drifted to Joey's expression, one that made it clear he was waiting for Tristan to return to the makeshift soccer game, and her smile became sincere. "He's missed you."

He reached over and ruffled the top of Joey's hair. The boy gave a squirm and disgusted face that spoke of how good today was going for him. He still wasn't speaking much, but actions said plenty. "He's a great kid. Aren't you, Joe?"

Joey's appalled look fell flat and his eyes lit as he looked up at Tristan, making it more than obvious just how much he admired him. "Yeah."

"Just a yeah? Nothing else?"

Joey lips compressed into a tight line and Cara caught Tristan's conspiratorial wink. He was trying to draw him out, she knew, to make him think beyond what he typically considered his limits. Joey's mouth lost the hard look and he smiled his broadest smile as he offered, "I'm smart."

That he was. Smarter than most teenagers and at times Cara believed smarter than she was where certain things were concerned.

The answer clearly wasn't enough for Tristan as he pressed Joey with a questioning look. "That's it? Just smart? You have to have a better reason than that."

Joey's lips regained their tight look while his eyes pinched closed. Pink blossomed on his cheeks and knots of anxiety formed in the pit of Cara's belly. Pushing him was one thing, forcing him to respond to a question clearly beyond his abilities was another. She opened her mouth to tell Tristan to stop. Before the words could come out, his own cut her off.

"How about because you can kick my butt at soccer?" Tristan asked.

Joey opened his eyes to reveal relief that quickly turned to playfulness. He darted behind Tristan and ran after the ball they'd lost in their earlier skirmish. Bringing it back, he stood in front of Tristan in what could only be called a taunting manner and waved the ball in the air. "Yeah. I can kick your butt."

Cara laughed at the confidence in his voice, and the startled look on Tristan's face. She'd never heard her brother talk that way before, with such bravado. She'd never seen him stand up for himself this way or come out of his shell so completely. It was wonderful, everything she'd wanted for so long, and caused by Tristan's presence.

"Yes, you can." Tristan stole the ball from the boy's hands with lightning fast reflexes, then shot Joey a grin. "That doesn't mean you can't still use some practice." He handed the ball back to him. "Take this out and do some footwork while I talk to your sister. Just look at her sitting over there all by herself...she's lonely."

Joey glanced Cara's way. His look spoke volumes to the fact he didn't think she looked lonely. He was right. She wasn't. At least she didn't feel that way until Tristan joined her on the bench and made it clear she might just have been lonely after all.

His arm came up on the back of bench and rested lightly against her shoulders. She shivered at the feel of his strong fingers brushing against her bare nape, spurring to life warmth and longing throughout her body. She wore her hair in a ponytail, and he lifted the long mass away from her neck. His touch turned more solid, his fingers caressing, stroking, rendering the kind of soul blistering heat the late morning sun could never provide. It might be almost eighty-five already, but she hadn't even felt warm until he sat down.

Now with just that touch, with his nearness, her nerves stood on end with awareness and her nipples beaded with the same. She swallowed against the sudden dryness in her throat, needing to talk, to end the intimacy of the moment, to remind them both they were just friends.

"Nice work," she finally said. "You're going to have him cocky in no time at all."

Tristan's hand fell away and he pulled back on the bench to pass her an agitated look. "He needs to have a strong self-esteem. He's one hell of a lot better than he used to be, but he still has a long road ahead of him."

If he *ever* fully overcame his problems, Cara added silently. She glanced to where Joey ran with the ball then back at Tristan. The frustration had come into his eyes so easily. That never would've happened in the past. Why had it now? Why so suddenly did it seem she could rile him with a simple sentence meant to be nothing more than teasing? "I meant that as a joke."

The temper left his eyes at the same time his hand returned to play along the sensitive skin of her neck. This time when he relaxed back he didn't look out at Joey, but directly into her eyes. "You haven't done that much lately."

"Joke?" she asked quickly, struggling to ignore the effect his potent gaze had on her. The even stronger effect that single unruly strand of sandy brown hair blowing across his forehead had. There was no point in even trying to deny the effect his mouth had on her when it split into a sexy grin. Desire pooled through her blood and deep into her loins. Heat centered her, rousing her heart into a hasty beat while her pussy grew damp and throbbed with a longing all its own.

"Joking...and smiling. It looks good on you."

Tristan's gaze was no longer tense, but dark and needy. His fingers ended their gentle caressing of her nape and slid beneath the wide neck of her T-shirt to massage her bare shoulder. His touch there was nearly as light, but not nearly so innocent. The ache within her grew, unleashing a rush of raw desire deep into her core and pushing a barely audible cry from her lips.

Barely audible, and yet he heard it. The proof was in his eyes, the sudden dilating of his pupils until the black infringed almost completely upon the brown, the hunger that burned there. His mouth moved, but no sound came out, and as his body drew nearer to her, the appetite in eyes flaming ever higher, the air surrounding them becoming almost excruciatingly hot, she realized it was because he wasn't about to speak, he was about to devour her.

Cara squeaked out another cry and forced herself to stand when all she wanted to do was sit here and let him have his way with her. Let him consume her kiss by kiss, lick by lick, thrust for demanding thrust. She couldn't do that. Not with Joey so close by. She couldn't do that even without Joey so close, not until she told Tristan the truth, and maybe not even then.

"Th—hanks for a—asking to s—see him," she managed.

She drew several calming breaths and pretended to study her brother's moves for a few seconds before turning back to Tristan. The heat was still evident in his eyes and the air around them, but not so much that she felt she couldn't control herself any longer. And yet as much as that might be true, she wasn't about to sit back down beside him and find out. "You're really good with him," she offered instead.

The words sent the throbbing in her sex to the back burner as self-disgust assailed her. Tristan *was* really good with Joey. He'd always been this good. That she'd become upset when Joey mentioned Tristan's name, the last time she'd been here, was ridiculous. She'd been truly disturbed that he might have seen Joey without her permission. While she'd found out from the school staff that Tristan hadn't been here since the last time they'd come together, she still loathed herself for ever being irritated with the idea he could've come alone.

"I've always had a thing for kids...we both have."

The way he droned out the words, the memories that filled his eyes, his emotions, she knew what he was thinking: about their past, when they'd first started dating, about how they'd planned their future and the family they would make together. The one she'd been too afraid to give him and had run away instead.

She'd been a coward in the past. She'd been afraid their children would turn out like her brother or possibly like their father. If they did turn out that way, then she would be one damned lucky woman. Joey even now was running and laughing, letting his happiness be known, and Tristan…Tristan was looking at her like he still wanted it all. Still wanted her in his life regardless of what he'd said about her not being his destiny.

She didn't deserve it, not after the way she'd left him behind, but if she told him she still wanted all that too, that she wanted his love, his hand, the children they would create together even if they weren't perfectly normal, would he still give it to her? Was he strong enough to walk away from Brandy, a woman he believed he was meant to spend his life with, and be with Cara instead?

It wasn't a question she wanted to ask, and it was also a question she had to know the answer to. Sinking back down onto the bench, she took his hand and met his gaze as warmth gravitated between them.

Awareness gathered in his eyes, across his face, and she knew he was reading her once again. Let him read her, she wasn't holding anything back this time. "Tristan—"

"Yes?" he cut her off in a rush.

A rush that stilled the words on her tongue and washed away every ounce of her courage. God, she couldn't do this, not here, not now. Maybe not ever. Biting down on the inside of her cheek, she glanced over to where Joey toed the soccer ball, then back at Tristan and forced a smile as she released his hand. "We should probably think about heading out for some lunch."

151

His eyes registered a disappointment she felt with every fiber of her being, making her ache to force the words out terrified of his response or not. Before she could do so, he stood and said, "Yeah. I guess we probably should." Then walked over to where Joey played and scooped both soccer ball and giggling boy into his arms.

＊ ＊ ＊ ＊ ＊

"We should have brought Amy along. If anyone can get into Joey's head and try to understand what's going on, it's her."

It was the first time either of them had spoken since leaving Joey's school over an hour ago. Silence had never felt so deafeningly painful in Cara's estimation. She grabbed onto his words now, yearning for conversation of any kind. "She works with kids a lot?"

"No, she's psychic."

The moment the words left his mouth, Tristan snapped his head around to stare at her. It was possible she might have missed the connection if not for his bug-eyed look, but now that she'd seen it everything fell into place.

That first morning they'd spent shopping together Cara had felt a bit uncomfortable around Amy and how she seemed to be able to read into her thoughts and feelings so well. Yesterday's excursion had lessened her discomfort to nearly nothing and she'd honestly felt they were developing a friendship. That Amy truly liked her and cared about her as a person.

Now she knew better.

Reality twisted her belly and squeezed at her heart. She'd never had many friends growing up in one of the seedier areas of Vegas, never any girlfriends. Brandy had been her friend for a while and in a way still was. Amy had never been her friend. She'd merely been doing Tristan a favor.

"You set her up, didn't you?" Cara tried to keep the anger from her voice, tried and failed. She didn't want to argue again, didn't want this nearly perfect day with Joey to end this way.

She just couldn't help herself or the rising note of anguish that filled her words. "She didn't want me as her maid-of-honor, she made that up so I would have to spend time with her and she could pick my brain. She doesn't even goddamn like me!

"And why should she? I'm nothing but a slut, right, Tristan? Nothing but a whore just like my mother was."

"*Scopata!* Don't say those kinds of things, Cara! That's not true!" He focused back on the road and his tone dropped to a calmer level "Yes, I asked her to listen into your thoughts, but I never suggested that she have you be her maid-of-honor. She honestly wants you to be. She told me this morning you're one of the first women she's liked in a long time and coming from her that's saying something.

"As far as you're being a—"

"Why do you care so much?" The question came out quietly and she knew it was because she feared the response. Her initial rush of anger had passed with his admission that he'd asked Amy to listen in, but not to befriend her for his purposes. Now she needed to know why he cared enough to want to know her thoughts—if he too wanted to say to hell with destiny and reclaim what they'd once shared before she'd allowed anxiety to rule her.

Tristan glanced at her and smirked. "That's a pretty obtuse question."

"Not really. It's not like I'm a part of your life these days. At least, not as anything more than a friend."

"I wish you were."

The honesty in his voice, in his eyes when he again glanced her way, had her heart pounding madly against her rib cage. She couldn't accept that single response to mean what she hoped. She needed more. She needed to know that when he was with Brandy it was Cara he thought of. "You have a funny way of showing it."

The flash of remorse in his eyes ensured she didn't need to expand on the words. He understood completely. Understood and if his look were to be believed, despised himself for it. "Cara...there's a lot you don't know. I know Amy filled you in on what happened with her and Lucas a couple months back, but there's more to it than that."

What did that have anything to do with this? The man who'd taken in Tristan and Lucas as teenagers had recently been murdered and somehow that tied into their situation? "You think the killer is still on the loose and that has something to do with your being here and the way you treat me? I don't understand."

"I don't know if Solaris' death is connected to what's happening right now. To be honest until a couple days ago, I never even considered it."

"What changed that?"

Tristan exhaled loudly, sounding more tired than she could ever remember him being. "A lot of things... Brandy. The Eye. The picture of—"

"Slow down. The Eye. What about it? I know the stories, but how does that affect anything? How does it affect us?"

He again glanced over. The weariness she'd heard in his voice was evident in his eyes, but also there was hope. "I didn't think there was an us."

"I don't know that there is," she answered honestly, wishing all the while that there could be, that it wasn't too late. That the night when she'd dislodged her emotions from their lovemaking and the vision it rendered, she also hadn't dislodged any chance of them having a future together.

"But there might be?"

"You're the one who said we don't belong together, Trist."

The hope she'd detected moments ago fell flat. "You walked out on me. Not once, but twice. How the hell was I supposed to feel after that?"

Cara narrowed her gaze on his hurt expression, the tumble of emotions she felt roiling through him. Is that why he thought they didn't belong together? Not because of Brandy at all, but because of her leaving him? Was she truly the one responsible for this divide between them? If she were, then she'd only opened this rift because she loved him. Because she'd wanted what was best for both of them and up until a very short while ago hadn't been able to see what that was.

She could see it now, see it as clearly as if it were a living, breathing thing. What was best for both of them was to have a future together, one as friends and lovers. Somehow she had to convince him of the same, regardless of what supposed destiny the Eye might ultimately reveal to him.

She settled her hand over the one of his that was reclined on the armrest between them. He glanced over at her with the action, and she used that moment to try to explain it all with her eyes, with the emotions that churned through her body, with the love she still felt for him and always would.

"I've always come back, Tristan, even though I probably shouldn't have," she said softly when he turned back to focus on the barren stretch of road and desert unfolding around them. "The only reason I ever left you in the first place is because I believed it was the right thing to do for both of us. If Amy listened to my thoughts at all, she should've been able to tell you that."

His attention remained directed ahead and silence filtered between them, weighting both the air and Cara's shoulders as empty seconds passed by. Then Tristan turned his hand over beneath hers, enveloping her palm with his own.

"She did," he said quietly. "She also told me that you still love me and the real reason you're afraid of us being together...because of how our children might turn out."

Cara sucked in a sharp breath with the admission, and yet at the same time knew relief. She'd planned to tell him tonight, tell him both her reason for leaving and that she was sorry and still loved him in a way time and distance could never change. Amy had saved her the trouble. "She was right...about both things. I'm sorry I didn't tell you myself, but then it doesn't really matter any more. We aren't meant to b—be..."

Hearing the tremor in her voice, Tristan pumped her hand and looked over at her, forcing a reassuring smile. "I don't know that for a fact, Cara. That's why I have to gain possession of the Eye. Brandy has it. She has the answers to everything."

"That's how you know she's your true destiny?"

His smile fell flat with the continual ache in her voice, the unshed tears that now clung to the backs of her eyes, diffusing their normally brilliant green shade. He wanted to fix it all, to make her not hurt any more, to make himself not hurt any more either. He couldn't. Not here, not now, and never with only a few simple words.

"No. That's not how," he said, telling her what little he could, what little he knew himself, to try to make her understand. "I believe she's my soul mate because not only does she have the power to stand strong and trust in me when she's frightened, but because of what happens when we're together."

Cara's hand went limp in his grasp and she looked away, mouthing an almost silent, "When you have sex."

"We've never had sex," he snapped back, refusing to allow her to think he would sleep with another woman while she still filled his heart. But then why shouldn't she believe it? He'd gone to Brandy less than a half a week before, seeking out that very thing — sex with another woman to erase the memory of the one he still loved.

She turned her head back and slitted her eyes. "I was there, Tristan. You can't deny what I saw with my own two eyes."

"You saw us *almost* having sex....just as I saw the two of you." He hadn't meant to add those last words, had known at the time something had been seriously out of perspective because Cara would never act that way around another woman.

As much as Tristan hadn't meant to say it and believed she hadn't been herself that night, he couldn't stop his mind from roaming back or his body from responding to the memories. Cara's hungry look as she went to Brandy, her throaty moans of desire when Brandy first began to finger her nipples, the way the breath panted from her mouth, hot and hazy, when Brandy finally stopped her ministrations only to slide her hands beneath Cara's shirt and fondle her naked breasts.

Merda, he'd never been so in tune with Cara's mind, her thoughts as he had that night. She'd been ready to give in, to sink into Brandy's arms completely and beg her to take her over the edge. She'd wanted her to bring an end to the torrent of heated pressure building with her pussy, to strip her bare and slice her tongue through her moist center until she was coming into Brandy's mouth.

His cock hardened painfully, pulsating with the clarity of the image, of how easily he could recreate the scene, of how badly he'd wanted to charge into Cara's apartment after she'd run off and taste the sweet arousal Brandy had stimulated in her sex.

Struggling to ignore his erection and how badly he still wanted to do that, place her back on his bed and lap at her juices until she was coming in his mouth, Tristan glanced over at Cara. Deep crimson stained her high cheekbones and when she felt his gaze on her, she jerked both her hand and face away from him to stare out the passenger's side window.

"I don't know what that was," she said in a low voice. "I've never done that before. I won't. I've told Mason over and over again I won't touch the other girls at the club. That night, I—I wasn't myself. I—"

"You don't have to justify your actions, Cara. I understand. It wasn't you who wanted it to happen, it was..." Who? Him? No, he hadn't wanted it to happen. He hadn't made an effort to stop it at first either, but that was because he hadn't been able to find his voice any more than his brain. The sight of them touching each other had been too erotic, too arousing to form thought. He'd managed though, for Cara's sake and the knowledge she'd live to regret her actions.

"I don't know what it is about Brandy," Tristan admitted. "There's just something about her, something that pulls you in even when all you want to do is run."

Cara wrenched her head back around to face him, her face no longer red, and eyed him speculatively. "If she can make me feel that way too, feel so connected to her on a level I've never even considered feeling things for another women, then how can you be so sure what you're experiencing with her is different than the way she makes anyone feel? And please don't tell me because she's strong enough to stick around when she's afraid. I stayed for four years and you've barely known her four days."

Six days, but it had felt far longer. Perhaps because the bulk of the days he'd also spent with Cara, making love, arguing, hating her, loving her.

Dio, she drove him crazy.

She made him ache for her even as he knew better than to do so. "I can't be certain, Cara. I can only guess that I'm doing the right thing here. I can't explain the way Brandy affects me, the way she makes me feel. It's almost painful at times..." Sometimes just one look at her face and his heart hurt so badly it felt as though it might burst. "I don't love her, but if she's the one, if that's what the Eye tells me, then I will learn to love her."

"What happens if you just forget about it? If you pretend you never knew it existed and so you couldn't follow its guidance? What happens if you never see Brandy again?"

Her eyes came more alive with each word, until energy spun visibly between the small, confined area that separated them.

Energy...and desperation.

Tristan knew without having to read into her emotions what she was feeling now, what she wanted. She wanted the same thing he'd once craved, that the parts of him that didn't feel honor bound to another, still craved. She wanted another chance. He knew deep down that given one she would never run from him again. He also knew he had an obligation to both his past and to himself. "I'll always wonder."

"But it won't kill you."

"No. I don't think it will kill me, but I doubt I will ever be completely happy until I know the truth."

Cara's left cheek sunk in and he turned back to the road, waiting for her thinking to draw to an end. Finally, she reached back across the armrest and took his hand, pumping it as he'd done to hers earlier. He glanced over at her and met with eyes no longer filled with tears but hunger. "It won't kill me to go home alone tonight either, but that doesn't change the fact I don't want to. Don't make me, Tristan."

His still hard cock throbbed with the desire that turned her voice breathy, the meaning behind her words, her hot look. She might not want to go home, but he wanted to take her there. Not to her rundown apartment, but to the home in Ashton they'd have made theirs in a couple years, after they'd begun adding to the family.

He couldn't take her to that place tonight, and maybe he never would be able to, but he could take her back to his hotel suite. He could show her one last time how much he loved her and always would. "I don't want you to be alone tonight, but I can't make you any promises if you stay with me, baby."

She nodded and a smile curved her lips, drawing his attention to their plumpness, making him remember just how good she tasted—like ripe strawberries, only better. He wanted to taste her now, to start with her mouth and work his way down, committing each inch of her lush body to memory.

"I know you can't make promises," Cara said, pulling his gaze back to the need in her eyes, but I also know I love you. I'm sorry that I get scared about things, "but you know my life tends to run to the negative. The good times are so hard to believe in."

The honesty in her words, her admission destroyed any chance Tristan had of escaping this night without having her one last time. The smart thing to do would be to take her back to her apartment and forget they ever had this conversation. But if there were even a chance that this might be their last night together, then he wouldn't be foolish enough to listen to intelligence.

The outskirts of Reno opened up around them and he was forced to concentrate on driving. He relied on his tone and the knowledge that while Cara might not be his soul mate, she could still read into his emotions to get his feelings across. "I love you, too. I love you in a way I will never love another woman, not even if she is my destiny."

"I can't make you any promises either, Tristan. I can't leave my job at the Red Room. I have to be able to pay for Joey's tuition. I know I could get a job in the art industry, but until we see how things turn out, I'm not ready to do that."

He stopped at a red light and looked over, knowing the reasons she'd kept her distance these past months well now. Not because she thrilled in stripping for strangers the way he'd accused, but because she hadn't been able to bear the thought of running into him. "Because if we don't end up together, you won't want to see me?"

"I just…" Her voice shook and she smiled tightly. "I can't. It's too much."

The light turned green and he accelerated, letting her words hang in the air for several long seconds. He glanced over at her then and his heart ached with the realization of just how much his accusations had to have hurt her. She honestly had been trying to fend for Joey via the only method she knew how. At least the only method that wouldn't chance running into him.

Tristan grinned at the irony. She'd chosen stripping to avoid him and yet somehow it was the exact reason they'd been reunited. His grin died as he said soberly, "I don't think of you as a whore, Cara. I never have and I never will. I'm sorry I said that. I'm sorry I've said a lot of things lately. You've always been able to rile me like no other, but the past week it isn't even about riling. You just have to open your mouth and tease me a little and I go from calm to heated in a second flat."

She laughed shortly and her eyes danced with the joyous sound, warming his heart. "That sounds to me like something only a true soul mate should be able to do."

"I hope so, *mio bello*. I hope so with all that I am." The lights of the Lazy Ace appeared in the near distance and he nodded toward the casino's flashing sign, then looked over at Cara. "Last chance to change your mind."

"I'm not changing it, Tristan. I love you and if tonight is all we have left, then I'll take it."

Chapter Eleven

Cara stood in Tristan's hotel suite bathroom, her stomach a bundle of raw nerves and energy.

Was it really less than a week ago that she'd stood in this same spot, desperate to gain her distance from Tristan only to end up making love with him anyway?

It seemed like so much more time had passed than that. She'd learned so much, about herself and others. Most importantly she'd learned that she'd been wrong where she and Tristan were concerned, about where their future lay.

He might have said he could make her no promises tonight, just as she'd told him the same, but in her heart she knew otherwise. She knew that tonight was the beginning of something wonderful, the conception of their new life together.

She smiled at the thought, at conceiving in more than the literal sense, of doing so physically as well. For so long she'd been frightened of marrying him, of giving him the children they both wanted, and tonight she practically laughed with the idea.

Her heart warming with the faces of children to come filling her mind, Cara let free her hair from its ponytail and reached for the brush in the shower kit on the back of the toilet seat. Tristan liked her hair down, so that he could run his fingers through it. Tonight was all about pleasing him, showing him how much they belonged together regardless of what destiny might ultimately dictate.

Yet as much as it was about pleasing him, it was her own pleasure that burst forth with the first stroke of the brush's firm beads against her scalp. The light of joy that filled her heart turned to the warmth of desire in very different parts of her body. There was one singular thing she wanted now. One thing she hadn't felt in too long.

Her body heated with anticipation as she turned to the bathroom door that had been left open a few inches. "Tristan?"

Seconds passed and the door was pulled open all the way. Tristan looked across the short distance, his gaze first falling on Cara's and then drifting to the brush in her hand. Heat registered in his deep brown eyes and a sexy grin broke out over his face. "Would you like some help?"

"Have I ever been able to say no?"

Unease flickered through his gaze, but then quickly passed as he crossed to her and took the brush. "Not when it comes to my brushing your hair anyway."

Or to him touching any other part of her body. That unease hadn't been about her response to his touching her, she knew, it had been about the months when she'd refused to be with him, when she hadn't even wanted to see him. Only she had wanted to, and he had to know that after all that had passed between them today.

Tristan stood beside her with the brush, but had yet to make any effort to use it. "Please," she said, uncaring how desperate she sounded. "I need this."

He stood still an instant longer and then moved behind her and brought the brush to her scalp. Slowly he eased its thin plastic fingers through the length of her hair and she sank back against his chest and all but mewled her bliss.

God, she could melt, turn into a puddle at his feet.

The brush continued its long, sinuous strokes, massaging her scalp, loosening the muscles in her neck and shoulders while those deep within her grew tight. The temperature of the room around them intensified and Cara closed her eyes and sighed with the knowledge that she wasn't the only one affected. He was feeling it too.

"You're beautiful, *mia bella signora*." Tristan's warm mouth skimmed over her neck and she shivered as a current of heat jetted from her nape to her core. His lips stilled, applying pressure at the point where her pulse thrummed. His tongue came out, laving over her flesh, and her pussy moistened and tingled. "You taste exquisite."

She thought she could melt, but there was no "could" about it. She was melting, sinking into his sinfully blessed touch. "Mmm..."

"Good."

She could hear his grin and she smiled back automatically. It was so much better than good. "Very good," she answered languidly.

He flicked his tongue over her neck once again and she jerked with his touch and the throbbing it delivered deep in her sex.

He laughed shortly. "You're so responsive. More so than any woman I've ever known."

Even Brandy? The question popped into Cara's head without warning, bringing her eyes wide open. She shook it and the resulting doubt away. She wouldn't ruin this moment with thoughts of Brandy or anyone other than the two of them.

Desperate to return to the moment, to the feel of the brush gliding through her hair, to that of Tristan's mouth on her heated flesh, she moved back against him and rubbed her ass against his groin. His low grunt reached her ears and she smiled.

He met her gaze in the mirror. "If you want your hair brushed, I suggest you stop."

She almost laughed at that. He, the one who'd been nibbling away at her like she was his favorite dish, was suggesting such a thing. Still, she did as he said and remained inert while he continued to fan the brush through her hair, curling the ends under with meticulousness few men would either understand or take the time for. But then he wasn't just any man. He was one with an eye for a beauty, for indulging in the finer things, for ignoring his own suggestions and dropping his lips back to her neck to nibble.

"Tristan!"

Cara laughed huskily as the effects of his nipping took their toll on her body, warming her blood and making her cunt ache to be filled.

She shifted back against him again. If she were to be made to feel needy, then so would he. The hard length of his erection pressed against her buttocks and a guttural groan filled the air.

Tristan set the brush on the sink basin and gripped her hips in his hands. He rocked against her, rubbing his cock against the seam of her ass. "You do this to me, Cara," he said, his voice rough, his look as he met hers in the mirror, famished. "Every time I walk in a room and feel your presence, you do this to me."

He did the same to her. Made her nipples bead and ache for his clever mouth, made her pussy wet and hungry to be filled with his solid cock. He made her want to come undone completely, to lose control. "Touch me, Tristan."

"Like this?" He slid his hands beneath the hem of her T-shirt and up over the soft flesh of her belly until they cupped her breasts through the lace of her bra. One thumb slid past the thin material to chafe over an aroused nipple.

She jerked at the intensity of the subtle contact. "Oh, yes, like that!"

Grinning at their reflections, he moved his hands from her breasts to pull off her shirt. He unfastened the back clasp of her strapless bra and the black lace fluttered to the bathroom tiling unheeded.

Cara watched her reflection, her pupils dilating, her face becoming flushed, as his skilled hands returned to her breasts, cupping their weight, teasing her nipples with a lightness that was slowly driving her mad. Her pussy pulsed with need and grew moist and heavy to the point of agony.

Tristan's gentle caressing stilled and he caught her nipples between his fingers, plucking at the stiff, deep pink points as painful pleasure sizzled through her body. Juices flooded her sex. She whimpered and slammed her buttocks back against his swollen cock. "More. Give me more, Tristan."

A deep growl rolled along her ear and she caught his ravenous gaze in the mirror for just an instant. Then he grabbed hold of her hips and swiveled her in his arms. He went down on one knee and his lips came down hard over a throbbing nipple. He took the aroused bud deep inside the wet, warm interior of his mouth and suckled.

The fire building within her flamed higher, the air around them crackled with life. He palmed the globes of her ass with his large hands and sucked harder on her nipple. She moaned at the jolt of raw desire that shot from his lips to her core. He had barely touched her and already she was on the verge of orgasm.

While he couldn't read her thoughts completely, he could clearly read them enough. His mouth still firmly latched on her nipple, he brought his right hand around to the front of her thigh. He slid his fingers up the inside of the cuff of her shorts and past the damp crotch of her panties to tease along the edge of her mound.

"*Dio*, you're so wet, Cara. I haven't even touched your pussy yet and you want to explode, don't you, baby?"

"Yes." She allowed her head to loll back and her eyes to once again close, sensation to override her. "I want to come, Tristan."

"Then do it."

She was so close...so close... If he would just move his fingers a little higher, stop taunting her with their nearness to her clit and touch down on the swollen bud. Just a touch... He didn't stop his taunting, didn't offer a touch. He only lifted his mouth from her breast, tipped back his head and laughed at her impatience. "I want this night to be perfect, *mio bello*. I want to go slow and remember everything."

So did she, but right now she needed release.

She'd never touched herself in front of him when the lights were on. At least no other time than the night she'd stripped for him and even then the lighting had been dimmed. That night he seemed to enjoy the show, seemed to indulge in her exploration of her body, the shock of arousal she'd felt upon fingering herself. Tonight he could indulge again, because she couldn't wait any longer.

Her pussy spasmed with growing expectancy, liquid heat flooding deep within her sex. Cara brought her hands up from her sides and unzipped her shorts, aching with the need to stroke the spasms into more. Tristan rocked back on his knees, removing his tongue from where he'd skimmed lazy, wet circles over her breasts. Her fingers stilled on her shorts. Anxiety filled her with the realization he was watching, waiting for her to remove her clothes and fondle herself. Anxiety that turned to accelerated excitement when he looked up at her with burning anticipation in his eyes.

Heat gushed through her, the pumping in her pussy quickening with the restless urge to let go. She hastily slid off her shorts and panties. Then, to the sound of Tristan's sharp intake of breath and her own rapid breathing, she parted the lips of her cunt and petted her swollen clit.

The bathroom was no place to be getting off, not when they had the whole suite for their pleasure, but at this moment Tristan wasn't going to complain. He remained rocked back on his knees, his cock throbbing and his balls excruciatingly tight as Cara continued to fondle herself.

The last time he'd seen her naked, she'd had her pubic hair trimmed neatly. Now the tight, red curls were gone completely and the sweet pink flesh of her cunt was bare and moist with arousal. He wanted to touch, to lick, to bury himself inside her. She never gave him the chance. Instead penetrating her pussy with her own slim fingers.

She cried out with the contact and her hips bucked at the urgent assault, exposing her dewy sex to him entirely. Her scent colored the air as she thrust against her seeking fingers, her cries turning to breathy moans and sighs.

His cock felt ready to explode within his briefs, his balls growing heavier, tighter. He wanted to remove his clothes, take his erection into his hand, and join her. It was too late for that. She was already falling over the edge. Her long red hair hung wildly down her back and her tongue licked repeatedly over her wide, plump lower lip. Shallow cries of ecstasy ripped from her mouth as her bucking hips moved faster.

An unseen wind picked up around them, the few items that weren't firmly latched down, lifting with the force of the orgasm coursing through her, of the crackle of life that flowed between them. He believed at that moment she would come undone. Instead, she lifted her head, opened her eyes and stared deeply into his, conveying more emotion, more feeling than what she'd ever before let show.

Tristan had never realized until now, but she'd always held a part of herself back in the past. The part that feared. That part was bared to him now, and he drank it in, drank in everything she gave to him and, when she came seconds later, he felt the force of her release tumbling through his own body and deep into his soul.

As her breathing evened out, Cara smiled down at him, the rapture that clung to her swollen lips and heavily-lidded eyes all feminine satisfaction. In her pride, he found his own. While they might not have been joined physically, she had given him the most precious gift that she ever could. She had given him herself unconditionally and without a single fear, including what the morning might bring.

Unable to remain idle any longer, he gathered her in his arms and buried his face in the sensual delight of her sex. He allowed himself one single lick of the juices that glistened along her pussy lips and against her inner thighs, then pulled back and grinned up into her eyes. "*Dio*, I love you."

She started to respond in kind, but before she could get the words out Tristan scooped her up and over his shoulder. To the sounds of her breathy laughter he carried her to the bedroom and placed her back on the bed.

Cara came up on her elbows and smiled as she glanced around the room at the service trays heaping with food, including her two favorites. "You've been busy."

He grabbed a plump strawberry from the fruit tray and reclined on the bed next to her. He took a moment to revel in the beauty of her naked body opened to him, concealing not a single secret, then he dragged the berry's fat tip up her belly and over the fullness of her breasts. He grazed an aroused nipple and she sucked in a breath.

He skimmed the berry across the rosy fullness of her lips, then pulled it back away. "I thought you might be hungry."

"I'm famished."

"Me too." He crushed his mouth to hers with a desperation that wasn't warranted. She wasn't going anywhere tonight. She was his and his alone. And yet he couldn't think about just tonight. Thoughts of tomorrow filled his mind and made him frantic to possess her now and again many more times before the sun rose.

He sank his tongue deep into her mouth, feeding from her sweetness, taking so much more from her than just a kiss. Her lips were at first soft, pliant, then they came alive, sucking at his, pulling at his tongue with an urgency mimicked in the sudden impatient lifting of her hips. When he sensed her pulling away, attempting to end the kiss, he regained control, plunging his tongue explosively deep, stealing her breath, her sanity. Destroying his own judgment until thought was no longer even a possibility. And when finally breathing seemed to elude him as well, he pulled his lips back and replaced them with the ripe berry.

Cara's tongue came out, sweeping over the fullness of the berry until it glistened a startling red. It reminded him of the way her pussy had looked moments ago. Moist and full and blood red with her need. Her tongue slipped back between her lips and she chewed at the berry's tip, nibbling off the end and then releasing it.

Tristan pulled the fruit back and juices streamed from its open end, leaking along her lower lip and running in lazy rivulets along the sensitive flesh of her neck. Those rivulets called to him, made him yearn to sweep over them with his tongue. He held back that urge and pressed the exposed berry against her collarbone.

She jerked with its first touch and he placed a hand on her arm, silently telling her to remain still. She did as he asked, watching with wide, hazy eyes and tight, puffs of hot breath as he dragged the berry back down along her breasts. He purposefully chafed it across the same erect nipple as he had before, and was rewarded with the bucking of her hips and a helpless erotic sound that was as much plea as bliss.

His cock responded to that sound, twitching violently, all but begging for release from his briefs and slacks. Soon, but not yet. He wasn't done creating his masterpiece and if he removed his clothes now he would never get to finish before he plowed into the warm, willing walls of her pussy.

He moved the strawberry lower yet, caressing it across the flatness of her belly and leaving streams of ripe red juice in his wake.

"You're making a mess," Cara murmured.

He smiled up at her and shook his head. "No, baby. I'm making my dinner. "Mmm… Here comes my favorite part."

Her eyes flared wide as she followed his gaze. "Tris—"

The word died as he pushed her bent legs farther apart and touched the cool berry to her open sex. He stroked her clit with the fruit's juicy edges and the small nubbin puffed up. He brought the fruit back and forth, staining the lips of her cunt a deep red. With each pass of the berry's tip over her clit her hips arched and her breathing grew more jagged, her eyes a more brilliant shade of jade.

Tristan pressed his thumb against the rear of her sex, opening her pussy lips wide, and pushed the berry inside to the sound of her shallow gasp. He bent his head and ran his tongue over the exposed part of the berry and the flesh of her cunt that surrounded it and then slid from the bed.

"Tristan?"

Her voice came out low, but breathy and he knew she was enjoying this every bit as much as he was. "Don't move, Cara. I want you just how you are."

Anticipation shone in her eyes and she bit down on her lower lip and nodded. Not about to leave her alone for long, he went to the serving trays and lifted the lid of the vat of warm chocolate. He ladled a spoonful of the sweet, rich substance from its container and then returned to the erotic sight of Cara waiting for him, her eyes dark and stimulated and her sex filled with the fruit.

His cock jerked impatiently and he pushed back his need once again. He wanted to drop down on his knees and eat the juicy fruit from her cunt. And he would. Soon. First he had to finish his work.

"A little chocolate here." Using his shoulders, he pushed her legs farther apart and settled between her thighs. Slowly, he drizzled the tepid sauce from the ladle. Her breath hissed in with the first contact of warm against cool and chocolate gushed in rivulets down her lips and around the plump berry.

"And now it's time to feast."

Taking her ass into his hands, Tristan brought her sex to his lips. The scent of her excitement filled his nostrils with sweetness and desire, and as he lapped his tongue over the chocolate, strawberry and pussy concoction he'd created, juices streamed onto his tongue that tasted much more like those of Cara's arousal than those from the berry.

He bit into the plumpness of the fruit and then skewered his tongue through the meat of its center. Breaking through to the other side, he tasted the readiness of her hot, eager body.

She arched up beneath him and the breath wheezed from her lungs as her fingers sank into his hair. "Please…"

"Please, what, Cara? Please kiss you? Show you how you taste? How excited this makes you?" He thrust his tongue deep into her sex once again, then rubbed his mouth over the chocolate sauce and remains of the strawberry.

Her hips arched and her pussy ground against his pelvis as he came up over her and buried his tongue between her lips. She latched onto him, suckling at his mouth, licking at his lips, reveling in her own taste with breathy sighs and delighted moans.

She wrapped her legs around his back, and her cunt rubbed against his cock through the layers of his slacks and briefs. His penis throbbed, his balls felt ready to curl into his body, and Tristan couldn't hold back any longer.

With one last hot, sticky kiss, he stood and quickly removed his clothing, aware her hungry eyes watched his every move. He settled back between her thighs then and buried his tongue deep into her cunt, licking away the excess juice and arousal that coated her lips. He ate at the remains of the berry and teased her clit with the edge of his teeth. Her nails returned to his scalp, pinching almost painfully, and when her body began to shiver, her clit to swell to the point of no return, he came up on his knees and, holding her belly and ass in place, plunged his cock into her pussy.

Cara's breath streamed out with the force of the entry and her hands fell at her sides. She attempted to sit, but he didn't allow it, continuing his long, solid thrusts into her slick sex until she could only recline boneless on the bed. Her nails bit into the sheets and finally she found a rhythm, sucking his cock deeper and deeper into her warmth with each sinuous thrust.

The air around them was torridly hot despite the swift breeze that ascended, sweat glistened over her skin and her breathing came out in short, breathy pants.

It wasn't enough. His balls were painfully tight to his body, his cock throbbing and his spine tingling. He could come at any moment, but he wouldn't do it without her.

Sliding his thumb between their bodies, Tristan found her clit juicy and swollen. He scrapped his nail over the tender bud and was rewarded with a spasm that jolted from her body and into his. Once more he dragged his nail across the distended nub and the spasm turned to chaotic trembling. She was close now, close enough he knew the moment he gave himself over to the power that now swelled between them, sizzling the air with its energy, she'd be right alongside him, swirling into the unknown together.

They had to go together.

Last time they'd been there together she'd left him. This time she would take him back. He knew it, and still as he finally allowed his orgasm to surface, shaking through his body and blinding him to everything but the woman in his arms, he reveled in the fact she was by his side.

They crossed into the golden lands. The place of rolling fields and love, of children and happiness and there he found Cara waiting for him. And when he reached out to her and gathered her close, she gave in to him as well. Calling out her love, her need, her yearning to be with him always. He impaled her in this vision land and she contracted around him, creaming onto his cock and milking forth a release of his own that left him shattered and breathless. And when their pleasure finally subsided and their breathing returned to normalcy, she took hold of his hand and she walked with him back to their people, to their place, where they belonged together for eternity.

"Tristan?"

He opened his eyes to the sound of Cara's anxious voice. Her head rested on his chest, her body circled in his arms and a mess of tangled and sticky bed sheets. She tipped back her head to look up at him and the worry he'd heard in her tone centered into her eyes.

Concern tightened his gut and, in turn, his hold on her. "What is it, baby?"

"Are you okay?"

"Yes. Why I wouldn't I be?" Was she not okay? Did she already regret returning to him? She couldn't. He'd felt her love in the vision, felt it long before the vision had even begun. She wouldn't regret this night. He wouldn't allow it.

She ran her fingers through the hair on his chest and, resting her head back, murmured, "You were gone for so long, I…I was worried."

The knots that had formed in his gut released and he breathed out a sigh. She didn't regret it. She only feared that he had. "I like it there, with you. Sometimes I can't help but think how much easier it would be just to stay there."

"I like it too."

"I thought you hated it?" he asked, stunned by her admission. "That it scared you?"

"It did. Not any more. Nothing scares me any more."

Even as she said it, he could feel her lying, see the proof of her dishonesty in the slight twitching of her nose. Something did scare her and he knew what that something was—the same fear that ate at him and that wasn't the fear of regret on either of their parts. It was the fear that come morning this temporary bliss they'd found would end and cold hard reality would stare them in the face.

"I love you, Cara. Nothing will ever change that."

She kept her face downcast, but snuggled closer to him and he could feel both the silent tears that flowed onto his chest and the helplessness of the emotions that tumbled through her. "I know you do," she said, her voice quiet. "And I think maybe that's the hardest part of all of this. For so long I never even had that, the love of anyone, and then Joey came along and then you. I finally had someone to love, to be loved by in return. And now this… Knowing that sometimes love really isn't enough."

Maybe not always, but it would be this time, Tristan thought, pulling her closer yet, sharing the warmth and happiness she evoked in him in the hopes of easing her mind. He wanted to do so aloud, to reassure her with promises of the tranquility and children, of the love and laughter that had filled their vision, but he couldn't. He couldn't tell her anything for a certainty until he possessed what he'd come to Reno to find. Not until he held the Eye, until he unleashed its secrets and met with the answers to his existence and those of his future could he give her anything but his love.

He would get those answers tomorrow.

Whatever it took he would hold the key to it all in his hands by nightfall.

He had to. He was already fighting that which he felt honor bound to discover, to follow through on. One more night with Cara and there would be no fighting involved. Destiny wouldn't mean a damned thing. Nothing would but proving to her that love really was enough, more than enough to build their future on.

* * * * *

"I wondered if you'd ever come back."

Tristan shrugged off the accusation that seemed to fire from Brandy's dark eyes. He was here to convince her to hand over the Eye by whatever means it took, including lying. "I haven't heard from you. I thought you might need distance."

"I wasn't sure you wanted to hear from me."

"Cara and I have worked things out. She understands about us." He forced himself to move into her apartment and a satisfied smile to claim his lips while inside his guts knotted. Cara and he might have reached an understanding of sorts, but he knew better than to believe she truly understood why he had to come here today and sacrifice everything they had for answers. "Besides we have still business to attend to."

Brandy crossed her arms over her chest and raised an eyebrow. Disdain coated her words. "Business...I see."

"I didn't mean it like that." Actually, he had meant it like that. He'd hoped she would accept he was here on business alone and keep this meeting impersonal. He'd been foolish to believe such a thing was even possible where the two of them were concerned. She held a power over him, a power over his mind and body that would take effect the moment they stepped any closer to one another.

"Then you aren't here just for business?"

"I'm here for you."

The words rolled off Tristan's tongue like the bitterest acid, but they obviously didn't sound acidic to her. She was in his arms before he'd even realized she'd moved. Her mouth latched onto his and her tongue slid past his parted lips, invading his senses with a carnal demand he ached to be able to deny.

He couldn't deny it. From the first touch of her hands on his body, her lips to his, the fire raced through him, hardening his cock and tightening his balls with an almost desperate need.

It made no sense that he could be this aroused, that he could want her so badly after having Cara numerous times less than twenty four hours ago. But he was aroused, painfully so, and he wanted her so badly he feared he might fuck her where they stood if they didn't move elsewhere fast.

Brandy's hands curled into his sides, her long nails catching in the material of his short sleeve polo shirt and nipping past to the muscled flesh of his abdomen. He pulled her flush against him, crushing her breasts between them, and drowned every one of his reservations in the feel of her supple ass cradled in his palms, the ridge of her mound riding against his rock solid erection, the electric heat that zapped the air around them and had his temperature rising to a dangerous level.

Her nipples speared at him through their shirts and he released his hold on her ass to bury his hands beneath her tank top. She wore a bra today, but one so sheer and lacy it hid nothing from the imagination or from his touch. He caught a hard nipple through the thin material and tugged at it. She growled into his mouth and pushed him back hard against the wall.

She followed him back, wrapping her legs around his waist and straddling his cock with her pussy. Even through their clothing, the grinding sensation had his penis on fire with the need to explode. He had to get her naked, had to feel her hot flesh against his, had to bury his cock deep into her warm, willing body and fuck her until they were completely joined, the way they were meant to be.

Tristan pulled his hands from her shirt and yanked at the hem, ready to tug it over her head and bury his face between the silken flesh of her breasts. Brandy's hands over his halted him mid-tug. Her touch was scorching, but more than that it was strong, cementing his palms in place completely.

He gave another tug, drawing on supernatural strength, but still her hands remained over his, stopping him from going any farther.

She shouldn't be so strong. She shouldn't be able to hold his powers at will. The thoughts pounced through his mind, but before he could fully digest them, she was removing her hands and pushing away from his chest.

They stood staring at each other for a long moment, both of them fighting for breath. Then her mouth curved in the naughty smile that beckoned to him like no other and he forgot every thought in his head but the one that told him he had to have her, had to end this madness she stirred in him once and for all.

"I'd like to take this somewhere else," Brandy said, her voice a husky murmur that edged over his raw nerves and pressed agonizingly at his heart. He fought the sensation that she was trying to hurt him, her voice could never do that, and glanced toward the back of the apartment where he guessed her bedroom to be.

Her eyes danced with rich humor and she laughed. "No. I mean somewhere else completely, somewhere we won't risk Cara walking in on us and anyone's feelings being hurt. I won't have that happen to her."

Once more Tristan's thoughts evaded him as Cara's loving eyes filled his mind.

Merda! Why did Brandy have to bring up her name? He had to forget about Cara, forget how deep his love for her ran. He had to because what he felt with Brandy was too explosive, too surreal to be anything but authentic. Brandy was his destiny. He couldn't change that, he could only embrace it. "That's very considerate of you."

"She's special to me."

As she was special to him, he thought sadly, knowing after tonight Cara would never again believe she was special to him. She wouldn't believe she was anything to him, not even his friend. And she was right. They could never be just friends. They'd both known it all along, even if they'd chosen not to admit it.

Aware he couldn't do anything about Cara now, he closed the short space Brandy had put between them and cupped her cheek. He brushed her lips slowly, tenderly, putting all the love that stirred through him into the kiss. That love might not have been brought forth by Brandy, but she could assume it had. "Cara's lucky to have you."

She pulled away from him, laughing shortly, and her lips curled into a knowing smile. "She's even luckier to have you."

The stiffness of her tone and her expression conveyed she knew what he'd tried to hide. Tristan owed it to her to explain that he couldn't help his thoughts, that Cara was and always would be special to him. Only he couldn't get the words out. He wasn't prepared to discuss Cara with anyone, even his soul mate.

Shrugging off her words, he held out his hand. "Are you ready?"

Warmth returned to Brandy's eyes. "Just let me grab my things." She disappeared into the hall at the back of the apartment, returning less than a minute later with a suitcase in one hand and a loaded down canvas bag in the other.

He narrowed his gaze on the items. She said they were going elsewhere, he never realized she meant somewhere outside of this town as her baggage seemed to indicate. Unless she planned to go back to his suite? No, she wouldn't go there. Not when she knew Cara was just as apt to walk in on them there as she was here. "Where exactly are we going?"

She passed him a coy smile. "Away, remember?"

That didn't answer his question and judging by that smile she'd purposefully responded obtusely. What did it matter, really? They could go anywhere so long as they were together. Still, he was curious. "I don't have any other clothes with me."

"You have your wallet though, right? Where we're going you won't need many clothes and if you do, you can always buy enough to last you."

He glanced at her hands, wondering why if he needed so little she needed whatever filled her bags. The answer came to him in an instant and he grinned as relief assailed him. The Eye, of course. One of those bags held the Eye, and the other was probably nothing more than a few essentials.

He took the suitcase from her and gathered her hand in his, bending down to kiss her on the cheek in the process. "So, I don't even get a hint?"

She tipped back her head in laughter and the dark silky strands of her hair slid against her pale neck, making his cock throb with an unnaturalness that momentarily alarmed him. He shouldn't be so responsive to such a simple action, just as Cara should never have been so aroused by the mere sound of Brandy's voice.

Her laughter died away and she rose on tiptoe to sink her tongue between his lips. His thought scattered away with that first lick, with the taste of her, hot and potent as the finest liquor, sliding through his mouth and burning its way downward.

She pulled back. "Quit trying to guess and let's get out of here before it's too late."

Too late for what? Tristan silently questioned as she tugged him through the door and down the dank stairwell to the bottom floor. Something told him whether he wanted to know the answer to that question or not, he'd be finding it out very soon.

Chapter Twelve

"This an okay time?"

Cara looked up from the rich chocolate cake waiting for her on the scarred coffee table and smiled at Amy, who stood with her head popped into the apartment doorway. "I'm about to stuff my face with a hundred pounds of chocolate, but if you don't mind being witness to it, I don't mind the company."

Amy came inside and settled on the couch across from Cara. She glanced at the cake and raised an eyebrow. "Damn. Now that's what I call a killer looking cake."

She laughed at her word choice, not missing the irony. Brandy had called it killer as well. Obviously the two of them never discovered just how soul soothing a good piece, or in this case ton, of chocolate could be. She leaned forward with the intentions of swiping a bit of frosting with her finger, but then changed route and started to cut the cake into pieces instead. No sense in acting like a completely uncivilized pig.

She sliced her knife through the center of the cake, then glanced up at Amy. "Brandy made it for me. Want some?"

"Brandy? That's...odd."

"Not really. We were friends before she and Tristan met." While Brandy had made it sound like they'd been seeing each other for weeks or possibly even months, Tristan had assured her to the contrary. "Besides it's not like it's her fault that he and I aren't together. She has something that I don't, something he needs." Something she couldn't even begin to put her finger on.

She'd seen the things that happened between Tristan and Brandy the night she'd walked in on them. It appeared no different than what happened with her and Tristan. Only it was different. Tristan had said last night when he was with Brandy it was almost painful at times.

"You're okay with that?"

Cara cut the cake into quarters before again looking at Amy. Was she okay with Tristan following what he believed to be his destiny? Did she have a choice in the matter? She'd done everything in her power to convince him the two of them belonged together. If he still needed to find out for himself, then what was she supposed to do about it but let him?

As much as she couldn't influence him any more than what she already had, it didn't stop her chest from tightening or the emotions from gathering in her throat. She pushed the sensations back to concentrate on the cake. The dark chocolate seemed to shout to her, offering up its secrets of sensual delight and her mouth watered in anticipation. "I'll be fine. Just give me five minutes."

Five minutes. You'll be in heaven in one minute, honey, the little voice in the back of her head said. She smiled as she grabbed a paper plate from the small stack she'd set on the counter and heaped a piece of cake onto it. Nirvana was almost hers.

Unfortunately, friendship came with the price of giving Nirvana to others first. She held out the plate in offering to Amy, who hadn't said a word in nearly a full minute. The woman's gaze seemed trained on the cake, her attention steadfast.

Cara frowned and waved the plate in front of her. "Yes? No? Lost in space?"

Amy remained silent and Cara's frown turned to a scowl. As much as Cara valued their newfound friendship, she was in dire need of some serious chocolate. "Last chance."

She waved the plate one last time, then shrugged and rested it on her lap. Her fork dug into the moist layers, and caramel and chocolate sauce ran in rich rivulets between its tines. Her nose twitched with the mouth watering intensity of the scent.

Oh God, this was going to be so good.

She pulled the fork to her mouth slowly, inhaling its intoxicating aroma the whole way, then opened her mouth just as slowly, determined to enjoy every bite to its fullest.

Her tongue touched against the cool edge of the fork's tine and —

"Holy shit, Mike!"

Amy's hand flew out in a wide arc and the plate on Cara's lap and the fork in her hand both went careening to the floor. The chocolate orgasm she'd been in the midst of died in an instant.

She glared at Amy's frantic look. "What the hell did you do that for?"

She looked baffled, sputtering out, "The c — cake it...talked to me."

"The cake talked to you? That's impossible."

The shock in Amy's eyes was replaced by frustration and an erratic tick started up near her left eye. "It's not goddamned impossible. I heard it. I saw it move!"

"Its lips?"

"No, not its lips." She stood and toed at the cake on the floor. "Its layers. They separated and I heard — I heard Mike." Her eyes widened and she looked back at Cara. "What the fuck...something isn't right here. Something's is very *not* right."

Possibly the company.

"Goddammit, this isn't about me! It's about that cake and whoever made — " She stopped short and her hand flew to her temple. Her eyes widened farther yet as she asked frantically, "Where's Brandy?"

"I have no idea. When she dropped my cake off earlier — " Cara glared at the floor, and back at Amy " — she said she would probably have plans later tonight and to enjoy it. Only I don't think I'll be enjoying it."

Amy rolled her eyes, then fixed her with a hard look. "I will make you another damned cake. You have bigger problems than that. Brandy is with Tristan."

"There's a good chance of it, yeah." And that's exactly the reason why Cara had needed the cake so badly, to drown her sorrows.

"There's no good chance about it, Cara. She *is* with Tristan. And she's going to kill him."

Cara was prepared to deny anything Amy suggested about Brandy and Tristan. Only she never guessed she'd suggest something like this. It was too much to digest, too much to take in. The blood drained from her head and her belly pitched into her throat. She swayed, catching herself on the arms of the chair and looked across at Amy.

She shook her head. "You're wrong."

"I'm not wrong! I saw it just now. She's taken Tristan somewhere. Somewhere you can't reach him, but I can."

The certainty in Amy's eyes, and the sudden telling pressure on Cara's heart were too much to deny. Still, it made no sense. "Why would she do that? How? He's too strong. If he uses his powers, no one can beat him, except maybe Lucas or another one of the Sons."

"Or Mike," Amy put in resolutely.

"Mike?" The name came back to her in an instant and terror she couldn't even begin to understand clawed at her insides. "The guy you put in the psych ward for murdering your uncle Solaris and then coming after Lucas and you? What does he have to do with this? Has he escaped? Is he after Tristan?"

"No. At least, I don't think so. I don't mean Mike the man, I mean his spirit. Or whoever's spirit it was that inhabited his body. I still don't remember who or what it was. I only know it's with Brandy now."

Cara gave her head a firm shake, needing to dislodge the muddle that had settled over it, to make some sense of all this. Only nothing made sense, not even after Amy's explanation. It was just too much, too bizarre to believe. "She's always been so nice to me. She…" *Made me want her in the most unholy of ways.*

"You didn't want her, Cara. She only made you think that you did to get close to you, to get even closer to Tristan. She made him believe she was his soul mate, enough so to walk away from his true destiny. Think about it. Tristan hasn't been acting like his normal, calm self lately. He's confused, yes, but he's also on edge all the time. Would he ever have called you a whore in the past?"

"No. He never would've said anything like that. He told me he was sorry. I—I should've known." Oh, God, she should have. If Amy was right—and Cara knew in her heart she was—and she was Tristan's soul mate, then she should've known something was wrong with him. She should've stopped this long ago. Instead, she'd let him go, right into the hands of the enemy.

Her belly lurched with the reality she'd okayed his going to Brandy. If anything happened to him, if she lost him, the man she was destined to spend forever with, if she never had the chance to give him the children they'd both wanted for so long…

She couldn't think about the ifs, because there were no acceptable thens. Nothing that could happen to her would be bad enough to balance the harm she'd allowed to befall Tristan. "Oh, God, Amy we have to find him. He can't die!"

"He's not gonna die," she growled, the harsh tone snapping Cara from her daze. "We have to find Lucas and Perry and then we have to find Tristan. Together we have the power to stop her. You just gotta be strong and trust me."

Cara looked at the cake on the table and then to the piece on the floor, the piece that had nearly taken her life and shivered. She knew just how evil the cake was now, knew instinctively one bite would have been her end. Amy had saved her and now it was up to them to save Tristan.

Forcing courage she couldn't begin to feel, she stood. "I do. I trust you."

"Good. Now let's get the hell outta here before it's too late."

* * * * *

Tristan glanced around the one-story house as they entered, more than a little shocked by its size and stylish decor. The place was located an hour north of Reno, set back in the woods and at the end of a path they'd had to tread by foot to make it down.

Brandy had been right about one thing, Cara would never find them here.

No one would.

His stomach tightened with unexplainable anxiety as he turned and asked, "So, this is your...summer place?"

Brandy swung the canvas bag from her shoulder and dropped it onto the floor of the living room, which opened up immediately from the house's front entrance. She took the suitcase he still held, rising on tiptoe to deliver a teasing kiss with just a sprinkling of tongue in the process.

"Weekend getaway," she murmured, sucking sensuously on his lower lip as she pulled away.

She sashayed to a door at the back of the room, and he forgot all about his sudden bout of anxiety as he fell victim to the hypnotic sway of her ass beneath her shorts. His cock sprung to life. The need to possess that had clawed at him back at her apartment returned full force, heating the air and his blood to fever pitch in an instant.

She opened the door when she reached it, then turned and called over her shoulder. "Make yourself at home, Tristan, I'll be right out."

He watched the continual mesmerizing motion of her buttocks until his view was cut short by the closing of the door, then groaned. She'd damned well better be right out. As hard as his cock was, he wasn't liable to last more than a few more minutes.

Needing to free his mind from thoughts of placing his hands and mouth all over her tight curves, Tristan sank down on a tan leather sofa that matched the one in his condo almost perfectly. He ran his hand over the material, expecting to find faux leather. Instead his palms met with the cool slide of the genuine article. It was the last thing he should have expected to find in a house in the middle of nowhere, particularly a house owned by a woman who had mismatched leftovers for furnishings in her city apartment, and yet somehow it fit perfectly.

Nearly a minute had passed when a sudden breeze picked up, lifting the short hairs on his head. He glanced up to find Brandy standing a few feet away. Her lips were curved in the naughty smile he'd come to know well these past days, and his body responded as it always did when she looked at him that way—his cock hardening further yet and his heart squeezing with almost painful pressure.

"Do you like it?" she asked, sinking down on the couch's armrest.

The naked flesh of her thigh grazed against Tristan's leg through his slacks and her arm pressed into his side. She was as close as she could be to him without actually being in his lap. He wanted her closer. He wanted to feel her rear pressing against his shaft, the cleft of her ass riding along his erection, hinting at the pleasures to come.

He'd started to reach for her, when her eyes stopped him. They'd always been gray in the past, the color of smoke. Now they were almost translucent, surreal. Something about that dreamlike shade beckoned to him, asking him to give in to it, to her. "It reminds me of something I would have decorated myself."

Brandy's smile drew wider and her tongue came out, the small pink tip making her lips glisten. "Does that surprise you?"

"I suppose, in a way." And he supposed, in an even bigger way, he didn't care.

Slipping deeper into her entrancing gaze, the shimmering appeal of her mouth, he reached for her. His hands barely made contact and she was in his lap, her ass twitching against his erection, her arm snaking around his back, her teeth nipping at his jaw.

"We have a lot in common, Tristan." The words seemed to float from her parted lips to dance on the air between them. "A lot more than you even know."

She lowered her mouth to his and sank her tongue between his lips, spilling her intoxicatingly sweet flavor and making his temperature fan higher yet. "Heat, for example." She rubbed the pad of her thumb over the beads of sweat that had formed on his brow in the last few seconds, then nipped a taunting kiss at each corner of his smile. "You make me so incredibly hot and yet it's not hot enough. I want to crawl inside your skin and become one with you."

Brandy's arm left his back, and she turned sideways in his lap and slid her palms under his shirt. Her long nails chafed over the muscles of his abdomen, eliciting a hiss of breath from deep within him. A hiss that grew all the louder when she shifted her ass against his groin and rubbed it the length of his swollen cock.

The breeze picked up, gusting with vigor as Tristan brought his hands to her face and touched his mouth to hers. She smiled. He could feel it against his lips, but more so deep in his heart. That unexplainable burning compression slammed at his ribs once again, and then she parted her lips and allowed his tongue to sink inside.

The pain passed and there was only warmth, need. Magic.

This had to be magic. The taste of her, the uncontrollable desire she stimulated in him was too enchanting for anything else. It *was* magic. The truth was in their kiss, the way he felt when they embraced. His wish to never move again, but simply sit here and be with her forever.

He took a long, leisurely sampling of the warmth and wetness of her mouth and then pulled away and met her eyes. Once more their translucency called to him, seemed to beg him to dive in and never look back. "Do you believe in destiny?"

"Oh, yes. I believe you've found your destiny."

The certainty in her tone was all the final persuasion he needed. She knew what they were to be to one another. Maybe she'd always known. Maybe this last week had been nothing more than a test to her. If it was, then it was one he planned to pass with flying colors. "I believe I have, too."

"I've been wanting you so badly, Tristan." Brandy's hands slid upward and she flicked her nails across his nipples, making them stand on end with raw nerves and energy. "Every time we've come so close, something's happened. First that picture, then Cara. I wanted to fuck you so badly that night it drove me crazy when she came in. I thought I might scare her off by coming onto her, but she liked it. I honestly thought I knew her, but I didn't know she was like that."

Cara wasn't like that. The words were on the tip of Tristan's tongue as were the feelings he'd buried at the back of his heart. Completely different words came out of his mouth and the emotions he'd almost touched on skirted away on the rising wind. "You have that effect on people. You make them want you. You make me want you. That day when you said I was a tiger, I thought you were wrong, I thought I could never be like that, but you make me like that, Brandy. You make me want to throw you back on this couch and fuck you until neither one of us can breathe."

The arousing circling of her nails came to an abrupt halt and she flashed wide eyes on him. "You can't! Not here, I mean," she added more calmly, her fingers returning to their drugging pace over his chest. "I have something else planned for us. You don't want to ruin my surprise, do you?"

"No. I never want to upset you." The words came out fast, automatic even, and he frowned at the desperation behind them. He hadn't wanted to say that, so why had he?

Brandy rose from his lap and offered an outstretched hand. "Come with me, Tristan, and I promise I'll make this an experience you'll never forget."

The heat in her nearly clear gaze, the electricity that sizzled between them, the visions of events yet to come that flashed before his eyes, all asked him to forget about his hasty response and do her bidding. He took her hand, thrilling in the bone deep jolt of sensual awareness that simple connection brought forth, and followed behind her.

They breached the doorway to the room she'd earlier disappeared to—a bedroom he saw now—and the wind blew faster, stronger, spiraling effects around them, littering the air with objects from papers to books to wall trimmings.

All but one wall trimming.

Tristan's gaze landed on the portrait hanging above the bed and his feet planted themselves where they stood. They had to have, because he hadn't stopped their progress. "Alana," the word whispered from his mouth.

Brandy jerked back to glare at him. "What?"

He didn't know. He hadn't meant to speak her name. He didn't know why he cared. He shouldn't care about anything, but finally joining with his destiny.

He shrugged. "I hadn't noticed the picture was missing from your apartment."

Her narrowed eyes slowly lifted. "I moved it so it wouldn't bother you any more. I didn't know you'd be here. We can go somewhere else if you'd prefer."

"No!" He took a step back with the force of his response, aware it had come from him, but not believing he'd spoken it all the same. He never yelled, never lost his calm. He never used to anyway. Something had changed in him this last week.

"You don't want me, after all?" Her gaze returned to its narrowed state as she looked at the picture of the woman who resembled Alana so completely. "Is it because of her? Did you love her, Tristan? Do you still?"

He shook his head at the lunacy of the questions. Yes, he'd loved Alana, but as a friend or brother would, nothing more. As far as his wanting Brandy… He might not understand what was going on with his mind right now, but wanting her wasn't something that involved thought. The need was alive within him, the pressure to possess building to an unseen height, boiling the blood in his veins.

Even as he thought it, his cock throbbed violently, his balls drawing excruciatingly tight against his scrotum. His fingers curled at his sides, then uncurled and lashed out, grabbing hold of her shirt and dragging her firm to his chest. The breath rushed from her lungs, slamming him in the face like the hottest current. Her nails dug into his flesh and the hard ridge of her mound ground against him.

Pain filled him, ate at his heart until he could barely breathe. Tristan didn't care. Breathing was no longer important. Only one thing was important.

"Brandy."

He needed her beyond reason, needed to strip off her clothes and push her to the floor, needed to bury himself deep into her pussy, and come all over her pale, smooth skin. He needed to make her his.

"I need you now," he growled.

Her lips twitched. "Patience, Tristan. We do this my way."

"Then do it fast."

Her nails left his flesh to gather in his shirt. With a hasty yank that she never should've been strong enough to execute, his shirt was gone and his chest bared to her touch. Her eyes lit with humor. "Fast enough?"

"Keep going."

It was meant to be challenge, a demand to make her tear at his slacks with the same zealous urgency, to force her to quit toying with him and allow him to fuck her the way they both ached to let happen. Instead, she walked around him, stalling at his back.

Brandy's fingers touched down on his spine and he released a shallow gasp at the branding heat of her touch. Slowly, she moved, tracing the shape of the glyph that lined his flesh, he knew.

"It's so perfect," she breathed.

The way she said it, or perhaps what she didn't say struck a chord within Tristan, making him momentarily forget their purpose here. How could she act so nonchalant? How could she not question why a man would have such a feminine symbol tattooed onto his back? Or did she already know it wasn't a tattoo, but a sign of his heritage that he'd been born with? "What do you mean?"

"It's just...beautiful."

He circled around, needing to see her expression, suddenly desperate to read into her more than what she was allowing, to unlock the emotions and hidden thoughts just beyond her smile. "You don't find it strange?"

Her smile grew as she stepped into him and twined her arms around his neck. "The only thing I find strange is that you want to talk about a marking on your back when we could be talking about each other, about all the ways I plan to fuck you." She leaned back far enough to snake a finger down his chest and her eyes danced with the shivers her touch evoked. "First with my breasts, then my mouth, then my pussy, then my ass. Before we're done, Tristan, you're going to be one very dead man."

The lazy way she stroked her tongue over her lips, punctuating her words, the spike in the room's temperature and the erratic squalling of the wind all joined together to make him forget about discovering her secrets any further tonight. There would be plenty of time for discovery, now was the time for more primal pursuits.

Now was the time to take.

"I want you now, Brandy. No more patience."

Pressing her hand flat on his chest, she pushed him toward the bed. "If you want me, Tristan, you'll lie down and let me strip you."

He could do that. He could be submissive for her. Not always, but this one time. He knew instinctively she'd make it worth his while.

She pushed at him again and Tristan allowed himself to fall on the bed. She covered him in a flash and her hands seemed to be everywhere at once, tugging, nipping, yanking at his slacks and briefs. Then her hands were gone and so were his clothes.

He stared down at his naked body. At the deep purple head of his cock inches from her mouth and her delicate hand wrapped so securely around his shaft. She licked her lips, then skimmed her tongue over the tip of his penis. His cock throbbed with that first lick and his hips jerked upward, thrusting the head of his shaft tight to her mouth.

She took another long, lusty lick, murmuring her pleasure over the pre-come gathering on the head of his cock and then pumped his hard, hot sex in her hand. The blood screamed through his body and his heart lurched in his chest, pain squelching any desire her touch elicited.

"God, you taste so good, Tristan. So sinfully good. I want to suck on your dick until you're coming in my throat. But I have to be patient. We both do." Brandy released her hold on his erection and he drew in a long breath as the pain subsided. She rose up on him and once more her palms were flat against his chest, pushing him back. He allowed his upper half to fall back against the mattress out of instinct, because he'd already decided she could have the control this first time. And yet something in her eyes made him doubt that move.

"Good," she said when he was flat on his back again. She came to her feet beside the bed, then reached beneath it and grabbed something. She crawled back onto him, her knees biting in his calves and thighs, and his wrist met with cold, hard metal.

"Now lie still and be a good boy."

Tristan snapped his attention on the objects she held and his gut knotted with anxiety when he realized they were handcuffs. She'd latched both his wrists into place along the bed's headboard before his voice caught up with him.

"What the hell are you doing?" he barked as she crawled back down his body and began to shackle his ankles.

She finished her work, and returned to take his face in her hands and kiss him softly. "Making this more exciting for you, Tristan. I want it to be perfect."

"But—"

"You trust me, don't you?"

The question was laced with underlying ache. The left side of her cheek sank in and the dazzling green shade of her eyes turned murky as they filled with tears. His heart squeezed with that look, with the way the tip of her nose trembled.

Dio, how could he allow Cara to think she had anything but his absolute trust? "Yes. I trust you."

"I wonder though, if you might not live to regret that."

The softness of her voice was gone and so were her features. No murky green eyes stared back at him, no trembling nose centered her face. Only an upturned smile and translucent eyes met his. Brandy. Not Cara. Never Cara. Only Brandy.

"You're not scared, are you, Trist?"

He blinked at the name, at the woman who smiled down at him. Her long red hair brushed over his body, tickling the bare flesh of his shoulders and chest. Her full lips curved in the brightest smile.

No, he wasn't scared. Cara couldn't scare him. Nothing but her leaving could do that. "I love you, baby. You can't scare me."

"But it won't it be fun trying?"

Rearing back on his thighs, she tugged at the hem of her shirt. She tossed it aside to reveal the enticing jiggle of her naked breasts. Her nipples peaked, a deeper brown than he remembered, and she slid down his body and buried his cock between her cleavage. She milked his engorged shaft, and his fingers curled helplessly, as his body drew tight, his balls tighter yet.

"Yes," he growled. "Fuck me, baby. Fuck me with those luscious tits."

She stopped suddenly and tipped back her head to look up at him. "Do you talk that way to Cara? Does she like it rough?"

Tristan's mind spun with the question, with the harshness of his words, with the woman looking at him. The woman who wasn't Cara. "What?"

Brandy's lips quirked and her words held a sardonic edge. "Cara. You know, the woman you love? Cara, your soul mate. *That* Cara."

That Cara. Not this Cara, because this wasn't Cara. This was Brandy. The woman who was his everything, the one he was meant to walk beside, to grow old with. "Cara's not my soul mate. You are."

"Am I?" She turned back to her pumping, squeezing his shaft with the fullness of breasts and her palms, spurring his blood to a burning crescendo and the wind that engulfed them into a torrent of fury. "Does this make you feel close to me, Tristan? Does it make you feel like we're bonding? Does it make you burn to fuck me?"

"Yes."

"And what about this?" She scooted farther down his body, dragging her cunt along his thigh. He felt the wetness that lined her pussy lips and his mind skipped with the realization she was completely naked.

But how could that have happened? When?

The questions died away as her tongue again settled over his erection. She laved at the bulging veins in his cock and his heart pounded madly against his ribs as pre-come gushed from the tip of his penis. Her hands fell to his balls, fondling, shaping, squeezing them within her palm. The pressure increased, the air around them grew weighty, and he fought for breath, for logic as the blazing need to possess, to be possessed slammed into him hard.

Bowing up on the bed, he yanked at his wrist bindings, cursing when they refused to budge. He was supposed to be strong, stronger than any mortal man and sure as hell stronger than a pair of dime store handcuffs. Yet Tristan couldn't break his chains. He only could vent his growing frustration.

Scopata! He wanted to cup the sweetly rounded curves of her ass, wanted to dip his fingers into the wet hole of her pussy and make her flame with the same need that scorched through him.

He wanted to take her to their special place. The place that was his and hers alone. "I want to go there now!"

He hadn't meant to yell, but it seemed to be what Brandy had been waiting for. She released his cock and rose up to straddle his groin. Her eyes were afire, a surreal shade of dazzling light that splintered into him and tensed his body with barely-there-pain.

Slowly her smile spread. "Thank you. You're making this so easy on me."

"Making what easy?" he questioned through his ache, his confusion.

"Killing you, Tristan. Why else do you think we're here?"

Chapter Thirteen

The pain that held Tristan's body victim intensified, turning from barely perceptible to barely tolerable. He fought at his shackles, yanking with a rage he didn't understand. The hard edge of the cuffs bit into his flesh, the sticky warmth of blood spilling down his arms and onto his feet. That rage and his struggles died when Brandy's words caught up with him.

Killing him? Had she really said that? No. He'd heard her wrong. He'd been confused. Again. Still. Nothing made sense any more.

Only, one thing did. His reason for being here. "We're here because we're meant to be, because we're destined. It's the reason we met. The reason that sometimes when you smile, I can't breathe it hurts so much."

She laughed at that, tipped her head back and laughed loud and long. "Like now? Does that hurt you? Does it hurt you when I laugh?" He nodded mutely, unable to speak, to think with the severity of pain that sliced through him. She continued on in a tone that was as amused as it was derisive. "That's the evil, Tristan. It's leaking into your soul, it's taking you over. It's making you see things that aren't there. It's making you believe I'm someone I'm not, that you actually want to be here with me."

Her tone calmed and she reclined against him to finger the lock of hair that fell across his forehead. Pointlessly, he flinched from the touch. It was a move Cara made. Part of his mind leaped at the thought, wanting to believe this was Cara. But the rest of him, those slim parts that still held on to judgment, knew better.

No matter how much Brandy might seem like Cara at times, even look like her, she was nothing like the woman he loved.

She sat back once more, the wetness of her pussy straddling his cock and spearing guilt through him too intense to take in. It was his fault that he was here. His fault he'd allowed himself to be led astray, to let Cara go. His soul mate. The woman he was truly destined to spend forever with, to grow old with.

Reality passed over him in waves of fathomless ache. He closed his eyes, trying to force out the pain that ate at his heart and threatened to leak into his soul. It only made the pressure worse. As did Brandy's nails when they buried into his abdomen an instant later.

Tristan's eyes snapped open with the agonizing sensation of flesh and muscle being torn into. He stared down numbly to where rivulets of steaming red liquid oozed from his stomach and onto her fingers. She smiled back at him, that naughty smile he'd so foolishly let win him over. The one that even now had his cock stirring against her hole in search of entry.

His body might want her, but not his mind. He would fight this in whatever way he could. He owed it to Cara, if not to himself.

"You're one of the lucky ones, Tristan. One of my favorites. I won't make this hurt too badly. In fact, I think you'll find it to your liking. Now lie back and be a good boy and let me fuck you to death. After all, you were so eager to get started."

Brandy's nails pressed farther into his torn flesh. He bit back a hiss of agony as her pussy lips pressed against the head of his cock, opening to him, beckoning him to sink in and fuck her. Only he wouldn't be the one doing the fucking. She would. She would fuck him to death just as she'd promised.

He had to do something, anything to stop that from happening. Even if that something meant killing himself before Brandy could, for even death was preferable to betraying Cara any more than what he already had. If death were indeed his only way out of this nightmare, then he would first get some answers.

Out of instinct, Tristan searched for them inside Brandy, seeking hidden warmth, emotions, fragmented thoughts, broken lines in her aura. Nothing he found told him more than what he'd already known. She was the evil that sought to destroy him. The monster that would tear him limb from limb given the opportunity to do so. He knew the "what" well, it was the "who" that remained elusive.

"Who are you?"

"Why I'm your destiny, Tristan." The fire in her eyes flamed higher and her laughter screamed through his ears. "Your destiny in hell, maybe."

Once more her pussy lips opened to him and slowly she began to sink onto his cock. He yanked at his bindings, at the shackles that threatened to be the death of him, channeling every ounce of his supernatural strength into breaking free and still they held tight. Refusing to give in, he twisted his body, struggling to force her away, to keep her from sliding onto his shaft completely, and when that too failed he resorted to words. "Get the fuck off me!"

To his astonishment, she lifted free of him and rose to stand next to the bed. She patted his cheek and stared down at him lovingly. "All you had to do was ask, sweetie."

The tone was too kind, the endearment unbelievable. Something was happening. The turbulent emotions that sizzled through him told him that something was horrific.

Brandy turned to the door. "I believe we have company, Tristan. Now who do you suppose could be scratching at my door? Could it by your beloved Cara?"

At first he heard nothing and then he heard a voice. Amy's voice. They were here, all of them—Cara, Amy, Lucas and Perry—and entering the house.

Dio l'aiuta. God help him, she would not hurt his family!

"If you so much as a lay a hand on them, I'll—"

"Yes, Tristan," she asked, smiling back at him. "What will you do? You can't break free, you've already tried. Your powers are useless compared to mine. You can't do anything, and neither will your precious family be able to. Your little whore will soon be mine to play with and we both know how much she likes it when I play with her. But don't worry, sweetie, I'll let you watch. And this time she won't go running, this time she'll stay until the end." Her lips twitched. "Her end, that is."

"Tristan?"

Cara. *Merda!*

"Tristan," Cara called through the door a second time. "We're here for you. We're coming in."

"Cara, no!" Tristan shouted.

"Yes, Cara! Yes!" Brandy's laughter cut through him, rattling his bones, his soul. "Come in and see what your darling's been up to in your absence."

"Don't do this, Brandy," he pleaded, praying weakness would prevail where strength had failed. "I'll give you whatever you want. I'll give you myself."

Her eyes glossed over for an instant, returning to the smoky shade he once knew well and then she tossed her head back and high-pitched laughter spiked through the room. The wind picked up, bringing with it an icy edge that bit into his flesh and chilled his body's warmth until he shook with it.

"You already have, you fool," she spat. "You've been mine for days. The second I contacted you in Ashton, I knew you'd come crawling to me on your hands and knees, begging for your precious Eye.

"The Eye," she repeated, her voice raising several octaves to a squealing hiss. "The Eye that I never even had. You're going to die, Tristan. Your adoring lover and friends are going to go right along with you, and for something that doesn't even exist."

He blinked with the bitter sting of her words. She didn't have the Eye? No. She had to have it! But why did she? He'd never seen it. In pictures yes, but nothing said those pictures were authentic or recently taken.

He'd been so thirsty for answers, so goddamned hungry to uncover the truth of his past, his future that he'd allowed himself to be strung along, to take Cara and the others right along with him.

"Son of a bitch!"

Brandy's laughter droned to his ears and then died abruptly as she turned from him. Opening her palm, she thrust her hand toward the door. It blew open in a wide arc, crashing back against the wall.

In that moment, as Tristan stared upon his worst nightmare—his destiny and the only woman he would ever love looking upon him with tears of hatred in her eyes—he forgot all about the Eye, about his hunger for knowledge, and felt only self-loathing.

Slowly the others' stunned faces came into view, but that's all he could see of them. Only Cara mattered now, for if he died Perry, Lucas and Amy would be able to forgive his sins, but Cara never would, not when he lay shackled naked and aroused with an equally naked and aroused woman standing mere feet away.

Cara's chin trembled and the side of her cheek sank in. Tristan's mind drifted back to his vision moments ago, when she'd looked at him that same way. He'd ached for her then, but it was nothing compared to his pain for her now. Emotions roiled through her, emotions so thick and intense they hurt more than Brandy's laugher and smiles could ever accomplish.

He had to make her understand, had to explain this wasn't his fault. That he'd been deceived. Once more he wrenched at the shackles that bound him. Once more his struggles were met with pain, tearing at his wounded flesh.

The hatred in Cara's eyes turned to cold fury and her aura flashed an acrid blue.

Tristan knew only words would help now, and then only cautiously spoken ones. Before he could get so much as a single one out, she wrapped her arms around herself and turned to run. Amy stopped her, holding her in place, turning her back to face him while she whispered soundless words in her ear.

Cara shook her head and those eyes he swore he saw smiling down at him, asking him if he was scared, filled with tears. He blinked back his own emotions, and silently begged her to hear him. She could communicate with him, maybe not in words, but in ideas, in emotions, if only she would listen.

The wind lifted again, funneling crystals of ice and snow, and faltering Tristan's efforts to make contact with Cara. The harsh gusts pushed at his skin, clotting the blood that leaked in thin streams from his wounds and rippling across his body to expose the structure of muscle and bone and the thin cord of veins. That same gusting wind lifted Cara from the floor. Her eyes lost their cold edge and she screamed as she was sucked through the doorway and dropped at Brandy's feet. The door slammed shut. The pounding weight of free flying oak meeting metal echoed through Tristan's head and shot pain so deeply into his chest it threatened to blind him.

Briefly he was cognizant of the others' frantic shouts, their efforts to communicate with him via thought, their fists pounding at the door, and then he heard nothing, saw nothing at all, but Cara's pale face as she pushed her way to her feet.

Tears streaked over her cheeks, tears that curled his guts. He wanted to blame Brandy again, to say this was all her fault, that she'd tricked him into coming here. He couldn't blame her, because he'd had a choice. He'd voluntarily walked away from Cara and the love they shared. At the time he'd believed it the right thing to do, that he had to reveal his true destiny, to unveil the Eye. Now he knew otherwise.

Now that it was too late, he could see the truth and ached to say anything he could to make Cara see it as well. "Ca—"

"Welcome," Brandy cut off his words in a singsongy voice. She bent before Cara and, pasting on a bright smile, offered her outstretched hand. "Welcome to my home, Cara love. You're just in time for the fun to start."

* * * * *

Remember, he loves you.

Cara strived to remember those words, the last Amy had spoken to her before she'd been sucked into this room and the door slammed shut behind her. Yet as much as she wanted to believe it, that Tristan could love her and still be here, engaging in sex with another woman, it was just too much.

She couldn't believe it. She also couldn't turn away.

Tristan might not love her. He might not be faithful to her. But she did love him and she would until the day she died. She prayed that day wasn't today.

"Take my hand, Cara," Brandy implored, waving her hand inches from Cara's face. "It won't bite. I promise."

"Unlike my cake."

Brandy grabbed her hand and wrenched her to her feet. She pushed her back onto the bed beside Tristan and stood with her hands on her hips, laughing. "So you liked it, did you?"

She almost had. She'd come damned close to liking it so much she'd died for it. She pushed up on her elbows and narrowed her gaze on Brandy. Fear curled tight in her belly, but she refused to acknowledge it. Panic would accomplish nothing. She had to rely on instinct. To do whatever it took to achieve what seemed the impossible—emerging from this room with both Tristan's and her own lives intact. "It was scrumptious. Killer, even. I ate every last crumb."

Brandy shook her head and laughed shortly. "You're not a very good liar, Cara love. Your nose twitches. Besides, I know you didn't eat a single bite. If so much as a morsel had touched your tongue, you would already be dead."

Cara's heart sped up with the reality of how close she'd come to dying. Too close to allow it to happen now. She forced a smile. One that felt so brittle it might crack at any moment. "Sorry if I disappointed you."

"Oh, but I'm not disappointed. I'm pleased. It will be so much more fun to watch you die, than just to know that it was happening."

Cara heard Tristan's breath catch and knew he was on the verge of saying something. She didn't trust him to talk. She had to keep the conversation going on her own. It was the only way. "What would it take for you not to kill me?"

Brandy tipped back her head and snorted. "You two really are made for each other. He said the same thing. For him the answer was nothing. For you though, I might just make an exception." Her voice turned to a gentle murmur and she approached the bed, stopping just shy of Cara's legs. Her eyes, which had been ablaze with light when Cara had first been pulled into this room, now darkened with flaming desire.

She inched the rest of the way forward and her legs brushed against Cara's, her naked mound and breasts inches from her face. Cara fought her revulsion, the bile that rose up in her throat and the fresh course of dread that filled her. "What do I have to do? What will take it for you to make an exception?"

Brandy's mouth twitched and she leaned down to run her finger up Cara's thigh, pulling away and laughing when Cara jumped at her touch. "I've seen your moves at the Red Room. I've felt those big, hot tits of yours in my hands. I want to see the rest. I want to feel all of you. I want to fuck you. Is that worth your life, worth poor little Joey still being able to say he has a big sister? Letting me fuck you?"

Oh, God. She couldn't do this. She couldn't allow Brandy to suck her back into her web, to make her believe she truly wanted her touch. But if she didn't do it, then what? This might be her only chance, her only way out. As much as the idea repulsed her, she had to do it. For Joey. For Tristan. For her newfound friends trapped outside the bedroom. She knew better than to think Brandy was done with the others. The moment she finished with Cara and Tristan, she would go after them as well.

"Cara. Don't do it!" Tristan shouted. "It won't be enough, you have to know that. She's trying to get into your head. She's trying to mess with your mind the same damned way she did mine. She wants to make you suffer, and when she has, when she's done laughing over your humiliation, she will kill you."

He was probably right, given the chance Brandy would kill her, but that wasn't the part of his words that spurred the anxiety in her belly to bitterness. That part was where he tried to make it sound like none of this had been his fault.

She turned back and glared at him, hating how beaten he looked, how his wounds made her heart ache and her tears threaten to resurface. Damn him for making her want to believe him. She couldn't feel pity. Not now.

"Is that what happened, Tristan?" she demanded, letting her disgust over his body's response to Brandy's handling show. How could she even consider he didn't want Brandy when his cock was hard as granite, the tip of his penis lined in the glistening essence of sex. "She got into your mind and made you think you wanted her, made you let her lead you here and shackle you to her bed? Made your cock so hard that even now when you know she's going to kill you and all those you've ever claimed to love, it still aches to fuck her?"

Remorse passed through his eyes and he mouthed, "Yes."

"The answer is no, Tristan. I know why you walked away from me and it wasn't because of Brandy's convincing. It was your own convincing. Your own needs. It was all about you, wasn't it? Tell me, goddammit," she snapped, allowing the hurt that filled her to come through in her words. "At the very least I deserve the truth."

He remained silent for just an instant and then he let his words out on a rush. "Yes. I did it all for me. I wanted answers. I just—I never thought it would lead to this. If I could go back, if I could do it all over again, I would never leave you, Cara. I love you, baby. I know you don't believe that now, but it's the truth."

"Enough!" Brandy barked, bringing Cara swiveling back around to face her. "Make up your mind, Cara love, and decide fast. I've already wasted too much time here. I won't waste any more."

Make up her mind to give her body to this monster. To make Tristan watch while she was possessed by someone other than him. It wasn't that difficult of an answer, though it was one based on survival more than she dared to let show. "Yes."

"Yes?" Tristan repeated on a heated breath.

She glanced back at his incredulous gaze. He'd made poor choices. He didn't deserve her help any more than her love. Still, she ached to explain, to make him see her true reasons. She couldn't do that. Revealing anything to him would mean revealing it to Brandy as well. "Yes, Tristan," she said, pushing anticipation into her voice while her belly shook with terror. "If she's good enough for you, then she's good enough for me."

Cara turned to meet Brandy's lust-filled eyes. Bile rose up in her throat and she choked it back and stood. Shutting out her feelings, her emotions, she pulled her T-shirt over her head and unclasped her bra. Her nipples peaked with the cold that still clung to the room and she lifted Brandy's hands to her breasts and squeezed them within her own. "I want you to fuck me. I want to feel your tongue on my nipples, buried deep inside me. I want Tristan to watch. I want him to pay for deceiving us both. He deserves death, but first he deserves to suffer."

Brandy's palms remained still on her breasts, but the heat that flamed in her eyes turning them from a nearly translucent yellow to a surreal orange spoke of her want, of giving in. "You're certain about this?"

"Yes." Cara squeezed the backs of Brandy's hands once more, brushing them over her breasts. Her nipples throbbed with the intimacy of that touch and she sucked in a breath as unexpected heat coiled deep in her pussy. This wasn't part of the plan. She wasn't supposed to fall back into Brandy's web, to let Brandy make her want. It was too late to go back, too late to say she'd changed her mind. She could only give in and pray it led to the outcome she'd intended.

"Oh, God, yes," she sighed, pressing her breasts harder against Brandy's palms. "Can't you feel it for yourself? Can't you feel the heat between us? The way my tits are swollen for you. My nipples standing on end?"

"I can feel it, but should I believe it. You wouldn't dare lie to me again would you, Cara? You wouldn't be making me think you want me just long enough to get away?"

Yes, she would. She would do whatever it took to escape this unharmed, physically if mentally wasn't an option. Out of desperation, she pushed Brandy away and unsnapped her shorts. She took hold of her hand again then and glided it past the open vee and into her panties. Their joined fingers touched down on her mound and she inhaled sharply at the juices that flooded deep within her sex. "Does this feel like I'm pretending?"

Brandy's gaze snapped back to her face and her smile tugged high at the corners. "That's all for me? Your pussy is dripping for me?"

No, she wanted to scream. It was dripping because Brandy was making it. She couldn't honestly feel this way about another woman. She couldn't even feel this way about another man. She only could feel this way for Tristan.

Cara blinked hard as the reality of that slammed into her. Oh, God, he really had been telling the truth. Brandy had made him deceive her. She'd made him come here and even now she had him lying on her bed in wait of her return.

She had to get them out of here and she had to do it now. There was only one sure way to accomplish that. As much it repulsed her, she would do it because she had to.

Bending her head, she pressed her body full against Brandy and ran her tongue over the other woman's lips. "I want to feel your tongue on me. I want to feel it moving inside my cunt. Please, Brandy. I need this."

"You want me so badly you'd beg for me? Tristan never begged."

"Tristan never realized how good he had it." Only he had.

Even as she spoke, Cara could feel the edge of his thoughts, of the words Brandy wouldn't allow him to speak, of the emotions that stormed through him telling Cara exactly how much he had realized it. How much he loved her even now, as she was doing her damnedest to make it clear to both him and Brandy that he mattered nothing to her. "He will," she said, her tone thready. "He'll watch us and he'll learn. You'll let him watch, right? You'll give me that much?"

Brandy rose on tiptoe and brushed her mouth across Cara's. "Yes. I will. It isn't what I'd planned, but it's so much better."

She pulled back in a blur of speed and pushed Cara toward the bed. Cara fell onto the mattress and scrambled into a sitting position. Brandy was already there, looming at her feet. Crawling between her knees, she grabbed her thighs and yanked them apart. "Undress for me, Cara. Take off the rest of your clothes and lie back on the bed. I want your legs spread just like this. I want to see what you're offering me."

"Please don't do this, Cara." The words hissed from Tristan's mouth, barely a whisper, and she knew how much it pained him to speak. "It's not worth it. All you're doing is giving away your self-respect. You're giving in to everything you hate, and for nothing. She's still going to kill you."

Cara swallowed back the words that lodged in her throat. The ones meant to reassure him. To set the concern that roiled through him, fighting with the knives of pain, at ease. Instead she laughed breathily and said all that she could. "Maybe so, but what a way to go."

The normally tanned flesh of his face grew pale and waxy and red lines streaked over his cheeks. "You don't mean that," he rasped.

"Oh, but she does, Tristan."

Cara wrenched her attention toward Brandy's laughing tone and felt the coolness of the woman's fingers on her legs. The heat in her gaze was directed at her widespread thighs. Cara followed her gaze and drew in a ragged breath of panic at the realization she was naked.

This wasn't possible! Brandy couldn't have undressed her without her knowledge. But the flash of her shorts and panties lying next to her on the bed and the cool touch of air at her sex ensured Brandy had and even now was staring upon her naked mound with open lust in her eyes.

"I wish you could see this, Tristan. I wish you could see just how wet your beloved Cara is for me. Her pussy is swollen. You can't see it, but you'll hear it when I make her come and she screams my name. You'll hear it when she's creaming in my mouth and begging me to fuck her harder. You're going to hear it all."

Cara's belly clenched, her heart pummeling fiercely. Her fingers wanted to curl, to tangle into the sheets. She kept them flat at her sides and laid back, opening her thighs farther yet and helplessly begged. "Yes, I want that. I want you to fuck me now!"

Brandy's palms moved up her thighs and then one slender finger found her hole. Wetness seeped through Cara's cunt, juices of arousal she wanted to deny. She wasn't really feeling this, it was Brandy making her believe it. Yet as much as she knew that, she couldn't stop her hips from arching against that assaulting finger or the moan of desperation that broke from her lips. "Oh, God! It's just too much."

Brandy's thrusting fingers stilled and she pinned her with a burning glare. "Would you like me to stop, Cara love? It's not too late to change your mind. I can stop this right now and kill you instead."

She would do it, Cara knew. If she asked for absolution right now Brandy would give it to her. She couldn't choose the easy way out. Too many people were counting on her. "No! I want more. I want your tongue in me. I want to come in your mouth."

With a high-pitched laugh, Brandy caught her thighs in her hands and sank down to breathe tepid air against her pussy. Tension licked through Cara, climax building at a blind pace. She held her breath, shutting out the sensations. She had one chance to escape this nightmare and that chance was nearly upon her.

Brandy's head bent further and then the wetness of her tongue was on Cara, stroking over her swollen cunt, teasing her clit with measured strokes. Cara pushed back the pressure, pushed back the burning desire to let go and explode. With a glance at Brandy's head to see that she was completely engrossed, she reached for her shorts and clawed mindlessly into her pocket. Her fingers pressed against the sponginess of the most unlikely of weapons. One that she'd grabbed while walking from her apartment for a reason she couldn't even begin to explain.

The weapon safe in her palm, she breathed out, "I'm so close. I need...I need..."

The thrusting of Brandy's tongue came to a standstill and she rocked back to stare up at her through deep red eyes. "Anything you need, Cara. Just say it."

Cara's stomach quaked with the extreme shade of her eyes, the realization her one chance at freedom was now upon her. She forced her nerves to settle, her heart to not beat out of her chest, and whispered, "A kiss. I need a kiss."

In a slow motion daze, Brandy drew up to her mouth. Fighting the sickeningly sweet taste of her, Cara parted her lips and filled Brandy's mouth with her tongue. For an instant she let the kiss deepen, to grow wetter, more elemental and then she jerked away from Brandy's lips and thrust her hand over the woman's mouth, crushing the moist chocolate cake in her palm past her tongue and deep into her throat.

The crimson shade of Brandy's eyes faded to yellow as comprehension dawned. She clawed at Cara's hand, her tongue pushing against her palm in an effort to relieve herself of the deadly cake. She was too strong for Cara to hold for long, but it was long enough. Brandy's mad sputtering, the bulging of her eyes, the crackling of the air all assured the cake was doing its job.

Brandy stumbled from the bed. She slapped at her chest and beckoned to Cara with engorged eyes.

Cara tipped back her head and laughed. As if she thought she would help her. As if she thought anything that had passed in this room had been real. Nothing had been real. Only one thing was... Brandy was dying.

Brandy faltered, swaying on her feet and Cara raced to her side and pushed her to the floor. The breath whooshed from Brandy's lungs, fogging the air with a thin green film. Her arms fell at her sides, her eyes snapped shut, and finally her struggles ceased.

Cara toed her motionless body, refusing to believe it was over until she had concrete evidence. And when she felt no movements, saw no more air leaving her mouth, she bent over Brandy's still body and laughed hysterically. "How's that for just desserts, you bitch?"

"Cara."

She turned at the sound of Tristan's voice. It was solid for the first time since she'd found him here, and her entire body sighed with relief. Her heart pounding against her ribs, Cara rushed to the bed. She grabbed a miniature key from the nightstand next to the bed and started to unhook the first of the handcuffs that held Tristan's wrists in place. A gushing noise halted her progress and brought her attention swiveling back around. Green air leaked from Brandy's still body, air that looked more like fog. It gathered in a thick condensation and then with a screeching hiss, lifted from the corpse and launched toward the bed.

Cara lurched back, falling onto Tristan's splayed body, and watched in awe as the green mass slammed into the picture that hung over the bed and disappeared.

She waited several long seconds, her heart playing a staccato beat, and then finally turned back to Tristan. His expression and the emotions that roiled between them, said he was as shaken as she was, though the words that came out of his mouth were anything but. "Were you really that close?"

It was Brandy, she knew. The magic within her, evil as it might be, that had allowed Cara to feel so much, to want her so badly. Too badly to admit it to Tristan. Even if his reasons for asking her were only to prove she'd been every bit as sucked into Brandy's power as he had.

She shrugged and glanced at his still swollen cock that rubbed against her thigh. As much as she knew it wasn't his fault, that Brandy had made him feel things he didn't want to, just as she had Cara, she couldn't stop the contempt from entering her voice. "That you'll never know, but I think it's safe to assume you were."

Chapter Fourteen

Tristan had put off this moment the entire day. He couldn't put it off any longer. He'd stood across from Cara at Amy and Lucas' wedding, more than a little aware that as two of his closest friends took their vows, the woman he loved ached to do the same thing. That truth was in the misty green shade of her eyes, the heat that filled the distance between them as they stood on opposite sides of the aisle, and the depth of emotions that burned through her at dinner.

That whole time he'd yearned to talk to her, to ask her the questions that had weighed on his mind the last two days. He hadn't done so because he didn't want to ruin Amy and Lucas' wedding day by pushing Cara into making a scene.

And that was a load of bullshit.

He hadn't approached her today or anytime in the past two days for the simple fact he was scared to death of her rejection.

She'd made it clear that day at Brandy's house she blamed him for what happened, for leaving her behind and chasing after his destiny. And she was right, it was his fault. But he was sorry, damn it. Sorry and sick to death of ridiculing himself for making the wrong choices. Just as he was sick of standing here, watching Cara from across the bar, and doing his damnedest to get her to turn and notice him.

She didn't turn, just kept up her discussion with Paul, Perry's twin brother, and the attractive blonde he'd come here with. The same blonde he'd seen Perry arguing with earlier tonight. Tristan had been able to feel the emotions raging through Perry, the hurt, the frustrations, the bitter ache, and he was able to guess that whoever the blonde was, she was at the source of Perry's mood swings. Since he hadn't seen the two brothers speak a word to one another since Paul arrived this morning, he was also able to guess the woman was responsible for whatever rift existed between them.

The part of Tristan whose greatest goal was seeing others happy ached to question the fracture in a relationship that had always been so strong. The selfish part of him, the part that only wanted one thing right now and it wasn't to mend other's feuds, refused to get mixed up in the middle of things.

He had more than enough of his own problems right now. And whether he liked it or not, the time had come to address them.

Tossing back the remains of his drink, Tristan set the rocks glass down and sidled across the bar. He came to a stop just behind Cara and tapped her shoulder. Heat charged through his fingertips. Heat she felt too, judging by the way she first jerked and then stiffened.

If he were to believe that reaction, then he would guess the answer to his next question would be no. He wasn't going to believe the reaction. He couldn't.

The conversation fell silent and she swiveled around to face him. Her emotions were masked now, more completely than she'd ever kept them from him before.

Laying his own on the line, he smiled at her and extended his hand. "Would you like to dance, Cara?"

Her left cheek sank in as her attention drifted to his hand, back to his face, and then again to his hand. Tristan inhaled a long breath and held it, waiting as time ticked slowly past, seconds feeling like hours. The silence around them grew and with it his certainty that she would say no. Then, just when he was prepared to retract his hand, his offer and walk away from this bar and her life in general, she smiled.

It wasn't a big smile, but it was a smile all the same.

"Yes," she said softly. "I'd like that."

Cara accepted his hand and heat jolted between their joined palms. The air whooshed from his mouth and he cursed under his breath for the way she affected him. One touch, just that one, that subtle brush of her fingers against his, and he was aroused in a way only she could accomplish. In a way that affected more than just his body, but reached deep within him and swelled his heart with hope and his soul with wonder.

Clinging tight to the desire that coursed through his veins and warmed his blood, he led her onto the dance floor and pulled her into his arms. He reveled in the feel of her, the softness of her body pressed against his, the energy that swirled like a tangible thing between them. Then she pushed back from his embrace and broke that revelry.

Humor glinted in her eyes as she lifted her hands to his mouth and pushed at the corners of his lips. "It's a reception, Trist. Now I realize we're sharing this bar with most of Reno, so it isn't a traditional one, but you should still try to be happy."

He wanted to laugh at the words, at the realization she'd only stopped dancing because in restraining his desire, he'd turned to scowling. He couldn't laugh, not when so much still went unanswered.

He caught her hands in his once again and twined them around his neck. Dropping his own to her waist, he soberly met her gaze. "You want me to try and be happy, but what about you? Are you happy, Cara?"

Her tongue slipped out of her mouth, wetting her lower lip, then retracted as she bobbed her head in response. "Yes. For the most part I am."

Tristan pulled his gaze from the glistening appeal of her rosy red lips to focus on her words. For the most part, she'd said, and that left room for more. "What would make you even more so? What would it take to bring the light back into your eyes?"

"Forgetting."

She answered so swiftly it took a moment for the word to sink in and when it did, his heart squeezed tightly with the reality she wanted the same thing he did. But how to get there from here? "I want that too. I want to forget the past couple months. Neither of us is liable to let that happen though, are we?"

Cara stilled in his arms and her eyes filled with what looked to be regret. But why would it be? She had nothing to regret. "Then how about forgiving, Trist? Do you think we might be able to handle that much?"

Emotions clogged his throat. He swallowed them back and they fell back into time with the music. "You could do that? You could forgive me?"

"I want to do that," she admitted in a quiet voice, then settled her head against his shoulder and pulled him tight against her.

The emotions rose up again. This time Tristan didn't try to push them back. He knew doing so would be pointless. He held onto her, fearing his embrace was crushing her and at the same time not about to let go.

"I want you to do that," he breathed near her ear.

She tipped back her face and the regret he'd seen in her eyes moments ago was back in full detail. "What about you? Do you want to forgive me?"

"For what, baby? You've done nothing wrong."

Her chin trembled and her eyes gleamed with unshed tears. "For what happened with Brandy. For the things I had to do to see her destroyed. For making you believe I actually wanted any of it to happen."

A tear slipped free, rolling down her cheek. His heart turned over for the remorse he now realized she'd been living with these past days. He wiped the tear away with his thumb and pressed a kiss to her forehead. "Everything you did, you did for me. You sacrificed your pride to save my life, to save both of our lives and probably those of everyone else I care about. How could I ever be upset with you for that?"

Cara bit down on her lip and closed her eyes. More tears joined that first one, rolling down her cheeks in earnest. He pulled her tighter to him and danced with her silently, aware they were in a room filled with laughter and music—music that no longer matched this dancing style—and completely uncaring. Let him look like a poor helpless fool in love. Let him look like anything so long as Cara stayed in his arms.

"It's been a long time since we've danced."

He smiled at her softly spoken words and drew in a breath of her sweet scent. It was light enough to barely be distinguishable and strong enough to have the desire he'd been fighting since leading her onto the dance floor taking full effect. His cock stirred and his pulse accelerated, beads of perspiration forming on his brow.

Taking a chance, he lowered his head and nuzzled the sensitive flesh just below her ear. A shiver rushed through and passed over into him. A shiver punctuated by a breathy sigh. "It's been too long," he finally responded, the thickness of his voice evidence of the state of the rest of him. "You feel incredible."

"So do you." She swayed against him and rubbed her pelvis against his quickly expanding erection. Tipping her head back, she met his eyes with hungry ones of her own. "Maybe we should see what else feels good."

"What are you saying, Cara?"

"There's a lot of leftover champagne. I've always believed second to chocolate, which by the way I've given up permanently, champagne is the best thing to dip your strawberries into."

A grin tugged at Tristan's mouth. One that when he let blossom, she returned wholeheartedly. Warmth filled his body, heat that had nothing to do with sexual chemistry, though he was feeling plenty of that too. This warmth was far more elemental, the kind he'd spent years chasing, the kind he'd only ever known with Cara, his soul mate, his everything. The warmth of love.

"Champagne is nice, but I can think of something even better to dip my berries into. Something far more appetizing."

Something that had the warmth of love blending with the warmth of lust, and making his cock throb with need.

"Mmm... That just might be something you'll have to show me."

The purr to her tone had every one of his nerves standing at attention. He stopped moving and held her back far enough to read her emotions. They reflected everything he felt, including his sudden desperation to leave this bar behind and retreat to the privacy of his suite. "When can I show you?"

"Now."

"Right now?"

Cara's smile spread into her eyes. "Right now. Unless you have better plans."

Dio caro, was she joking? "Nothing could ever be better than spending time with you, *mio bello*. Nothing could ever mean more to me. I—"

She placed her fingers to his mouth, cutting him off short. "Shhh... You can tell me upstairs. Let's leave now when no one's watching."

Laughter bubbled up inside him. Everyone was watching, and she had to know that. He didn't bother to ask, but took her by the hand and whisked her from the room.

* * * * *

"I love you."

Cara laughed while her heart squeezed with joy. She slid back beneath the covers and into the warmth and security of Tristan's strong arms. "If you tell me that one more time, I swear I'll be forced to strangle you."

"Well, then my lips are sealed. But only for the next few minutes."

And that was fine by her. He'd done nothing but express his love both vocally and physically since they'd come upstairs several hours ago and while she'd told him she didn't need to keep hearing the words, each time he spoke them it thrilled her.

She held everything now, everything she'd once had and never realized how perfect it was, and everything she wanted for the rest of her life. Almost everything, anyway. She placed a kiss to Tristan's chest, then rose up on her elbows. "Were you serious about Joey? What you said before I distracted you?"

The deep brown of his eyes lit with humor. "You didn't distract me, baby, I distracted you. And, yes, I was serious. We'll find a school near Ashton. There has to be a good one within a couple hours from there. Until we do find it, we'll just have to put the company jet to use and make weekly trips in to see him."

He was so good to her, this man she'd come so close to losing because they'd both been too blind to see the truth for so long. They weren't blind anymore. The truth was in front of them and she wouldn't let it fade away ever again.

She brushed her mouth over his softly, delighting in the magical warmth even that subtle touch swelled between them. "Thank you."

"Don't thank me. I plan to have you spend every plane trip mulling over the chaos your leaving caused. There's at least a month's worth of back work waiting for you."

A month, a year's worth, she'd take it. The mere thought of returning to Manseletti Art International and putting those skills Tristan taught her years ago back into action filled her with boundless joy. "Gladly."

"You won't be saying that after you see Janice's mess. The poor thing couldn't seem to keep her eye off the boss long enough to get her work done."

Cara laughed softly and lowered to his mouth to nip a corner at each side. "Well, her boss is quite a catch."

"Was," he corrected, wrapping his arms around her and rolling them until he lay on top. "I called and let her go this morning. It was inevitable." His cock chafed against her inner thigh and her pussy heated with the knowledge he wanted her again. He bent to her chest and his tongue blazed a path over her naked flesh and across the top of her breasts. "And, for the record, this boss is already caught with no intention of ever escaping."

She started to respond, to say that he had no choice in the matter because she wasn't letting him go ever again, for destiny or any other reason. The shrill ring of the telephone cut her off short.

Tristan glanced at the clock. "It's after two in the morning. As much as I don't want to interrupt this, I should take it."

She nodded and he picked up the phone, growling a greeting into the phone.

She laughed at his surly tone, stopping abruptly when it changed to one of open disbelief. "You're kidding me?"

She couldn't hear what was being said on the other end, but she could feel its effects on Tristan's body. Whoever it was, whatever it was about, it wasn't good.

"And there was nothing there?" he asked. "No trace of anything? A struggle? What about the blonde? The one who was with him most the night?" He paused as a muffled voice sounded on the other end, and then laughed. "Nice. Leave it to him to steal his own brother's date." The humor left his tone once more and he nodded at the unseen caller. "Yeah. I will. You too. Thanks for letting us know."

Tristan set the phone down and crumpled back on the bed. Anxiety poured from him in waves.

Cara came up on an elbow. "What's the matter?"

"Nothing."

"Don't tell me nothing, Tristan. I can see there's something wrong. I can feel it. Your emotions are a jumbled mess."

He rolled back over her and slid his arms under her back. "I should know better than to try to keep something from you, shouldn't I? It's Paul."

"What about him?"

"He wanted to get back to Vegas tonight so he'd be there for his morning meeting. He'd agreed to take that painting that resembles Lucas' sister along and drop it off with one of his friends who specializes in paranormal forensics, only he never made it."

Tension spiked in Cara's body and she jerked in his arms. "*What?*"

"His car was found halfway between here and Vegas. There's no sign of him and no sign of the painting."

"Maybe the car broke down and he had to walk. He probably took the painting because he knew how important it is to us."

Tristan brushed a kiss over her mouth. "It's a nice thought, but the car didn't break down, baby. It was still running when the cops came across it."

"So, he's just gone?"

"Yes. And unfortunately there isn't a thing we can do about it right now. Lucas said the cops wouldn't even let him know anything further until morning and, while this might not be his jurisdiction, he's one of them."

"So, we're just supposed to forget about it for now?" Cara was aware of her rising voice, the fact her belly tightened a little more with each question, but how was she supposed to feel? How could Tristan act so calm?

The answer to that last one was simple, of course. He could act calm in the face of danger because it was his calling. He was a man who prided himself on remaining tranquil regardless of the situation and now that the evil Brandy instilled in him had passed, he was back to living up to his calling completely.

"We're supposed to do our best to relax and get some sleep while the people who are trained to look into these kinds of things are looking into it. I hate this too, Cara, but I promise you tomorrow we'll find some answers."

He shifted against her and the hard length of his cock caressed her slit. She closed her eyes on a wave of ecstasy and her pussy grew damp with desire. He was right, she knew, even if she hated having to accept it. "You're right. There's nothing we can do tonight. I just don't like knowing that painting's free or that it might be out to hurt Paul or...come back after one of us."

"It's only a picture, *mia bella signora*."

"It's *not* only a picture." It was evil. It was where whatever had possessed Brandy now resided. She'd seen it go into that painting with her own two eyes. They both had.

"Did I ever tell you you're as pretty as a picture?"

The somberness of Cara's thoughts faded slightly as laughter drifted from her lips. "Oh, God, Trist. That is the absolute worst line I've heard come out of your mouth."

"It's also a lie. You're far prettier than a picture. You're beautiful and you're mine." His mouth crashed down over hers, his tongue spilling past her lips, coaxing, teasing, taunting the air from her lungs.

Tristan's hand moved between them and then touched down between her legs. One finger stroked her mound and her pussy pooled with wetness. She needed more than that one finger. She needed to feel him inside her, needed to feel his cock filling her, taking her to their special place.

As much as she needed, she didn't miss his motivation for moving on her so quickly. He was trying to help her to relax, to forget her fears if only momentarily. She pulled from his mouth, gasping for breath, and feigned a glare. "Are you trying to distract me again?"

The corners of his mouth tipped up and his lips broke out into the sexy grin that would forever be her undoing. He tipped his hips and brought the head of his shaft to her hole, rimming her pussy lips with playful pleasure. "I don't know, is it working?"

She opened her mouth to respond, and he chose that moment to thrust into her. All that came out from her parted lips was a sigh of pure bliss. Maybe it was wrong to give in to their pleasure while someone they cared about could be in trouble. Wrong or not, she needed this connection right now more than anything. Giving in to that need, she wrapped her legs around his back. He cupped her ass and lifted her hips higher yet, pumping into her with measured thrusts she felt all the way to her womb.

"Oh, it's working," she breathed out raggedly. "Like you wouldn't believe."

He laughed hoarsely. "Then you'd better make me believe."

Once upon a time not so long ago, Cara might have doubted her ability to make him believe, because she herself didn't. That time had long since passed. She believed in him, in them, and their future together. A future not so unlike the shared vision that flashed through their minds as the winds stirred and the air heated.

The electric crackle of light and energy brought forth by their lovemaking was left behind then and they lay together on the golden fields of their special place, twined as one, hearts, bodies and souls. And as he came into her and she gave to him her own release, they joined in minds as well. Giving their love, their life, their everything, aligning forever with the destiny they'd found in each other.

About the author:

Jodi Lynn Copeland resides on 30-acres of recreational woodland and farmland, minutes from Michigan's state capital. Since writing her first book more than a decade ago, she has completed numerous novels that span the range of genres and sensuality levels. Jodi's books have received various awards and commendations, including 4½ Star Top Pick reviews from RT BOOKclub Magazine, Recommended Reads from The Road To Romance and Reviewer's International Organization (RIO), and nominations for such awards as the National Reader's Choice Award, the EPPIE Award, the Scarlett Letter, and the Lauries Bookbuyers Best. A Central Michigan University graduate, she holds a degree in Industrial Supervision and has minors in Business Administration and Engineering.

You can visit Jodi online and learn more about her and her novels at: http://www.jodilynncopeland.com or subscribe to her newsletter at: PassionPress-Subscribe@yahoogroups.com.

Jodi welcomes mail from readers. You can write to her c/o Ellora's Cave Publishing at 1337 Commerce Drive, Suite 13, Stow OH 44224.

Why an electronic book?

We live in the Information Age—an exciting time in the history of human civilization in which technology rules supreme and continues to progress in leaps and bounds every minute of every hour of every day. For a multitude of reasons, more and more avid literary fans are opting to purchase e-books instead of paperbacks. The question to those not yet initiated to the world of electronic reading is simply: *why?*

1. *Price.* An electronic title at Ellora's Cave Publishing runs anywhere from 40-75% less than the cover price of the <u>exact same title</u> in paperback format. Why? Cold mathematics. It is less expensive to publish an e-book than it is to publish a paperback, so the savings are passed along to the consumer.

2. *Space.* Running out of room to house your paperback books? That is one worry you will never have with electronic novels. For a low one-time cost, you can purchase a handheld computer designed specifically for e-reading purposes. Many e-readers are larger than the average handheld, giving you plenty of screen room. Better yet, hundreds of titles can be stored within your new library—a single microchip. (Please note that Ellora's Cave does not endorse any specific brands. You can check our website at

www.ellorascave.com for customer recommendations we make available to new consumers.)

3. *Mobility.* Because your new library now consists of only a microchip, your entire cache of books can be taken with you wherever you go.

4. *Personal preferences are accounted for.* Are the words you are currently reading too small? Too large? Too...**ANNOYING**? Paperback books cannot be modified according to personal preferences, but e-books can.

5. *Innovation.* The way you read a book is not the only advancement the Information Age has gifted the literary community with. There is also the factor of what you can read. Ellora's Cave Publishing will be introducing a new line of interactive titles that are available in e-book format only.

6. *Instant gratification.* Is it the middle of the night and all the bookstores are closed? Are you tired of waiting days—sometimes weeks—for online and offline bookstores to ship the novels you bought? Ellora's Cave Publishing sells instantaneous downloads 24 hours a day, 7 days a week, 365 days a year. Our e-book delivery system is 100% automated, meaning your order is filled as soon as you pay for it.

Those are a few of the top reasons why electronic novels are displacing paperbacks for many an avid reader. As always, Ellora's Cave Publishing welcomes your questions and comments. We invite you to email us at service@ellorascave.com or write to us directly at: 1337 Commerce Drive, Suite 13, Stow OH 44224.

Discover for yourself why readers can't get enough of the multiple award-winning publisher Ellora's Cave. Whether you prefer e-books or paperbacks, be sure to visit EC on the web at www.ellorascave.com for an erotic reading experience that will leave you breathless.

WWW.ELLORASCAVE.COM

Printed in the United States
28158LVS00008B/67-183